THE NIGHT WATCH OF ELDORIA

MICHAEL L MROWIEC

MAGIK LAMP PRESS

Electronic Book ISBN: 978-1-0691278-1-5
Paperback Book ISBN: 978-1-0691278-0-8
Hard Cover Book ISBN: 978-1-0691278-6-0

A Magik Lamp Press Novel.
www.magiklamppress.com
Magik Lamp Press is a division of Madole Labs.
www.madolelabs.com

Publisher's Note: This is a work of fiction. Names, characters, places, and incidents are a product of the author's imagination. Any resemblance to actual people, living or dead, or to businesses, companies, events, institutions, or locales is entirely coincidental.

"In the darkness, the line between the hunter and the hunted blurs, and the shadows reveal not only monsters but the fears we bury deepest within ourselves."

— Unknown Chronicler of Eldoria

FOREWORD

The journey to bring *The Night Watch of Eldoria* to life has been filled with shadows and revelations, much like the story itself. Writing this book allowed me to explore the boundary between fear and courage, how our past can haunt us, and our choices when faced with unimaginable darkness. Eldoria is not just a cursed city—it is a mirror reflecting our own struggles, our resilience, and the fragile alliances we form to survive.

This story is about more than monsters lurking in the dark. It is about the darkness within ourselves and the strength we find when we dare confront it. Every character in this book represents a fragment of that struggle—facing loss, doubt, and their own past mistakes as they navigate the dangerous labyrinth that is Eldoria. Enjoy walking beside Ethan, Lily, and the others as they grapple with the choices that define them and perhaps find a piece of your own story in theirs.

Thank you for stepping into the shadows with me. I promise you a journey full of twists, secrets, and moments where hope feels as fragile as a flickering light.

— Michael L Mrowiec

CONTENTS

PROLOGUE

The wind howled through the empty streets of Eldoria, carrying with it the scent of decay and the distant echoes of forgotten voices. The city had long been abandoned to its fate, a labyrinth of crumbling buildings and dark alleys that twisted upon themselves like the nightmares of those who once called this place home. A place where shadows danced and whispered secrets to anyone foolish enough to listen.

In the heart of the old quarter, a solitary figure moved with purpose. His cloak billowed behind him, the fabric worn and tattered from countless nights spent under the oppressive weight of the curse. The sigil etched into his arm pulsed with a dim, silvery glow, a reminder of the burden he bore—a mark that tied him to this place and the ancient ritual that demanded completion.

Father Gabriel paused before a shattered fountain, its once-proud statue now a broken remnant of a forgotten age. He knelt, his fingers brushing over the runes carved into the stone, their edges worn smooth by time.

The symbols were old, older than the city itself, and they spoke of a power that had lain dormant for centuries—waiting, watching.

He closed his eyes, murmuring a prayer that had been passed down through generations, a plea for guidance, for strength. The wind seemed to answer, swirling around him in a gust that carried the faintest hint of warmth—a promise or perhaps a warning. The sigil on his arm burned brighter for a moment, the pain sharp and insistent, forcing his eyes open.

Gabriel knew what he had to do. The Night Watch would soon begin again, and this time, the stakes were higher than ever. The relics had to be found, the ritual completed, or the curse would consume not just Eldoria but everything beyond its crumbling walls. He rose to his feet, his gaze fixed on the horizon where the first hints of twilight began to fade into darkness.

Somewhere in the distance, a bell tolled—a mournful sound that marked the beginning of another night. Another chance to break the cycle, or to fall victim to the endless shadows. Gabriel turned away from the fountain, his steps echoing against the cobblestones as he disappeared into the depths of the city, the weight of countless lives resting on his shoulders.

The Night Watch had begun. And with it, the hope of salvation—or the certainty of doom.

MARKED BY MIDNIGHT

The shadow of the clock tower stretched across Eldoria, shrouding the city in an unsettling gloom. Midnight approached, and the air thickened with a sense of unease. The usually vibrant streets lay silent and deserted, only the occasional flicker of a neon sign and the rustle of wind cutting through abandoned alleys broke the stillness.

In the Old Quarter, gothic spires jutted into the night sky, their weathered stones in stark contrast to the gleaming glass and steel of downtown's skyscrapers. The two faces of Eldoria—old and new—stood frozen in time, waiting for the inevitable strike of midnight.

A lone figure hurried down the cobblestone streets, footsteps echoing off ancient walls. He glanced over his shoulder repeatedly, his eyes darting from shadow to shadow. The weight of the city's curse clung to the air, an oppressive force that seemed to press down on everything.

The clock tower loomed ahead, its face barely visible in the darkness. As the figure approached, grotesque carvings of gargoyles and twisted figures seemed to shift in the dim light, coming alive under the faint glow. The carvings were remnants of a time when Eldoria's past merged seamlessly with its haunted present.

A cold wind swept through the narrow streets, bringing with it the scent of decay and despair. Windows rattled, shutters creaked, and the city seemed to hold its breath—waiting. The massive clock hands edged closer to midnight, each tick resonating through the stillness. Behind closed doors, the people of Eldoria waited, bracing themselves for what was to come.

With each passing second, a low rumble built up from deep within the clock tower, reverberating through the cobblestone streets. The city trembled as if in anticipation. The lone figure paused, feeling the ground beneath his feet quiver, the hairs on his neck rising from an unseen charge in the air.

The ancient clock tower began to chime, deep, resonant tones ringing out across the city. The figure froze, heart pounding as the first bell echoed through the empty streets. He looked up, his face pale under the eerie glow that seemed to come alive around the tower.

With each toll, vibrations would shake loose bits of debris from crumbling facades. The sound was all-consuming, resonating with a bone-chilling quality that carried a message—The Night Watch had begun.

Panic clawed at the man's chest, squeezing the air from his lungs. He ducked into an alleyway, pressing himself against the cold bricks, trying to disappear into the shadows. He knew what was coming—he had heard the stories whispered in hushed tones at Eldoria's taverns, the tales of those chosen for the Night Watch.

A sudden burning sensation spread across his wrist. He gritted his teeth, hissing in pain as he clamped his other hand over it. The glow beneath his palm was unmistakable. He slowly moved his hand away to reveal a mark etched into his skin—an intricate sigil glowing with an unnatural blue light. Its lines seemed to pulse in rhythm with his own panicked heartbeat, casting faint shadows on the alley walls.

He was marked. Chosen. A player in this twisted game.

Fear rooted him to the spot, his vision narrowing as if the shadows were closing in. His legs gave out, and he sank to the ground, the damp cobblestones cold against him. He squeezed his eyes shut, praying it was a nightmare, but the searing pain in his wrist was real. The sigil glowed relentlessly, a beacon in the dark, mocking his futile hopes of escape.

He had to move. He had to find shelter before they found him. The mist was already starting to seep from the cracks in the pavement, a ghostly presence creeping closer. He forced himself to his feet, legs trembling as he pushed away from the wall. The streets stretched out before him like a labyrinth, each alley and corner promising either safety or doom.

A scream pierced the silence—close, too close. The man's breath caught in his throat, his eyes widening in terror. He could hear the deliberate, heavy footsteps approaching, echoing ominously through the empty streets. He stumbled forward, fear propelling him as the mist snaked around his ankles, its cold touch spreading dread through his body.

There was no turning back now. He had to survive until dawn. The Night Watch had begun, and Eldoria's shadows had come alive.

CHAPTER TWO

BURDEN OF FAILURE

E than Marlowe slouched in his worn leather chair, the dim light of his desk lamp casting long shadows across the cluttered office. The clock on the wall ticked past midnight, each second punctuated by the rustle of papers as he flipped through case files.

He rubbed his eyes, bloodshot from hours of pouring over documents. The coffee at his elbow had long since gone cold, forgotten in his relentless pursuit of... what? Justice? Redemption? He wasn't sure anymore.

His gaze drifted to a framed photo, half-buried under a stack of reports. He reached out, hesitated, then pulled it free. Two faces smiled up at him—his own, years younger and unburdened, next to a beaming Lily. His sister's green eyes sparkled with a joy he couldn't remember feeling in ages.

Ethan jogged his memories. How long had it been since they had a real conversation? Not the obligatory small talk during family gatherings, but a genuine conversation. A memory surfaced—he and Lily sitting in a small café near the university. Lily, animated as ever, her hands moving wildly as she tried to explain her latest theory. The curse. She had been obsessed with it even then. He remembered the look in her eyes—earnest, almost pleading.

"Ethan, it's real. The stories, the sigils, all of it. I know it sounds crazy, but I've done the research!" Her voice had been insistent, her hands clutching a thick notebook filled with scribbles and old texts. Ethan had leaned back in his chair, arms crossed. "Lily, it's just folklore. Urban legends. Eldoria's a mess, sure, but you can't actually believe a curse is behind all of it."

She frowned, her enthusiasm dimming under his skepticism. "It's not just stories, Ethan. People are dying. And the symbols—the sigils—they match up with ancient runes. This isn't just random violence."

He sighed, rubbing his temples. "Look, I get that you're passionate about this, but I deal with real threats. Gang violence, corruption, missing persons. I can't waste time chasing fairy tales."

Her face had fallen, the light in her eyes flickering out. "You think I'm wasting my time."

"I think you should focus on things you can actually solve," he'd said, harsher than he intended. He saw the hurt in her eyes but didn't take it back.

She had closed her notebook, her expression hardening. "One day, you'll see I was right. And when that day comes, it might be too late."

***

The case file before him blurred, the words swimming together. Another dead end, another case that would likely join the growing pile of unsolved mysteries plaguing Eldoria. The city's darkness seemed to seep into everything, corrupting even the simplest of investigations. He leaned back, the chair creaking in protest. His mind drifted to Lily again. She'd be in her final year of college now, still chasing dusty old legends and folklore. He had scoffed at her interests once, dismissing them as childish fantasies. Now, in the depth of Eldoria's long nights, he wondered if there wasn't some truth hidden in those ancient stories.

A siren wailed in the distance, jolting Ethan from his reverie. The night wasn't over, and neither was his work.

With a sigh, he turned back to the files. The weight of unsolved cases, of lives he couldn't save, pressed down on him. But beneath it all, a spark of determination still burned.

His gaze drifted to the window, the neon lights of Eldoria's downtown casting an eerie glow through the grimy glass. Ethan remembered a time when those lights meant life, vibrancy, and a city pulsing with energy. Now, they were just feeble beacons in a sea of darkness, flickering reminders of what once was.

He stood, his bones creaking in protest, and moved to the window. The streets below were empty, save for a stray newspaper tumbling along the cracked pavement. His reflection stared back at him, a ghost haunting the glass.

"Damn this city," he muttered, his breath fogging the window.

Eldoria had been his home, his battleground, his entire world. He had walked these streets as a boy, full of hope and ambition. As a detective, he had sworn to protect them. Now, as a washed-up PI, he watched helplessly as the curse of The Night Watch slowly choked the life out of every corner.

The once-bustling Downtown district was a hollow shell of its former self. Skyscrapers loomed like tombstones, their windows dark and lifeless. The Old Quarter, with its cobblestone streets and Gothic architecture, had always held an air of mystery. Now, it reeked of decay and despair.

Ethan's fists clenched at his sides. How many had they lost? How many more would fall victim to the curse before it was done? The mist rolled in each night, and with it came the hunt. The chosen, marked by glowing sigils, ran like prey while the rest of the city cowered behind locked doors. And for what? Some ancient grudge? A twisted game played by powers beyond their understanding?

His eyes found the distant silhouette of the clock tower, its face glowing ominously in the night. The epicenter of their nightmare, tolling out their doom with each passing hour.

His eyes drifted back to the pile of case files on his desk. One folder stood out, its edges worn and frayed from countless nights of obsessive review. He pulled it from the stack, his hands trembling slightly as he opened it. The face of a young woman stared back at him, her eyes wide with terror. Andrea Bondy, age 24. His partner. The first victim of The Night Watch he'd encountered as a detective. The memory hit him like a physical blow. It had been a night much like this one. The fog had rolled in, thick and oppressive, carrying with it the stench of fear. Ethan had been on patrol, still green and full of misplaced confidence. The call had come in—a woman, marked with the sigil, cornered in an alley off Blackthorn Street. He had arrived too late. Andrea's body lay crumpled against a dumpster, her skin still glowing faintly with the cursed mark. She had been more than just a colleague—she was someone he had trusted with his life. And he had failed her. Ethan had stood there, gun in hand, useless. He had sworn to protect and serve, but what good were those words against an enemy he couldn't see or understand?

Ethan slammed the folder shut, his jaw clenched tight against the surge of emotions. Andrea's face haunted his dreams, a constant reminder of his failure. How many others had met the same fate since then? How many more would fall before this curse was lifted?

***

Could anyone marked by the sigil truly be saved? The question gnawed at him as it had for years. Those who survived often did so by becoming monsters themselves, sacrificing friends, family, strangers—anyone to stay alive until sunrise. Was that survival worth the cost?

Ethan's mind wandered to Lily, her passionate belief that there was a way to break the curse. He had dismissed her theories before, but now... What if she was right? What if there was a way to end this nightmare without more bloodshed?

The clock tower's bells began to toll, their deep, resonant sound echoing through the streets of Eldoria. A sudden tension gripped Ethan's body, his shoulders stiffening as if bracing for an unseen blow. His hand froze midway through, turning a page in Andrea's file. Each somber chime sent a shiver down his spine, a visceral reminder of the horrors about to unfold.

One. Two. Three.

He stood, moving to the window again. The mist was already creeping along the streets, tendrils of fog curling around lampposts and seeping into alleyways. Somewhere out there, people were running, hiding, praying they wouldn't be marked for tonight's twisted game. Four. Five. Six.

Ethan's eyes squinted. Every instinct screamed at him to act, to do something. But what? He had tried before, countless times, and accomplished nothing but adding to his collection of nightmares. Seven. Eight. Nine.

He turned away from the window, his gaze falling on the photo of Lily. Her smile, frozen in time, seemed to mock him. She believed there was a way to end this. He wanted to believe it, too, but years of failure had worn away at that hope.

Ten. Eleven. Twelve.

The final toll faded, leaving an oppressive silence in its wake. Ethan stood there, fists clenched at his sides, wrestling with the urge to grab his coat and hit the streets. But what good would it do? He had seen how this played out before. Getting involved now wouldn't change anything.

With a heavy sigh, Ethan returned to his desk. He pulled another case file from the stack, forcing himself to focus on the details of a missing person's report. It was safer this way, he told himself. Stick to the cases he could solve, the problems he could fix.

But even as he immersed himself in work, the unease lingered. The weight of The Night Watch pressed down on him, an ever-present shadow he couldn't quite shake.

Ethan's footsteps echoed in the empty hallway as he locked up his office. Another name etched into his failures, another ghost on his conscience.

He pulled his worn leather jacket tighter, bracing himself for the outside chill.

The streets of Eldoria were eerily quiet, save for the distant sound of sirens and the occasional scream. Ethan kept his head down, hands shoved deep in his pockets as he walked. The mist swirled around his feet, seeming to reach for him with ghostly fingers.

A sudden commotion broke the silence. Rapid footsteps slapped against the wet pavement, growing louder by the second. Ethan looked up just as a figure burst from an alleyway ahead.

The person stumbled, nearly falling. In the dim light of a flickering streetlamp, Ethan caught a glimpse of wild, terrified eyes and dishevelled clothes. But what made his breath catch was the glowing sigil on the stranger's forearm, pulsing with a ghostly blue light.

For a moment, their gazes locked. Ethan saw the desperate plea in the marked person's eyes, the silent cry for help he'd seen so many times before. His muscles tensed, and years of instinct urged him to act, to help.

But he didn't move.

The marked person hesitated for a split second, hope flashing across their face. Then, seeing Ethan's lack of response, they bolted down the street, disappearing into the mist.

Ethan stood frozen, his heart pounding. He could still hear the fading footsteps and the terror in those eyes.

But even as he spoke the words, something deep inside him rebelled. The encounter left him shaken, stirring up memories and regrets he'd tried so hard to bury.

CHAPTER THREE

KIN OF THE CURSE

Dawn crept over Eldoria's skyline, pale light barely piercing the fog that clung stubbornly to the streets. Ethan's boots scuffed against the cracked pavement, the quiet murmur of the waking city pressing down on him. The usual morning bustle had lost its energy; everything was muted as if the night's horrors still hung in the air. A newspaper vendor huddled in his booth, his eyes flicking nervously from side to side. He barely acknowledged Ethan's passing, lowering his gaze like everyone else who had learned to avoid eye contact these days. Across the street, a coffee shop sat half-empty, a shadow of its former liveliness. Ethan caught sight of a woman inside, clutching her cup with white-knuckled hands, her eyes staring into the steaming liquid as if she could divine answers in its depths.

The streets were stirring, but even the schoolchildren who hurried past did so in eerie silence, their parents hovering protectively beside them.

No laughter, no chatter—just the soft shuffle of feet, accompanied by the occasional glance over a shoulder.

Ethan turned onto Blackwood Avenue, where gothic spires and twisted gargoyles watched over the streets, their stone faces frozen in grimaces that mirrored the city's anguish. A businessman in a sharp suit quickened his pace, his polished shoes echoing against the pavement as though even daylight offered no reprieve from the shadow of The Night Watch. The city felt like a wound that refused to heal. Every face Ethan passed was marked by the same haunted expression, whether they bore the cursed sigil or not. They all carried the weight of the night, the heavy knowledge that the darkness was never far away.

A bus rolled by, its windows fogged with the breath of silent passengers. Some of them clutched protective charms—useless trinkets sold by vendors who preyed on fear, promising safety that would never come.

***

As Lily's apartment building came into view, Ethan's steps slowed. The red brick facade, dark with grime and age, loomed before him like a reminder of everything that had fractured between them. Each visit was a reminder of the gulf that had grown wider with each passing year, a chasm of unsaid words and unhealed wounds.

Ethan's knuckles rapped against the weathered door, the sound hollow in the empty hallway. Paint peeled from the frame, revealing layers of history beneath—much like the city itself.

"Just a minute!" Lily's voice carried through, followed by the rustle of papers and a muted thud.

The door swung open. His sister's hair was tied back in a messy bun, dark circles under her eyes matching his own. Books and papers littered every surface of her small apartment, post-it notes creating a maze of connections on the walls.

"You look terrible." Ethan stepped inside, scanning the chaos.

"Nice to see you too." Lily cleared a stack of leather-bound books from a chair. "Coffee?"

"What's all this?" He picked up a page covered in her cramped handwriting. Symbols and dates filled the margins, arrows connecting seemingly random events.

"I found something in the university archives." Lily grabbed the paper from his hands, smoothing it on her desk. "These patterns in the city's history—they're not random. The curse follows a cycle, Ethan. If we can understand it—"

"Stop." He pressed his fingers to his temples. "Not this again."

***

Lily's eyes flickered with frustration but also something softer—disappointment, maybe. She'd been down this road with him before.

"You saw it yourself last night. The sigils, the mist—"

"What I saw was another victim I couldn't help." His voice cracked. "Lily, I don't want to get into this again. I can't... I can't go down that rabbit hole with you. I've seen what happens when people believe in that stuff. Your theories won't save anyone."

Lily's face hardened. "And what will? Pretending it's not happening? People are dying, Ethan. If there's even a chance—"

"There isn't." He turned away from her hopeful expression, from the wall of evidence she'd gathered. "You're chasing fairy tales while real people need help."

"Fairy tales?" Lily's voice rose slightly, not in anger but in disbelief. "You think I'm wasting my time? What if I'm right, Ethan? What if there's something here that can stop all of this? You're not the only one who's lost someone." Her words were quiet but sharp. "At least I'm trying to understand why."

Ethan stood frozen, his back still to her. He could feel the weight of her words, sharp and cutting but also full of the same pain he carried. His fists clenched at his sides, a reflex he couldn't control.

The silence between them stretched, filled with the weight of shared grief and different ways of carrying it.

***

Lily crossed to her desk, pulling out a leather-bound tome with brass clasps. The book's spine bore no title, just a series of intricate symbols that matched the ones scattered across her research papers.

"Look at this." She laid it on the coffee table, careful not to disturb the brittle pages. "Dr. Vane lent it to me from her private collection."

Ethan's eyes narrowed. "Dr. Vane? The psychology professor?"

"She's more than that." Lily traced her finger along the symbols. "She's been studying The Night Watch for decades. These are her personal notes, observations of the patterns, the way the curse manifests."

Ethan picked up the book, its weight pressing into his palms. He wanted to dismiss it, toss it back on the table like every other crackpot theory he'd heard. But there was something about the precision of the notes, the meticulousness of the sketches, that made it harder to turn away. The pages revealed detailed sketches of the sigil, annotations in neat handwriting filling the margins. Dates, locations, and names created a web of connections that made Ethan's head spin.

"Dr. Vane's dedicated her life to this. Too much, if you ask me," Lily said, her voice softening. "She's not exactly... mainstream anymore, but that's because she's closer than anyone."

Ethan frowned. "Closer to what?"

Lily flipped to a marked page. "The Ritual of Severance. It's mentioned in fragments throughout Eldoria's history, always connected to periods when the curse weakened."

Ethan leaned closer despite himself. The sketches showed circular arrangements of symbols, similar to the sigil but broken and fractured.

"She believes the curse can be broken, Ethan. She's dedicated her life to understanding it. This isn't just folklore or superstition—she's approached it scientifically, documented everything."

"And what makes her different from every other crackpot who's claimed to have answers?"

"Because she's seen it happen. She's treated survivors and studied the psychological effects. She knows things about The Night Watch that aren't in any public records."

Ethan picked up the book, the weight of it substantial in his hands. Dr. Vane's precise observations filled page after page, each entry dated and cross-referenced. This wasn't the work of a conspiracy theorist—it was methodical, academic, thorough.

"She thinks we might be able to help each other," Lily continued, her voice soft but insistent. "Dr. Vane needs people who've been close to the curse, who've seen it firsthand. And we... we need answers."

Ethan snapped the book shut, the sound echoing through Lily's cramped apartment. "Academic fantasies, that's all this is. Some professor who's lost touch with reality, dragging you down with her."

He tossed the book onto the coffee table, scattering a few loose papers. The sketches of the sigil stared up at him, mocking his attempts to ignore their implications.

***

He wanted to believe her, to believe that the curse could be undone. But he'd seen too many bodies and promises of hope turned to dust. It's better to shut it down now before it could destroy her, too.

"You don't understand." Lily reached for the book, cradling it like something precious. "Dr. Vane has proof—"

"Proof?" Ethan's laugh came out harsh. "There's no proof that matters. The Night Watch takes who it wants when it wants. No amount of research or theories change that." He gestured at the wall of connections she'd built. "This obsession of yours—it's going to get you hurt."

"But if there's even a chance—"

"There isn't." His voice cut through her protest. "The curse isn't some puzzle to solve. It's not going to bend to your theories or Dr. Vane's research. It's a force of nature, like gravity. You don't negotiate with it; you don't outsmart it. You just try to survive it."

Lily's shoulders tensed. "That's not good enough."

"It has to be." Ethan paced the small space between her desk and the window. "Stop chasing these foolish ideas. Stop letting people like Dr. Vane fill your head with false hope. The only thing that matters is staying alive, keeping your head down."

He looked at the paper in his hand, his fist trembling for just a second.

CHAPTER FOUR

COST OF KNOWLEDGE

E than's boots scraped against the cracked pavement as he walked past the shuttered storefronts of downtown Eldoria. The morning sun barely pierced the haze clinging to the towers, casting the city in a sickly gray.

A news van sat parked outside the corner bodega; its satellite dish pointed skyward. Through the store's grimy window, Ethan caught fragments of the morning broadcast. Three bodies found. Two in the Heights, one downtown. The reporter's voice carried a familiar strain - the same tone they all used when discussing the victims of the Night Watch.

"...marks consistent with previous cases..." The store owner cranked up the volume. "...authorities advise residents to remain vigilant..."

A small crowd had gathered around the TV, their faces drawn and pale. An elderly woman clutched her shopping bag closer as the camera panned across one of the crime scenes. Yellow police tape fluttered in the background, a sight as common to Eldoria now as traffic lights.

Ethan pushed past the crowd, their whispered conversations barely registering. This city wasn't the one he grew up in—this place was hollow, filled with shadows and whispers of people who no longer trusted each other.

"My nephew worked with her," someone whispered. "At the bank on Fifth."

"Did she have the mark?"

"They all do, don't they?"

Ethan pushed past them, his shoulder brushing against a "For Lease" sign hanging in the adjacent window. Another business is gone. The whole block was dying slowly, store by store. Even the holdouts had started closing early, their hours shrinking as if trying to hide from the night itself.

The broadcast droned on, the same grim script repeated every morning. Ethan clenched his jaw, pushing past the growing sense that something bigger was at play—that this curse, this darkness, wouldn't leave him behind for long.

A bus rumbled past, nearly empty, despite the morning rush hour. The few passengers stared straight ahead, dark circles under their eyes. No one made eye contact anymore. No one lingered on street corners or stopped to chat. The curse had turned neighbors into strangers, each person wrapped in their own bubble of fear.

The sound of breaking glass echoed from somewhere nearby, followed by shouting. No one turned to look. No one rushed to help. They just walked faster, heads down, as if they could outpace the darkness that waited for nightfall. Ethan's steps slowed, a chill prickling the back of his neck. He scanned the street, eyes narrowing as his hand instinctively moved to his side—where his service weapon had once rested. Whatever had shattered the glass... it wasn't far.

Ethan's fingers brushed against the rough brick of a nearby building as the sound of breaking glass faded into the distance. His thoughts circled back to Lily—her determined face, the ancient texts scattered across her apartment floor. The sight of her, surrounded by dusty volumes and cryptic symbols, twisted a knot in his gut.

She'd always been the smart one, the one who charged headfirst into mysteries while he stood back, watching. But this wasn't just an academic puzzle—people were dying.

"It's all connected," she'd said, her green eyes bright with that familiar intensity. "The sigils, the victims, even the timing of the bells."

Ethan kicked a crumpled can down the sidewalk, its metallic clatter echoing against the empty storefronts. He had seen the marks himself—the strange glow creeping over innocent skin. But believing in Lily's theories meant accepting a world where ancient curses were real. A world where all his detective work—everything he'd believed in—meant nothing against forces he couldn't see or understand.

A gust of wind stirred a scattering of old newspapers at his feet. One page caught against his leg, a headline screaming about the Night Watch victims. Ethan tore it away, crumpling it in his hand. What could he do? Arrest a curse? Chase down shadows?

"You can't fix this one, Lil," he muttered, tossing the paper into the gutter. "Some things just are."

The words tasted hollow; each one weighed down with doubt. He pictured Lily hunched over her research, pushing deeper into that darkness with Dr. Vane by her side. He could almost see her getting closer to something—too close. His chest tightened. She was going to get herself killed, and he was choosing to stand back, just like with Andrea. The morning crowd shuffled past, their faces gray and drawn. Ethan joined their flow, letting the routine of the city pull him along. Better this way, he told himself. Better to stay in the world he understood, where problems could be solved with evidence and logic. Let others chase fairy tales and ancient curses.

But even as he told himself that, the weight of his choice pressed down like a stone, heavy and cold.

***

Ethan climbed the narrow stairs of the Victorian brownstone that housed Dr. Vane's practice. The wooden stairs creaked underfoot, each groan amplifying the silence of the empty stairwell—third floor, suite 312. The brass numbers were worn, and the shine long faded over time.

The door stood ajar. Leather-bound books filled the shelves, their cracked spines showing years of use. Papers and diagrams cluttered every surface, spilling across the antique desk in a chaotic order. Pale morning light filtered through the dusty windows, casting stretched shadows over the cluttered floor.

Dr. Vane sat behind her desk, silver-streaked hair pulled back in a tight bun. She didn't look up from the document she was studying. "Mr. Marlowe. I wondered when you'd come."

"Doctor." Ethan remained in the doorway, taking in the organized chaos of her office. Red strings connected newspaper clippings on a corkboard, mapping out patterns he couldn't decipher. "Lily's been spending time here."

"She has." Dr. Vane set down her pen and met his gaze. Her blue eyes carried the weight of too many sleepless nights. "Your sister's mind is sharp—perhaps sharper than most."

"That's what worries me."

"Afraid she might be right?" Dr. Vane gestured to the leather chair in front of her desk.

Ethan stepped inside but didn't sit. His attention caught on a familiar symbol sketched in the corner of her notes—the same mark he'd seen glowing on that terrified man's arm.

"You're pushing her." The accusation slipped out before he could stop it.

"I'm guiding her, not leading her astray. There's a difference." Dr. Vane stood, her movements precise and controlled. "The curse is real, Mr. Marlowe. Your sister understands that better than most. She's not chasing fairy tales—she's documenting patterns that could save lives."

Dr. Vane pulled a thick leather-bound journal from her desk drawer, its pages worn and riddled with colored tabs, a testament to years of obsessive study. "Your sister's research has taken a dangerous turn." She opened to a marked page filled with twisting symbols and dark diagrams. "This isn't just academic curiosity anymore, Mr. Marlowe."

Ethan's stomach knotted as he recognized the ancient script from Lily's apartment. The symbols seemed to writhe on the page, making his eyes ache just to look at them.

"The Ritual of Severance." Dr. Vane's finger hovered over the diagram. "It calls for blood sacrifice, Ethan. Willing sacrifice. Your sister's been cross-referencing celestial alignments, looking for the right moment."

"She wouldn't—"

"She would. She already has the founding relic." Dr. Vane snapped the journal shut. "That medallion she wears? It belonged to Eldoria's first mayor. She spent months tracking it down."

Cold sweat beaded on Ethan's neck. He'd noticed the old bronze medallion hanging from Lily's neck last week and assumed it was just another vintage piece she'd picked up.

"It gets worse." Dr. Vane reached for another set of notes, scribbled in Lily's frantic handwriting. "She's researching something called the Eye's Offering. Even my colleagues won't touch these texts. The last scholar who studied them disappeared three years ago."

"Why are you telling me this?"

"Because The Night Watch doesn't choose randomly, Ethan. It's drawn to those who dig too deep, to those who dare uncover its secrets." Dr. Vane's gaze sharpened. "And your sister? She's not just digging—she's using dynamite."

Ethan's hands clenched at his sides, knuckles white. The room felt smaller, the air thicker. His gaze drifted to the window, where the Clock Tower loomed in the distance, its shadow stretching across the city like a dark finger.

"She won't listen to me," he muttered, the bitterness coating every word. "Not after—" He stopped, Andrea's face flashing in his mind.

"Then make her listen," Dr. Vane said sharply, her chair scraping against the hardwood as she stood. "You're her brother."

"And what good has that done?" Ethan paced the cramped space between bookcases. His reflection fragmrented across the dusty glass cabinets—like a broken man trying to piece together a puzzle with missing parts. "I couldn't save Andrea. I couldn't protect this city. What makes you think I can protect Lily from something I don't even believe in?"

"Because you're afraid." Dr. Vane's words cut through his spiral. "And fear means part of you knows this is real."

The truth of it hit him like a physical blow. Every night since he'd seen that glowing mark, every scream that echoed through Eldoria's streets, every shadow that moved wrong in the corner of his eye—he'd buried it all under a mountain of denial.

"Even if—" Ethan's throat tightened around the words. "Even if it is real. What can I do? Chase shadows? Fight fairy tales?"

He slumped against the bookcase, the weight of his helplessness crashing down. The curse, the Night Watch, Lily's research—it all felt too big, too impossible. His badge hadn't saved Andrea. His gun wouldn't stop whatever stalked Eldoria's streets.

"I can't fight what I can't see." The admission hung in the air between them. "And I can't lose her too."

Dr. Vane watched him, her expression unreadable. The clock on her wall ticked away precious seconds, each one bringing the night closer, bringing whatever horror awaited his sister nearer to reality.

Dr. Vane pulled another journal from her shelf, this one bound in cracked leather with brass clasps. The metal caught the light as she laid it on her desk.

"The Ritual of Severance appears in fragments across different texts. Most were destroyed centuries ago, but I've managed to piece together the core elements." She opened the journal, revealing pages of meticulous notes and diagrams. "It's an ancient rite, predating Eldoria's founding. The ritual creates a metaphysical tear—a way to break Nyxmar's hold on our reality."

Ethan leaned forward despite himself, studying the intricate draw-ings. Circles within circles, marked with symbols that seemed to shift when he tried to focus on them.

"These markings match the ones in the clock tower," he said, his voice quieter now.

"Yes. The tower was built as a focal point, a channel between our world and whatever realm Nyxmar inhabits." Dr. Vane's finger traced one of the symbols. "The ritual requires specific conditions—a celes-tial alignment, certain artifacts, and..." She hesitated, her gaze sharp-ening as she met his eyes. "Blood freely given by someone marked by Nyxmar's sigil."

Ethan's chest tightened. The implications sank in like ice water. "How many have tried this before?"

"Seven attempts are documented." Dr. Vane's voice dropped to a near whisper. "The most recent was in 1987. They found pieces of the par-ticipants scattered across three districts. Some of the remains... well, some were still moving." She closed the journal with a heavy sigh. "The one before that, in 1932, ended with an entire family burning alive in their home. Their screams..." Her eyes darkened. "Witnesses said they kept screaming long after their bodies had turned to ash."

"And Lily knows about this?"

"She's been asking questions about the ritual for weeks. But she doesn't have all the details yet." Dr. Vane met his gaze, her blue eyes as cold as the journal in her hands. "The true horror isn't in the failure, Ethan. It's in the success. The last documented successful attempt was in 1784. The ritual worked—for three days, the curse lifted. Then something worse took its place. Something that made the survivors beg for Nyxmar's return."

She looked past him toward the distant fog-shrouded skyline. "They wrote about it in the darkest terms. Some of the words... don't even have translations."

Dr. Vane pulled a small cloth pouch from her desk drawer. The fabric was stained dark, and the sharp scent of metal hit Ethan's nose before she even loosened the drawstring.

"Your sister brought these last week." She emptied the pouch onto her desk—three tarnished copper coins, their surfaces etched with symbols Ethan recognized too well. "They're grave offerings from Eldoria's founding families. She found them in the cemetery behind St. Michael's."

Ethan's hand shook as he picked up one of the coins. The metal felt wrong against his skin, too warm, too alive. "She's been grave robbing?"

"The coins are just the beginning." Dr. Vane spread out a series of photographs—ancient artifacts laid out on what looked like Lily's bedroom floor. "The medallion, the coins, dried herbs that only bloom during the dark moon. She's collecting components faster than any researcher I've worked with."

The room seemed to grow colder. In the photos, Ethan recognized Lily's familiar bedspread, the corner of her desk where she'd once done her homework. Now, it was covered in symbols—crudely drawn and unmistakably marked with what looked like blood.

"When did she bring these to you?"

"Three days ago." Dr. Vane's fingers drummed against her desk. "She's already mapped the celestial alignment for next month's eclipse. She's not just researching anymore, Ethan. She's preparing."

Ethan's chest tightened. He should storm into her apartment, burn the research, and drag her out before she got herself killed. But he knew

Lily—she wouldn't stop, and he wasn't sure he had the strength to face her resolve. But the thought of confronting her, of seeing that determined look in her eyes—the same look she'd had when their parents died when she'd refused to let anyone help her through the grief—paralyzed him.

"I need time," he managed, though the words tasted like ash. "To think. To figure out how to handle this."

Dr. Vane's expression hardened. "Time isn't something we have in abundance, Mr. Marlowe. Your sister's racing toward something she doesn't understand, and she's not slowing down."

Ethan's hand tightened around the brass doorknob, his knuckles turning white. The floorboards groaned beneath his feet as he hesitated, ready to leave.

"Mr. Marlowe." Dr. Vane's voice cut through the silence. "There's something else you should know."

He paused, not turning around. The weight of the copper coins in his pocket felt heavier now, like a brand searing through the fabric.

"The Night Watch isn't just a game of chance." Papers rustled as she stood from her desk. "Those who dig too deep, who pry into the curse's secrets—they attract attention. And not the kind you want."

Ethan's shoulders tensed. Through the dusty window, the Clock Tower's shadow stretched across the street below, darker than it should have been in the morning light.

"Your sister's research," Dr. Vane continued, her heels clicking against the hardwood as she approached. "The medallion, the coins, the ritual preparations—each piece she uncovers, each secret she exposes... it's like lighting a beacon in the dark. And the darkness always notices."

"You mean—"

"The Watch notices those who notice it, Mr. Marlowe. And Lily?" The sound of Dr. Vane's pen tapping against her desk punctuated the silence. "She's been noticing quite a lot lately."

A chill crept up Ethan's spine as he remembered the glowing sigil on that terrified man's arm, how it had pulsed like a living thing. He thought of Lily's apartment, walls covered in research, ancient symbols drawn in blood.

"How long has she been in danger?" Ethan's voice cracked, the weight of the truth pressing down like an invisible hand around his throat.

"Since she started collecting the artifacts?" Dr. Vane's pause stretched thin. "She's been on its radar for weeks, Mr. Marlowe. Maybe longer."

Ethan's boots scuffed along the cracked pavement as he left Dr. Vane's office. The coins weighed down his pocket, an uncomfortable reminder of what Lily had set in motion. The sky above had turned that peculiar shade of orange, the one that always signalled sunset in Eldoria—too bright and unnatural, like the city was trying to hide something.

He passed boarded-up storefronts, their windows plastered with layers of old newspapers and missing person posters, the faces behind the faded ink blending into one another. A woman hurried past, clutching her bag close, eyes fixed on the ground. The city felt wrong like it was fading away piece by piece, slowly dissolving under the weight of the curse.

The conversation with Dr. Vane replayed in his mind. Lily wasn't just researching anymore—she was collecting pieces of something ancient and terrible. Each artifact, each blood-drawn symbol, brought her closer to whatever darkness lurked beneath Eldoria's surface.

His hand brushed his phone. He could call her, try to reason with her. But how could he admit that everything she'd warned him about—the 'crazy theories'—were becoming all too real? That ignoring them had been his mistake? That he'd failed her by ignoring the very danger she warned him about? That he'd failed to protect her by dismissing the very danger she'd tried to warn him about?

The shadows lengthened across the street, swallowing the fading daylight. Store owners flipped their signs to 'CLOSED,' metal gates rattling down over darkened windows. The exodus before sunset had begun—Eldoria's collective retreat from whatever hunted its nights.

Ethan's steps slowed as he approached the intersection leading to Lily's apartment. The coins weighed heavier with each step like anchors dragging him down. He'd seen that glowing mark and heard the screams that echoed through Eldoria's nights. He knew the truth now, but instead of clarity, it brought only helplessness. Knowing what lurked in Eldoria's shadows made the darkness feel all the more suffocating.

The Clock Tower loomed ahead, its shadow impossibly long for this time of day. It seemed to watch him with cold, patient eyes, a predator waiting for its prey to stumble into its jaws.

The sun dipped lower, painting the buildings in shades of blood and rust. Time was slipping away, but Ethan's feet refused to move. He stood frozen at the crossroads, paralyzed by the weight of his failure. The sense that something terrible was already moving toward him—it pressed against his chest like a vice, tightening with every second he hesitated.

Chapter Five

WEIGHT OF PROMISE

The sun bled across Eldoria's skyline, painting the city in shades of crimson and amber. Ethan watched from the corner of Maple and Fifth as storekeepers yanked down their metal shutters, the harsh clanking echoing through emptying streets. A mother hurried past, dragging her crying child by the hand, keys already clutched between white-knuckled fingers.

The city transformed with the fading light. Shadows stretched longer than they should, twisting into shapes that seemed to writhe just out of sight. The air grew thick and sticky, carrying that familiar metallic tang that always preceded nightfall.

Through gaps between buildings, the Clock Tower's spire pierced the darkening sky. Its face glowed with an unnatural light, hands creeping closer to the hour when the curse would take hold.

Doors slammed in rapid succession down the block. The click of locks and rattle of chains created a desperate symphony of fear. A cat darted across Ethan's path, fur bristling, and vanished into a storm drain. Even the animals knew what was coming.

The last rays of sunlight withdrew from the tallest windows, leaving a purple twilight pulsing with something dark and watchful. The temperature dropped sharply, raising goosebumps on Ethan's arms. His breath fogged in front of him, though the air was far from cold, adding to the unnatural feel of the evening.

An old man shuffled past, muttering prayers under his breath. The rosary wrapped around his gnarled fingers caught the dying light, beads clicking together like tiny bones. Above them, neon signs flickered to life, their harsh glow unable to pierce the gathering gloom.

The coins in Ethan's pocket grew colder, seeming to vibrate with an energy that matched the city's mounting tension. The few remaining pedestrians moved like frightened animals, backs pressed against walls, eyes darting between shadows. Their footsteps quickened with each passing minute, a desperate race against the approaching darkness.

A low hum filled the air, more felt than heard like the city was holding its breath in fearful anticipation. The curse was coming. Everyone could feel it, that creeping dread that marked the start of another Night Watch.

***

Ethan paced his apartment, wearing a path in the threadbare carpet between his desk and the window. The case files he'd tried reviewing lay scattered across his desk, forgotten. Dr. Vane's warnings echoed in his mind, mixing with fragments of Lily's excited theories about ancient rites and forgotten magic.

He grabbed the whiskey bottle and poured two fingers into the glass, leaving it untouched. The amber liquid reflected the light from his desk lamp, too much like the eerie glow of the Clock Tower's face.

"The Ritual of Severance," he muttered. The words felt wrong on his tongue, foreign and thick, like speaking a dead language.

His sister's voice played back in his memory: "Dr. Vane found references to it in texts dating back to Eldoria's founding. She thinks it was attempted once before, in 1892."

Ethan ran his hand through his hair, gripping it tight enough to hurt. Years of detective work and his instinct for logic screamed at him to dismiss it all. Ancient rites didn't break curses. Hell, curses weren't even real. But the weight of his detective badge pressing against his chest was a cold reminder of all the unsolved cases—the ones that never made sense and gnawed at the edges of reason.

The sound of breaking glass outside made him jump. It was just a cat knocking over trash, but his heart wouldn't slow down. The darkness pressed against the window, thicker than usual—heavy, almost alive, as if the night itself was waiting for something.

Dr. Vane's office came back to him—papers everywhere, but organized in their chaos. The way her hands had trembled when she spoke about the failed ritual, about how it had twisted something in the city's foundations. Made the curse stronger, hungrier.

"It's folklore," he said to his empty apartment. "Stories to explain what we can't understand."

But the words rang hollow, like lying to himself in a mirror. His reflection in the window looked haunted, older than his years. The city's lights flickered beyond the glass, and for a moment, he could have sworn they pulsed in rhythm with his racing heart.

The whiskey glass stayed untouched as Ethan's mind drifted to that morning outside St. Michael's. Father Gabriel had stood on the church steps, his thin frame backlit by the stained glass windows. A small crowd huddled around him, shoulders hunched, eyes darting toward shadows.

"The darkness tests us," Father Gabriel's voice carried across the square, steady despite the weariness etched in his face. "But even the smallest flame can pierce the deepest night."

A woman in the crowd broke down, mascara trailing black tears down her cheeks. "My son—he's marked. The sigil appeared last night."

Father Gabriel descended the steps and placed weathered hands on her shoulders. "Then we shall pray together, sister. Not just for survival, but for the strength to face what comes."

The priest's eyes had met Ethan's across the square. There was something in that gaze—not just compassion, but a fierce determination that made Ethan look away first.

"The curse feeds on fear," Father Gabriel had said, his fingers tracing the silver cross at his neck. "But more than that, it thrives on surrender. Each time we turn away and ignore a neighbor's cry, its grip tightens."

Ethan shifted in his chair, the memory gnawing at him. He'd done exactly that, hadn't he? He turned away from the marked man in the alley and told himself it wasn't his fight.

"There are worse things than death, Detective." Father Gabriel's words had pierced Ethan's cynicism. "To live without hope, without purpose—that is the true darkness. Sometimes the greatest act of faith is simply standing your ground when everything tells you to run."

The clock on Ethan's wall ticked, and each sound was like a hammer strike in the quiet apartment. Father Gabriel's words seemed to hang in the air, heavy with meaning he wasn't ready to face.

The first toll of midnight hit Ethan like a physical blow. He stood at his apartment window, watching darkness pool between buildings. The bells continued their count. Two. Three. Four.

The usual city sounds—distant sirens, the hum of traffic, even the whir of his ancient heating unit—faded with each resonant strike. By the eighth toll, the silence pressed in, suffocating his eardrums.

His fingers brushed the cold glass. "A great personal sacrifice," he whispered, the words vanishing into the void between bells. Nine. Ten.

Dr. Vane's office flashed through his mind—papers scattered across every surface, her steady hands trembling as she pulled out a weathered journal. "The ritual failed because they weren't willing to give up what mattered most," she'd said. "Not just blood or life, but something deeper. The heart's truth."

Eleven.

Lily's voice overlapped in his memory: "The relic's just a focal point, Ethan. The real power comes from what we're willing to lose. What we choose to surrender."

The final toll struck, catching Ethan's breath in his chest. The darkness outside seemed to thicken, gathering like ink in water. Street lights flickered and dimmed as if drawing back from what prowled the night.

He pressed his forehead against the cool window. Logic screamed that none of this was real—no curses, no rituals, no ancient relics with the power to save or damn a city. But the silence that gripped Eldoria spoke of things beyond reason, beyond the safe boundaries of what he'd always believed.

His reflection stared back at him, ghost-pale against the glass. The same look he'd seen in Dr. Vane's eyes when she'd warned him about the ritual's price. The same expression Lily wore when she pored over her research, searching for answers in centuries-old texts.

A great personal sacrifice. The words echoed, mocking his attempts to dismiss them as fairy tales and desperate hopes.

***

Ethan's phone shattered the silence, its sharp ring pulling him away from the window. Lily's name flashed on the screen.

"I need you." Her voice cracked, stripped of its usual confidence. "The sigil—it appeared on my arm. I can see it glowing through my sweater sleeve."

The floor seemed to tilt beneath his feet. His throat tightened, a deep fear twisting inside him. "Where are you?"

"My apartment. Ethan, listen—this isn't just about me anymore. Dr. Vane and I found something in the archives. The Ritual of Severance... it's not just theory. It's our only chance to end this."

Papers rustled on her end. "The relic acts as a focal point for the ritual. If we can find it before—" Her breath hitched. "Before whatever hunts the marked finds me, we can break the curse. Not just for me—for everyone."

"Stay where you are. I'm coming—"

"No! You don't understand. The mark chose me because I was getting close. Dr. Vane said the curse adapts and targets threats. But that means we're right. The ritual works."

Ethan grabbed his jacket, keys already in hand. "How can you be sure?"

"Because the last time someone attempted the ritual, they almost succeeded. The curse weakened. That's why it's choosing people connected to the research now—it's protecting itself."

The pieces clicked together—Dr. Vane's warnings, the ancient texts, the victims. All of it pointing to this moment, this chance to end the nightmare gripping Eldoria.

"I'm on my way. Don't move, don't—"

"Just hurry," Lily whispered. "Please."

Ethan's hand trembled as he stared at the phone, its screen dimming before fading to black, reflecting the hollowness in his own eyes. His sister—marked. The thought hit like shards of ice, cutting through the fog of disbelief.

The familiar walls of his apartment seemed to close in on him. Andrea's mangled body flashed in his mind, crime scene photos burning like fire behind his eyes. The same fate awaited Lily if he failed her, too.

He paced the worn floorboards, fingers clawing through his hair—the Ritual of Severance. Days ago, he'd scoffed at it—just another of Lily's obsessions. But now it pulsed in his mind, a terrible possibility. What if she's right? What if all those deaths, all that blood and horror, could have been prevented if someone had just believed?

His eyes fell on the scattered case files. Every victim was found at dawn; bodies twisted in ways that defied reason. No witnesses. No suspects. The only link between them was the sigil—a death mark as constant as it was unexplainable.

"Think," he muttered, pressing his palms to his temples. The clock tower's shadow stretched across the wall like a dark finger pointing toward an inevitable doom. Lily had the research. Dr. Vane had the knowledge. But the relic—where would they even begin to search?

His chest tightened. The curse was adapting, targeting those who posed a real threat. It had chosen Lily because she was getting too close to the truth. The realization terrified him, but in an odd way, it also steadied him.

Ethan's hand traced the scar above his eyebrow, a reminder of past failures. But this wasn't just another case. This was Lily. The one person he'd promised to protect—now caught in the same nightmare he'd been powerless to stop before.

He pulled his gun from the drawer, checking the clip even though he knew it was already full. But would bullets even work against whatever hunted the marked? The weight of the gun felt like false reassurance as his mind spun with possibilities—each one more terrifying than the last.

****

Ethan burst through Lily's apartment door, his heart hammering against his ribs. Books and papers covered every surface, creating a maze of research that led to her hunched figure by the window.

She turned, moonlight catching the silver-blue glow on her forearm. The sigil's serpentine eye seemed to pulse, its ancient glyphs dancing across her skin.

"We don't have much time." Lily's voice trembled, but her eyes blazed with purpose. She grabbed a weathered journal from her desk. "Dr. Vane decoded part of the text. The relic—it's an obsidian mirror, carved with the same symbols as the sigil. She thinks it's hidden in the catacombs beneath the Old Quarter."

"Lily, we need to get you somewhere safe—"

"There is no safe!" She slammed her palm on the desk, her voice tinged with desperation. "Don't you get it? Everyone who's been marked... they all died hiding. But the ritual..." She thrust a page of translations at him. "Dr. Vane found references to it working before. Someone almost broke the curse a century ago."

Ethan's fingers brushed the sigil on her arm, its unnatural chill seeping into his skin, igniting an instinct to pull her away from this madness. But seeing her conviction, that same fierce spark their mother once had, kept him rooted.

"Please." Lily gripped his sleeve, her hand trembling slightly. "I know you think I'm crazy, but I'd rather die trying to end this than wait for whatever's coming for me. And if we succeed..." Her voice steadied, and a glint of hope surfaced in her eyes. "No one else will have to face this. No more Andrea Bondys. No more marked victims."

The determination in her eyes reminded him of their mother—the same stubborn set of her jaw, the same unflinching courage in the face of impossible odds. His protective instincts roared to shield her, yet he knew now that he couldn't hold her back from this.

"Dr. Vane left markers in the catacombs," Lily continued, squeezing his hand tighter. "She's been mapping them for months, preparing for this. But I can't do it alone." She looked up, eyes pleading. "I need my big brother. One last time."

The clock tower's shadow stretched across her floor like a sundial, counting down their remaining hours. Ethan looked at the sigil again, its glow an ominous reminder of how little time they had left.

He took a deep breath. "Tell me everything Dr. Vane found."

***

Ethan's hand rested on Lily's back as they descended the apartment stairs, each step echoing in the empty stairwell. Her research journal clutched against her chest, Lily moved with purpose despite the tremor in her hands.

They slipped into the alley behind her building. The narrow passage trapped the night air, thick and heavy around them. Moonlight caught the sigil on Lily's arm, its glow casting strange shadows on the brick walls.

"The catacombs entrance is through St. Michael's," Lily whispered, her breath visible in the cold. "Dr. Vane left markers—symbols that'll guide us to the relic's chamber." She opened the journal, pages rustling. "See these patterns? They match the sigil's outer rings."

Ethan studied the drawings, forcing himself to focus past the supernatural horror of it all. The familiar weight of his gun pressed against his side, useless as it might be.

"How long?" His voice came out rougher than intended.

"The marked never survive past dawn." Lily's fingers traced the glowing pattern on her arm. "But that's not what scares me. Whatever hunts us—it usually finds its victims within hours."

The truth of what they faced hit Ethan like a physical blow. His sister was marked for death, their only hope lying in ancient tunnels beneath the city. Part of him still wanted to grab her, run, hide—but he'd seen how that ended for others.

"I know this is hard to believe," Lily said, touching his arm. "But I need you with me—really with me, not just following to protect me."

Ethan looked at her—really looked. Gone was the little sister who'd needed his protection. In her place stood someone stronger, braver than he'd allowed himself to see.

"I'm with you." The words came easier than he expected. "All the way."

The clock tower's bells rang out, marking the hour. Lily grabbed his hand, squeezing once before letting go.

"Then let's move. We've got a ritual to complete."

CHAPTER SIX

PATH OF NO RETURN

The distant wail of sirens pierced the night as Ethan and Lily crept through Eldoria's darkened streets. Shadows closed in around them, every faint noise making Ethan's hand twitch toward his gun. The cursed city loomed, oppressive and watchful, as if it could sense their fear.

His eyes struggled to focus as Lily consulted her journal at each turn. The sigil on her arm pulsed, casting an eerie glow across her determined face. She moved with purpose, her steps confident and sure, while he trailed behind, each of his steps weighed down by a doubt he couldn't shake. Andrea's face flickered in his mind, a ghost he couldn't escape. He'd missed the signs and hadn't been there when she needed him most. And now, with Lily marked... was he doomed to repeat his greatest failure? His hands trembled at the thought of history repeating itself.

"Left here," Lily whispered, but Ethan barely heard her through the thunder of his own heartbeat.

A cat knocked over a trash can three blocks away. Ethan shoved Lily against a wall, shielding her with his body. His breath came in sharp bursts as memories of other marked victims surfaced—their mangled bodies, the terror frozen on their faces.

"Ethan." Lily's voice cut through his spiral. "You're crushing me."

He stepped back, shame burning his cheeks as Lily steadied herself. Some protector he was, rattled by shadows while she, marked and hunted, remained composed. The weight of responsibility pressed down on his shoulders, threatening to crush him.

The sigil pulsed again, brighter this time. Lily didn't flinch, but Ethan's stomach lurched. What if he couldn't save her? What if all his determination, all his promises amounted to nothing more than empty words?

He'd spent years building walls, convincing himself that distance meant safety. Now, faced with losing her, those walls crumbled to dust.

His hand found hers in the darkness, gripping it like a lifeline. She squeezed back, strong and steady—everything he wasn't feeling. Her hand, steady and warm, anchored him, while his own heartbeat pounded like a war drum, every beat pulsing with a fear that felt as old as the curse itself.

***

The familiar streets of the Old Quarter had twisted into a distorted version of themselves, as if the city's bones had shifted in the dark, reshaping alleys and corners into something hostile and predatory. Ethan's feet caught on cracked pavement that hadn't existed hours ago. Ancient brownstones curved inward, their windows watching like hungry eyes.

The city itself seemed to breathe around them, transformed by whatever dark force powered the curse.

Lily stopped abruptly, her hand tightening on his arm. "Look at this."

Deep gouges ran along the brick facade of a nearby building, each groove wide enough to fit Ethan's arm. The marks raked downward, carving through solid stone as if it were butter. Below, the sidewalk bore massive impressions, each footprint sinking inches into the concrete, large enough to swallow his own twice over.

"Those weren't made by any person," Lily whispered, her voice tight. The sigil on her arm pulsed brighter, as if responding to something in the air. Ethan ran his fingers along one of the grooves. The edges were sharp, fresh. "Could be structural damage from—"

A low, guttural rumble rolled through the streets, cutting him off. It wasn't thunder—it was deeper, primal, vibrating through his chest like the growl of some ancient predator stirring from slumber.

Lily pressed closer to him, her eyes scanning the twisted streets ahead. "There's something else out here. Something watching." Her breath hitched. "Can't you feel it?"

He wanted to dismiss it as paranoia, to lean on logic and reason as he'd always done. But the patterns in the destruction—the sharp, fresh edges of the claw marks—told a story no rational explanation could unravel. Whatever had torn through these streets wasn't human. The systematic nature of the damage, the deliberate way it marked its territory—this was something hunting them.

The sigil's glow intensified, casting strange shadows across the warped buildings. Another rumble rolled through the streets, closer this time. Ethan's hand found his gun, though he doubted it would do much good against whatever was stalking them.

"We need to move," he said, tugging Lily's arm and quickening his pace. The rumbles echoed behind them, closer, as if urging them to run.

***

The air grew thicker as they moved deeper into the Old Quarter, and Ethan's mind drifted to his last conversation with Dr. Vane in her cluttered office. Her voice, calm and measured, cut through his present fear. "The Night Watch isn't just about physical survival," she had said, organizing her scattered notes with practiced precision. "It's designed to break you mentally. The curse feeds on fear, doubt, guilt. Every shadow will twist into your worst nightmare, every sound will echo with past failures."

An inhuman growl rippled through the streets, vibrating through his bones. Ethan's vision blurred, and for a heartbeat, Andrea's bloodied face replaced Lily's. He blinked, forcing himself back, heart pounding against his ribs.

"The curse will use your memories against you," Dr. Vane's words echoed. "It will make you question what's real. Trust becomes your greatest weapon, but also your greatest vulnerability."

Lily stumbled, and when Ethan caught her arm, her skin felt ice-cold. The sigil's glow pulsed erratically, casting strange patterns on the fog around them. For a split second, her face morphed into a grotesque mask of death, eyes hollow and skin gray. Ethan jerked back, Dr. Vane's warning ringing in his ears.

"Your mind will try to protect you by rejecting what you see," she had explained, her blue eyes piercing through him. "But denial is dangerous.

Acknowledge the fear, but don't let it control you. The curse wants you to doubt everything—especially each other."

The memory of her words steadied him. Ethan forced himself to look at Lily—really look at her. Past the tricks of light and shadow, past the curse's attempts to distort her features, he found his sister's determined green eyes staring back at him.

"You okay?" Lily whispered, her hand finding his in the darkness.

"We need to reach St. Michael's before dawn." Lily's voice cut through the fog of Ethan's fear. She pulled out a worn journal, its pages covered in cramped writing and strange symbols. "The mirror won't work anywhere else. The church sits on a convergence point of old ley lines."

Ethan's mouth went dry. The thought of crossing half the city with that thing hunting them made his skin crawl. But Lily's steady movements as she traced their route on a wrinkled map grounded him. Her hands didn't shake. Her voice remained clear and focused.

"See these markings?" She pointed to symbols sketched along the church's foundation in her notes. "They're not just decorative. They're part of an ancient warding system. Dr. Vane found references to them in texts predating the city's founding."

The sigil on her arm pulsed, but she barely seemed to notice. Instead, she flipped through more pages, comparing notes with the intensity he remembered from her college studies. Even marked for death, she approached this like any other research project.

"The Ritual of Severance requires three components—the mirror, the marked one, and consecrated ground. St. Michael's is the only place where the energies align properly." She snapped the journal shut. "We have five hours until dawn."

Her certainty steadied his racing thoughts. While his mind spun with memories of mangled bodies and blood-splattered walls, she focused on solutions, on survival. The curse might have marked her, but it hadn't broken her spirit.

***

The night air hung thick around them as they navigated through the twisted streets. Ethan's footsteps matched Lily's, their synchronized movement born from years of shared blood and history. The sigil's glow cast dancing shadows across the crumbling walls, but for a moment, the rumbles in the distance faded.

Lily paused to check her bearings, and Ethan studied her profile in the dim light. The determined set of her jaw, the focused gleam in her eyes—he saw echoes of their mother there. The same stubborn strength that had carried their family through the darkest times.

His chest tightened. When had his little sister grown so fierce? He remembered her first steps, her scraped knees, the way she'd clutch his hand during thunderstorms. Now she faced down ancient curses with unwavering resolve while he struggled to keep his fears in check.

She caught him staring and raised an eyebrow. "What?"

"Nothing." He cleared his throat. "Just... you remind me of Mom."

The words hung between them, delicate as spun glass. Their mother had been gone for fifteen years, but her absence still ached like a fresh wound.

Lily's expression softened. She reached out and squeezed his arm—the same gesture their mother used when words failed. "She'd be proud of you, you know. The way you've always looked out for me."

"Even when I'm being overprotective?"

"Especially then." A ghost of a smile crossed her face. "That's what big brothers are for."

The moment stretched between them, filled with years of shared memories and unspoken fears. For a heartbeat, the curse fell away. They weren't marked prey or desperate survivors—just a brother and sister, facing the darkness together.

Then the rumble returned, closer now, and reality crashed back. But something had shifted. Ethan's fear hadn't vanished, but it felt different now. More focused. This wasn't just about protecting Lily anymore—it was about standing with her, trusting her strength as much as his own.

***

A figure stumbled out of the shadows ahead, moving with jerky, unnatural motions. The sigil on Lily's arm blazed bright enough to illuminate her face—a middle-aged woman, her cheeks streaked with blood, eyes wide and darting, but strangely unfocused.

"Please," she whispered, her voice cracking as she looked past them. "He's in my head. Make it stop."

Ethan's hand moved to his gun, but Lily grabbed his wrist. "Wait," she hissed, her voice taut. "Something's wrong."

The woman's head snapped up, her neck craning at an unnatural angle. Her gaze fixed on them, but her eyes reflected something else—a cold, calculating intent that didn't match the fear on her face.

"Like puppets on strings," she said, her voice dropping to a deeper, unnatural tone. "We dance for his amusement."

She staggered forward, producing a knife from her coat with disjointed, puppet-like movements, as though someone else controlled her limbs. Ethan shoved Lily behind him, but the woman's attack was aimed at herself. She dragged the blade across her own arm, carving the flesh as if compelled.

"He watches," she snarled, her hand trembling against her own will, forcing the knife higher. "He pulls the threads. Makes us hurt. Makes us kill."

The sigil on her arm pulsed in eerie synchrony with Lily's, casting strange, looping shadows in the darkness. For a brief second, Ethan's gaze lifted to a window above, where a tall, cloaked figure stood watching, his presence radiating a chilling, controlling authority.

"Stop fighting," the woman whimpered, her original voice bleeding through. "Please. He'll only make it worse." Her body jerked, caught in a twisted battle between resistance and submission, her limbs contorting as though something unseen pulled them tight.

Lily took a step forward, her own sigil flaring in response. "Who's controlling you?"

Recognition flickered in the woman's eyes—not of Lily, but of something within her words. "The Architect," she whispered, the terror stripping her voice raw. "He shapes our pain. Builds his power from our fear."

Her body seized, spine arcing back at an impossible angle. When she straightened, her eyes had gone empty, all traces of humanity erased. She raised the knife again, with a dreadful, mechanical precision, as though controlled by the hand of someone high above.

The sigil on Lily's arm flared with sudden intensity, casting strange patterns across the crumbling brick walls. She gasped, clutching her marked skin as the ethereal light pulsed in rhythmic waves.

Ethan's stomach twisted. "What's happening?"

"It's... pulling me." Lily turned in a slow circle, her arm extended like a compass needle. The light dimmed when she faced certain directions, but blazed brighter toward others. "This way. Through the alley."

The narrow passage she indicated was barely visible in the darkness, wedged between two ancient buildings that seemed to lean together overhead. Ethan's instincts screamed at him to grab Lily and run the opposite direction. Every case he'd worked, every victim he'd found—they'd all started with someone following strange compulsions into dark places.

"Lily, wait—" He reached for her, but she was already moving, drawn forward as if tethered by an invisible thread. With each step toward the alley, the sigil's glow intensified, casting ghostly shadows across the narrowing path.

"Can't you feel it?" she whispered, pressing her hand against the wall, tracing patterns only she could see. "The energy here... it's like veins running through the city, channels of power connecting everything."

"What I feel is that we're being herded." Ethan caught up to her, his hand hovering near his gun. "Whatever this thing is, it's leading us somewhere."

"Or showing us the way." The sigil pulsed again, and Lily winced. "The mirror we need—what if the mark is trying to guide us to it?"

Ethan watched the light dance across her skin, unsettling memories surfacing of how similar marks had guided others to their deaths. Yet, something was different in the way it responded to Lily, almost as if it acknowledged her understanding of its nature. The glow felt less like a lure to destruction and more... purposeful.

His sister had always seen patterns where he saw only chaos. What if she was right? What if this was their only chance to break the curse? But if she was wrong...

The sigil flared again, brighter than before, its light catching on a symbol carved into the bricks—a pattern Ethan recognized from Lily's research journals.

***

Ethan's grip tightened on his gun as they moved deeper into the alley. Every shadow held potential threats, and his mind raced with possibilities. He'd seen what desperate people did when cornered—how survival stripped away humanity layer by layer until only the animal remained. The thought of Lily facing that kind of violence made his chest constrict. He'd already failed to protect Andrea. The memory of finding her body, broken and discarded like trash, still haunted his dreams. Now Lily bore the same mark that had sealed Andrea's fate.

"There must be others," Lily said, studying her glowing sigil. "The curse never chooses just one person for The Night Watch."

A faint scrape sounded behind them, too soft to be a misstep of their own but close enough to make Ethan's hand tighten on his gun. He shot a glance over his shoulder, his eyes sweeping the rooftops and shadowed windows. Nothing. Just flickering streetlights and the hum of the city. Yet, a prickle ran down his spine, like invisible eyes tracking their every move.

That's what worried him. Other marked ones could be anywhere—hiding in doorways, crouching behind dumpsters, watching from windows.

Would they band together against whatever hunted them? Or would fear turn them against each other?

He'd heard whispers about a mercenary in town, someone who specialized in supernatural threats. Marcus Voss. The name kept surfacing in his investigations, always connected to violence and death. If someone like that got marked...

Another sound—a rustling from an open window a few stories up, as if someone was leaning just out of sight. He met Lily's gaze and saw the same question in her eyes: Are we alone?

"We can't trust anyone," Ethan muttered, scanning the rooflines. "Not everyone marked will want to break the curse. Some might try to use it, try to control it."

"Or they might help us." Lily's optimism cut through his dark thoughts. "We're stronger together."

But Ethan had seen too many alliances shatter under pressure. He'd watched partners turn on each other when fear took hold. The curse wouldn't just test their courage—it would test their trust, their loyalty, their humanity itself.

And in a game where everyone was marked for death, who could they really trust?

***

Ethan watched Lily check her notes against a crumbling street sign, her movements precise despite the sigil's pulsing glow. No trembling hands, no panicked breathing—just the same focused determination she brought to her research. The mark that had reduced others to terrified wrecks seemed to fuel her instead.

She caught him staring and raised an eyebrow. "What?"

"Nothing." He shook his head, studying how she held herself. Gone was the little sister who used to hide behind him during thunderstorms. In her place stood someone who faced down ancient curses with squared shoulders and steady hands. "Just... you're handling this better than most."

"Better than you expected?" A hint of amusement crossed her face as she traced another symbol in her journal. The sigil flared, but she barely flinched, just adjusted her grip on the pen and continued writing.

"Better than anyone would expect." Ethan remembered the woman they'd encountered earlier, how the mark had twisted her into a puppet of fear. Yet here was Lily, using its light to illuminate her notes, treating it like just another tool in her research.

She glanced up from her work, expression softening. "I've been studying this curse for years, Ethan. I'm not going to let it control me now that I finally have a chance to break it."

The quiet conviction in her voice struck him. While he'd been drowning in guilt and denial, she'd been preparing, learning, building her defenses against this very moment. The mark hadn't caught her unprepared—it had found her ready for war.

"The sigil's pulling stronger now." She rolled her shoulder, adjusting to another pulse of light. "We should keep moving."

Ethan nodded, falling into step beside her. The curse might have marked her for its game, but Lily had turned the board in her favor. She wasn't running from the danger—she was walking straight toward it, armed with knowledge and an unshakeable will to survive.

The empty streets stretched before them like the bones of a dead city. Ethan's boots scraped against broken concrete, each step echoing off brick walls. He'd walked these roads countless times during investigations, but tonight they felt alien, hostile.

A window creaked somewhere above. Lily's hand shot to his arm, freezing them both in place. They waited, muscles tense, but only the wind whispered through the gap.

The sigil's glow cast strange shadows as they moved, transforming familiar doorways into gaping mouths, window frames into hollow eyes. Even the rats had gone quiet, as if nature itself held its breath.

Distant footsteps echoed from three blocks over—too measured to be random, too deliberate to be safe. Ethan guided Lily into a shadowed alcove, pressing close to cold stone as the steps faded away.

"Listen," Lily whispered, barely audible.

He did. Beyond the usual night sounds—the settling of old buildings, the hum of distant power lines—something else threaded through the darkness. A rhythm, almost subliminal, like the city itself was breathing. The air grew thick, pressing against his skin. Each breath felt heavy, loaded with anticipation. They were being watched—not by eyes, but by something older, something woven into Eldoria's very foundations.

A bottle rolled across the street, the glass scraping concrete. The sound cut through the silence like a gunshot. Ethan's hand found his weapon, but nothing emerged from the shadows. Just another empty street, another moment of tension stretching tight as piano wire.

They moved on, each step calculated, each breath measured. The night pressed closer, transforming familiar landmarks into twisted versions of themselves. Even the streetlights seemed dimmer, as if the darkness was slowly consuming them.

Chapter Seven

THE SIREN'S CALL

Ethan's legs burned with each step, his calves twitching, vision blurring at the edges from the endless pace. The weight of his gun pressed against his side, a constant reminder of dangers lurking in every shadow. He glanced at Lily, noting the sheen of sweat on her forehead despite the cold night air.

"We need to rest." His voice came out rougher than intended.

"Can't." Lily winced, rubbing her marked arm. "The sigil - it gets worse if we stop moving," she muttered, looking at her arm where the sigil's faint glow pulsed, a heartbeat that seemed to throb in her bones, driving her forward. Dark circles ringed her eyes, the confidence she'd shown hours earlier now worn down to bare determination. She stumbled on a broken piece of sidewalk. Ethan caught her arm, steadying her.

"Five minutes." He guided her toward a recessed doorway. "Just five minutes to catch our breath."

Lily slumped against the wall, sliding down until she sat on the cold concrete. Her hands trembled as she pulled out her water bottle, the plastic crinkling too loud in the empty street. She took a sip, then offered it to him.

Ethan shook his head. "Keep it. You need it more."

"Don't go all big-brother on me," she muttered, though her tone lacked bite, replaced with resignation. "We both know who led us here."

The sigil flared again, making Lily hiss through clenched teeth. She pushed herself up, swaying slightly. "We have to keep moving. North. It wants us to go north."

"Following that thing's directions doesn't seem smart."

"You have a better plan?"

Ethan didn't. His body ached, his mind felt fuzzy from lack of sleep, and every shadow held potential threats. He'd tracked suspects through these streets for days at a time, but this was different. The city itself seemed to drain their energy, each step requiring more effort than the last.

Lily started walking again, her movements stiff and mechanical. Ethan followed, fighting the urge to close his burning eyes. The night stretched endlessly before them, shadows pooling like ink around broken street lamps, each corner inviting danger and darkness.

A sharp, metallic click echoed off the brick walls; each beat cutting through the night with surgical precision. Ethan's hand moved to his holster, fingers wrapping around cold metal. Another click—deliberate, measured footsteps on concrete.

"Keep walking," he whispered to Lily. "Don't look back."

The footsteps maintained their steady rhythm, neither speeding up nor slowing down. Not the frantic pace of someone running from the curse, or the stumbling gait of its victims. These steps carried purpose.

Lily's breath caught. "They're getting closer."

Ethan guided her around a corner, ears straining. The follower matched their turn, maintaining distance. The sound bounced off walls, making it impossible to gauge exactly how far behind they were.

A car alarm blared three blocks away. Ethan seized the moment, shifting into position, instinctively placing himself between Lily and their pursuer. Years of tracking killers told him that this wasn't a mindless chase—it was a game of dominance. The footsteps never faltered, never changed their calculated pace.

"This way." He pulled Lily into a narrow alley, pressing against the wall. Their follower's boots scraped against loose gravel, still maintaining that methodical rhythm.

Lily's sigil pulsed brighter, casting blue shadows across their hiding spot. She pressed her marked arm against her jacket, trying to dim the glow.

The footsteps stopped.

Silence pressed against them, thick and stifling, stretching unbearably between each heartbeat. No shuffling, no breath—just the unmistakable presence of someone lurking in the darkness, watching, waiting. A predator's patience.

"They're playing with us," Ethan whispered, his throat tight. He'd tracked enough killers to recognize the difference between prey and hunter. Their pursuer wasn't running from anything—they were stalking.

The footsteps resumed, closer now. Each step precise, intentional, as if the hunter wanted them to feel every inch of his approach. Each click of heel against pavement a statement of control.

The sigil blazed without warning, searing through Lily's sleeve with an unnatural cold that made her flinch. She gasped, stumbling as an invisible force yanked her arm toward a narrow side street.

"This way," she breathed, taking a step in that direction. "It's never been this strong before."

Ethan grabbed her shoulder. "Wait." The calculated footsteps behind them had stopped.

A figure emerged from the shadows, his polished shoes reflecting the sigil's glow. Tall, broad-shouldered, with salt-and-pepper hair and an expensive coat that seemed untouched by the night's grime. He glanced calmly at the shadows around them, adjusting his cuff as if entirely unperturbed by the cursed streets.

"The pull gets stronger near midnight," the man said, his voice carrying a hint of amusement. "Though it's not always honest about where it wants to take you."

Lily's hand tightened around Ethan's sleeve. "Who are you?"

"Marcus." He stepped closer, hands open at his sides. "And that mark on your arm—I've worn it three times now. Survived each game."

Ethan shifted, keeping himself between Marcus and Lily. "Nobody survives multiple rounds."

"Nobody you've heard of." Marcus smiled, the expression never reaching his eyes. "If I wanted you gone, Detective, you'd never have seen me coming."

"The sigil's quite particular about its directions. Sometimes it leads you to salvation." He paused, studying Lily's glowing arm. "Sometimes to slaughter."

"You're saying we shouldn't trust it?" Lily's voice wavered.

"I'm saying I can help you navigate its... quirks." Marcus gestured toward the direction the sigil pulled. "That path, for instance—looks promising, doesn't it? But I know these streets. Know what waits in the darkness ahead."

Ethan's fingers brushed his holster. Marcus noticed, his smile widening slightly.

"No need for that, Detective Marlowe. I'm offering assistance, nothing more. Though time's rather short, and that mark won't wait forever." Marcus extended his hand. "What do you say?"

The sigil pulsed again, more insistent. Ethan exchanged glances with Lily, reading the same uncertainty in her eyes that churned in his gut.

Marcus stood waiting, patient and composed—either their salvation or their executioner.

Ethan studied Marcus's outstretched hand, catching a glint of an expensive watch peeking from beneath his sleeve. His pulse quickened—a composed man in these cursed streets wasn't natural.

"The Ritual of Severance." Marcus lowered his hand, unbothered by Ethan's hesitation. "Your research has led you down that path, hasn't it? Ancient rites, forgotten magic." His gaze shifted to Lily. "But did your books mention the price of breaking such bonds?"

Lily stepped forward. "You know about the ritual?"

"I know many things about this city's darker nature. The ritual itself..." Marcus adjusted his collar. "Let's say I've seen what happens when people attempt to sever ties they don't fully understand."

"You're saying it won't work?" Ethan caught the slight curl of Marcus's lip.

"I'm saying survival requires pragmatism, Detective. The curse operates on rules—brutal ones, but rules nonetheless. Breaking them..." Marcus glanced at the sigil on Lily's arm. "Well, that tends to have consequences."

Ethan's shoulders tensed as he stepped forward. "We don't need riddles. Either help us or don't."

"Direct, aren't you?" Marcus's chuckle was low and humorless before he pointed down a narrow street. "The sigil pulls you north, but two blocks that way lies a nest of those puppet-things you encountered earlier. We go east first and circle around. Slower, but safer."

Ethan's fingers drummed restlessly against his side. Every instinct screamed not to trust this man, but Lily's sigil pulsed again, making her stumble.

"Fine," Ethan said. "But I'm watching you."

"I'd be disappointed if you weren't." Marcus smiled, cold and practiced. "Shall we?"

They fell into step behind him, Ethan keeping one hand near his gun. Marcus moved with precise steps as if the city's corruption couldn't touch him. Each calculated movement reminded Ethan of predators he'd tracked—the ones who played with their prey before striking.

Lily froze mid-step, her hand brushing against the brick wall. Ancient markings caught the glow of her sigil, their shapes seeming to ripple under her touch as if stirred by unseen currents. The symbols formed a pattern that stretched along the building's facade, disappearing into shadows.

"These markings." She traced one with her finger. "Dr. Vane showed me similar ones in her research. They're part of an old binding ritual."

Marcus glanced back, his expression neutral. "Graffiti. Street artists love their mystical symbols."

"No." Lily pulled out her phone, fingers shaking as she swiped through photos. "Look. The same pattern, the same curves. Dr. Vane said they appear where the curse's influence is strongest."

Ethan studied the wall, noting how the symbols seemed to absorb the sigil's light rather than reflect it. "You've seen these before?"

"They're everywhere once you know where to look." Marcus's tone remained dismissive, but Ethan caught the slight tension in his shoulders. "Remnants of old superstitions, nothing more."

Lily shook her head. "Dr. Vane traced their origin to an ancient text. They're control markers, used to channel and direct supernatural energy." She pointed to a specific curve. "This one represents binding. And this—it's about dominion over will."

"Your professor seems to have quite the imagination." Marcus checked his watch. "We should keep moving."

But Ethan noticed how Marcus's eyes lingered on the symbols, his casual dismissal at odds with his careful attention. The markings were too precise, too deliberate to be random graffiti. They spoke of calculation, of purpose—someone marking territory with ancient warnings.

"They're fresh," Ethan said, running his finger along a groove. The stone was newly cut, edges sharp and cold under his fingers as if the markings had only recently been carved. "Someone's maintaining these."

Marcus's smile tightened, but there was a pause before he gestured down the street. "Fascinating theory. But theories won't keep you alive tonight."

Lily photographed the symbols before following, her expression troubled. "Dr. Vane said someone was using these to control the curse's flow through the city. Directing it like water through channels."

Ethan watched Marcus's every move as they approached another intersection. Something about the man's confidence set his teeth on edge—no one should be this composed during the Night Watch.

Marcus held up his hand, stopping them. "We need to head west here."

"The sigil's pulling north." Ethan stepped closer to Lily, whose mark continued to glow steadily in that direction.

Marcus's eyes narrowed as he nodded toward the shadows ahead. "That path north is a feeding ground. Three nights ago, I watched the mist swallow five marked ones. Not even screams made it back."

"And we're supposed to just take your word for it?"

"You're welcome to test my theory, Detective. Though your sister might not appreciate the experiment."

Lily touched Ethan's arm. "Maybe we should listen. If he's survived this before—"

"That's exactly what bothers me." Ethan kept his eyes locked on Marcus. "Nobody survives multiple marks. The odds are impossible."

"Impossible?" Marcus's laugh was sharp and cold. "You still think this is about odds? About probability?" He gestured at the darkness around them. "This is about knowledge, Detective. About understanding the rules of the game."

"Right. And you just happened to find us when we needed guidance."

"Stop it, both of you." Lily stepped between them, though her voice shook. "We don't have time for this. The sigil's getting stronger, and—"

"Your brother's instincts serve him well," Marcus cut in. "But his skepticism will get you killed tonight. I know these streets, know their patterns. West is our only viable option."

Ethan's hand drifted to his holster. "And if we disagree?"

"Then I wish you luck." Marcus's smile didn't reach his eyes. He waited a beat, letting his words sink in. "Though I doubt you'll live long enough to regret your choice."

Marcus brushed a speck of dust from his sleeve, his movements precise and unhurried despite the growing tension. "The marked ones who died last week—they thought they could outrun it. Quite the mess they left behind."

Ethan's stomach turned at Marcus's casual tone. The man spoke of death like discussing weather patterns.

"Those were people," Lily said, her voice tight. "They had families, lives—"

"They had the mark." Marcus cut her off with a wave. "And now they don't. That's the nature of the game—survival requires certain... compromises."

"Compromises?" Ethan stepped forward, jaw clenched. "You're talking about letting people die."

Marcus's lips curved into a cold smile. "I'm talking about understanding priorities. Sometimes, Detective, the only way to get through is to let others fall behind. Your sister's mark?" He nodded toward Lily's arm. "That's your priority. Everyone else is just... collateral."

The word hung in the air, stark and cruel. Lily flinched, wrapping her arms tightly around herself as if to shield against Marcus's calculating gaze.

"That's not how this works," Ethan growled, though doubt crept into his mind. How many times had he turned away from marked victims, telling himself he couldn't help?

"No?" Marcus raised an eyebrow. "Then tell me, Detective—how many marked ones have you saved? How many lives have your noble intentions preserved?" He straightened his cuffs, the gesture almost bored. "The curse demands its toll. Fighting that only gets more people killed."

The casual dismissal of human life made Ethan's skin crawl. This wasn't the perspective of someone trying to help—it was the cold calculation of a survivor who'd learned to step over bodies.

Ethan's neck prickled as they followed Marcus down another winding street. The man's footsteps remained precise, measured—a metronome counting down to something Ethan couldn't see. Three times now, Marcus had redirected them away from Lily's sigil-guided path, each detour leading them deeper into the maze of Eldoria's Old Quarter.

A scream pierced the air—human at first, then warping into something else. Marcus paused at an intersection, head cocked. "Interesting. They're hunting in packs now."

The casual observation made Ethan's stomach turn. He grabbed Lily's arm, pulling her closer as Marcus led them down an alley cluttered with broken furniture and discarded trash. The path narrowed, forcing them to walk single file between towering brick walls.

"Wait." Ethan caught Marcus checking his watch again—the third time in ten minutes. "Why are we stopping?"

"Timing is everything." Marcus glanced at the sky, then at Lily's sigil. "We need to be precise."

"Precise for what?"

Marcus ignored him, consulting his watch once more. The gesture clicked something in Ethan's mind—the way Marcus kept time, his calculated paths, how each detour pushed them further from their original destination. This wasn't guidance. This was choreography. Each detour felt like a nudge into something unseen, and Ethan's instincts buzzed with warning.

"Lily." Ethan kept his voice low. "How's the pull?"

She rubbed her marked arm. "Stronger. But... different. Like it's fighting against itself."

Marcus smiled, the expression sharp in the darkness. "The mark responds to proximity. The closer we get—"

"Closer to what?" Ethan cut him off, noting how Marcus positioned himself between them and the alley's entrance. "Because it seems like you're herding us."

"Such suspicion, Detective." Marcus spread his hands. "I'm merely ensuring we arrive at the right moment."

"The right moment for what?"

Before Marcus could answer, Lily's sigil flared brilliant blue, illuminating the walls around them. Ancient symbols identical to the ones they'd seen earlier covered every surface, their patterns spiralling inward like a web.

Ethan's fingers tightened around his gun as he watched Marcus study the glowing symbols. Every instinct screamed at him to get Lily away from this man, but her hand on his arm held him in place.

"We need him," Lily whispered, her eyes darting between the two men. "Look at how he moves through these streets. He knows things, Ethan. Things that could keep us alive."

"Or get us killed." Ethan's jaw clenched as Marcus traced one of the symbols with practiced familiarity. "Nobody survives three marks, Lily. Nobody."

"Then how else do you explain his knowledge?" She gestured at the markings. "He navigates the curse like... like he helped write its rules."

The thought sent a chill down Ethan's spine. He'd seen that kind of confidence before—in killers who knew every detail of their crimes, who revisited the scenes to relive their moments of power.

"Time to move," Marcus called out, checking his watch again. "The next window opens soon."

Lily tugged at Ethan's sleeve. "Please. Just until we understand more."

Ethan met her gaze, seeing the same determination that had driven her research all these years. He nodded once, sharp and reluctant.

"Lead on," he told Marcus, keeping his hand near his weapon. "But I'm watching every step."

Marcus's smile flickered in the sigil's light. "I'd expect nothing less, Detective."

They followed him deeper into the labyrinth of Eldoria's streets, each turn taking them further from familiar ground. Ethan memorized every corner, every possible escape route, tracking Marcus's movements with the focus of a hunter studying his prey.

The night pressed closer, and with each step, Ethan felt the weight of his decision. He'd let a predator guide them into darkness, gambling with Lily's life on the hope that Marcus's knowledge would prove more valuable than his obvious dangers.

CHAPTER EIGHT

SHADOWS OF REASON

Four hours of constant movement through Eldoria's maze had drained Ethan, and even Lily's determined stride had devolved into an unsteady shuffle. The wet cobblestones threatened to trip them with every footfall.

"We need to rest." Ethan steadied Lily as she stumbled against a brick wall. Her skin felt clammy under his touch.

"Can't." Lily's breath came in sharp gasps. She clutched her marked arm close to her chest, the sigil's glow pulsing like a trapped heartbeat. "It's getting stronger."

Marcus circled back from his position ahead, his movements still precise despite the hours of walking. "The pull doesn't care about human limitations. It will drive you until you break or arrive."

"Arrive where exactly?" Ethan's words slurred at the edges, fatigue clouding his thoughts. The buildings around them had taken on a darker character—weathered stone facades with broken windows that gaped like hungry mouths. The street ahead disappeared into a wall of mist that seemed to absorb all light.

Lily's sigil flared, yanking her forward. She cried out, grabbing a lamp-post to steady herself. "God, it's like hooks under my skin."

The air here was colder, heavy with an acrid, lingering smell, as if the blood spilled on these streets had never fully faded.

"This area." Ethan scanned the decrepit structures, recognition cutting through his exhaustion. "The Butcher's Row murders happened here. Three victims in '89, never solved."

"History has power in Eldoria." Marcus checked his watch again. "The mark knows where old blood was spilled."

Lily swayed on her feet. "We have to keep moving. The pull—"

"The pull is leading us straight into a killing ground." Ethan caught her shoulders as she stumbled again. "Everything about this feels wrong."

The sigil's light intensified, casting harsh shadows across Lily's face. Each pulse drew a fresh wince of pain. Ethan watched her struggle against its invisible grip, knowing they couldn't maintain this pace much longer. But the alternative—stopping here, in this blood-soaked part of the city—felt like walking willingly into a trap.

Marcus stepped in front of them, blocking their path with an outstretched arm. "The sigil wants death. Nothing more." His eyes fixed on Lily's marked arm. "I've seen it drag others straight to their executioners."

"You said you'd help us find the mirror." Ethan's hand drifted toward the gun beneath his jacket.

"And I will." Marcus's face remained impassive in the ethereal glow. "But not by following that mark. There's a safer route through the old maintenance tunnels. They run parallel to these streets."

Lily doubled over, fighting against the sigil's pull. "How do you know about the tunnels?"

"Three cycles of the Watch. You learn things when you survive that long." Marcus pointed to a rusted grate set into the wall of a nearby building. "That entrance will take us beneath the killing grounds. The hunters rarely venture down there."

Ethan studied Marcus's steady movements, the practiced way he scanned their surroundings. No sign of fatigue or fear showed in his posture. Just the same unnerving calm he'd maintained since they'd met.

"Your sister won't last another hour fighting that pull." Marcus crouched by the grate, working at its corroded edges. "The tunnels are our best chance."

"And we're just supposed to trust you?" Ethan positioned himself between Marcus and Lily.

Ethan's fingers tightened around his gun. Every instinct told him not to trust Marcus, but Lily's ashen face and labored breaths forced his hand. They couldn't keep this up.

"Trust that I want to live." The grate came loose with a grinding screech. "Which means keeping you both alive too. The Watch doesn't spare survivors who lose their charges." His voice was cold, matter-of-fact, as if the risk of loss were as simple as checking his watch.

The tunnel's mouth gaped, dark and cold, its depths swallowing the faint light from Lily's sigil. A path into the unknown—safer, perhaps, but equally unforgiving.

The sigil flared again, drawing another pained gasp from Lily. Ethan caught her as her knees buckled.

"Your choice, detective." Marcus gestured to the dark opening. "Follow the mark's path straight to the slaughter, or take a chance on someone who's beaten this game before."

***

A sharp whistle cut through the darkness ahead. Ethan's hand flew to his weapon, but Marcus held up a palm.

"Hold." Marcus pressed against the tunnel wall. "Someone's coming."

Heavy boots scraped stone, and a beam of light swept across their faces. Ethan squinted against the glare.

"Hands where I can see them." The voice carried the weight of command. A figure emerged from the shadows, flashlight trained steady on their group.

Ethan recognized the short gray hair and weathered face. "Captain Marsh?"

"Marlowe." She kept the light on them, her other hand resting near her service weapon. "Should've known you'd be mixed up in this." Her gaze locked onto Lily's glowing arm, then shifted to Marcus. "And who's your friend?"

"Marcus. I'm guiding them to—"

"Save it." Marsh cut him off. "I've worked these streets twenty years. Never seen you before tonight."

Marcus's jaw tightened briefly, the confidence in his gaze faltering before he regained composure. "The tunnels aren't safe for—"

"These maintenance passages were part of my beat." Marsh's eyes narrowed. "I know every corner, every exit. And I know when someone's feeding me a line."

Lily stumbled, the sigil's pull growing stronger. Marsh noticed immediately, her tactical assessment shifting. Her gaze shifted from Lily to the tunnels around them, calculating distance and visibility.

"How long has she been marked?"

"Four hours," Ethan answered.

"We need to move." Marsh holstered her weapon but kept her flashlight trained on Marcus. "There's a secure checkpoint two blocks north. Better defensible position than these tunnels."

Marcus stepped forward. "The mark is pulling her south—"

"Because that's where they want her." Marsh's voice carried steel. "I've watched three groups follow those pulls tonight. None came back."

The authority in her voice made even Marcus pause. Ethan saw the calculation in his eyes, the subtle shift in his stance.

"Your call," Marcus said to Ethan, but his gaze never left Marsh. "Trust a cop who couldn't stop the Watch, or someone who's survived it."

Ethan felt the weight of the decision pressing down on him, caught between Marsh's steely authority and Marcus's practiced confidence. Trust was a luxury he couldn't afford—but neither was a mistake.

Ethan's head pounded as three voices competed for his attention. He watched Lily brace herself against the tunnel wall, her marked arm trembling.

"The sigil isn't just pain." Lily's voice cracked but held firm. "It's showing us where to go. The obsidian mirror has to be close—I can feel it."

"That's exactly what it wants you to think." Marcus stepped closer, his calm facade cracking. "I've seen dozens fall for this trap. The mark creates a compulsion and makes you think you're closing in on something important. Then it delivers you straight to the hunters."

"Both of you, enough." Marsh swept her flashlight between them. "I've got three dead bodies topside that followed their marks tonight. We move to the checkpoint, regroup, and figure this out properly."

The sigil pulsed again, and Lily grabbed Ethan's arm. "We don't have time to regroup. The mirror is the key to ending this—all of this. Dr. Vane's research proved—"

"Dr. Vane is dead." Marcus's words cut through the tunnel. "Found her in her office this morning. They didn't want her sharing whatever she discovered about the ritual."

Lily froze, her face draining of color. "Dr. Vane... she was the only one who understood this curse," she whispered. A moment later, her jaw set, the grief in her eyes hardening. "Then we have to finish what she started. We're closer than ever."

Ethan felt Lily's grip tighten on his sleeve. He looked at her face—pale, determined, scared but certain. Then, at Marcus, whose practiced confidence had given way to raw urgency. Finally, at Marsh, whose years of experience radiated from her stance.

The sigil flared again, stronger this time. Lily doubled over, but her eyes remained fixed on Ethan. "Trust me. Please."

"Blind faith is just a shortcut to the grave." Marcus shook his head. "We need to be smart, not faithful."

"What we need is to get off these streets." Marsh's hand returned to her weapon. "Whatever's hunting her will find us soon enough."

Ethan felt the weight of three paths before him—his sister's desperate certainty, Marcus's hard-won experience, and Marsh's tactical wisdom.

Each choice carried its own dangers, its own promise of either salvation or destruction.

***

Ethan looked at his sister's determined face and made his choice. He met Lily's gaze, seeing both fear and fierce determination in her eyes. He'd promised himself to protect her, but the only way forward was to trust her instincts. "We follow the sigil."

Marcus cursed under his breath. Marsh's expression hardened, but she kept her weapon holstered.

"Your funeral," she said, backing away into the shadows. "Don't say I didn't warn you."

They stepped deeper into the tunnel's twisted darkness, the air thickening with each step. Shadows seemed to stretch and breathe, pressing against Ethan's skin as if testing his resolve. Each footfall echoed like a heartbeat, blending with the relentless pull of the sigil as it drew them through the winding passages.

A crash echoed ahead, followed by rapid footsteps. A figure burst around the corner, nearly colliding with them. Blonde hair disheveled, glasses askew, notebook clutched to her chest.

"Bennett?" Ethan recognized the reporter from his detective days.

Sarah's chest heaved as she looked up, blinking frantically in the dim light. She clutched her notebook, her knuckles white, as though it was the only thing tethering her to reality. "Marlowe? Oh god, you have no idea..." Her professional armor cracked, and raw fear flashed across her face. "I've been tracking the pattern of attacks, trying to understand the selection process, but—" She swallowed hard. "I lost my crew an hour ago. Something took them."

"We need to keep moving." Marcus glanced over his shoulder, his gaze cold as he assessed her trembling frame. "Useful or not, she'll slow us down. This isn't a research expedition."

"I have information." Sarah's voice steadied as she flipped through her notebook, her hands shaking. "Police reports, witness accounts, patterns in the sigil appearances. Things they tried to bury." She thumbed through the pages, each one filled with scrawled notes and redacted statements. "There's a logic, Marlowe, a method to the madness. City records, council minutes, patterns no one wanted to admit—until now."

Lily grabbed Sarah's arm. "What do you know about the obsidian mirror?"

Sarah's eyes widened. "The artifact from Dr. Vane's research? I interviewed her last week. She hinted it was more than an artifact—a conduit, a... bridge, almost." Sarah's voice dropped to a whisper. "She called it a 'key' to navigating the curse's traps, but she didn't have time to finish her work."

"We don't have time for this," Marcus cut in. "Every minute we waste puts us all at risk. Leave her."

"She comes with us," Ethan said, his tone leaving no room for argument. He recognized the terror behind Sarah's professional facade—the same fear he'd seen in countless victims. "Her research might help us understand what we're walking into."

The air in the tunnel grew heavier as Marcus stepped toward Sarah, his face twisted in a sneer. Ethan moved between them, his hand instinctively reaching for the gun at his hip.

"Back off." Ethan's voice echoed against the stone walls. "She stays with us."

Marcus's laugh held no warmth. "Playing hero now, Marlowe? In case you forgot, your sister's the one marked. Every second we waste—"

"Is a second we might need." Captain Marsh emerged from the shadows, her badge catching what little light filtered through the tunnel. "Bennett's research could save lives."

The words triggered a memory in Ethan's mind—Father Gabriel's weathered face in the soft light of St. Michael's confessional. "Even in the darkest times, we are judged by how we treat the weakest among us," the priest had told him. "That's what separates us from the monsters we fear."

Ethan had dismissed it then, too wrapped up in his own cynicism. But now, watching Sarah clutch her notebook like a shield, those words rang true. He remembered how he'd walked away from that marked victim in the alley. Not again. A sliver of doubt crept in, but Ethan pushed it aside. Some things mattered more than survival.

"She comes with us," Ethan said, steel in his voice. Sarah's shoulders relaxed, her eyes shining with a mixture of gratitude and fear as she looked up at him. "And if you have a problem with that, Marcus, you're welcome to find your own way through these tunnels."

Marcus looked away, muttering something under his breath, his expression twisting with barely concealed disgust. He glanced at Lily's glowing sigil, then at the darkness ahead. "Your funeral." He spat the words. "But when something catches us because she can't keep up, remember—I warned you."

The tension crackled between them, thick as the darkness pressed in from all sides. The tunnel pressed in around them, shadows gathering like watchful eyes. Ethan felt the weight of Father Gabriel's words echoing in his mind. He'd failed too many people already. He wouldn't fail another, not even if it meant facing whatever horrors lurked in Eldoria's depths.

Captain Marsh stepped between Ethan and Marcus, her weathered face set with determination. Her posture shifted, shoulders squared as she pulled a folded map from her jacket pocket and spread it against the tunnel wall.

"We're here." She jabbed her finger at an intersection. "Service tunnels branch north and east. North leads to maintenance access, east to the storm drains." Her eyes flicked to Marcus. "Which route did you suggest?"

"North," Marcus said, crossing his arms.

Marsh's lips tightened. "Wrong. That tunnel flooded last month. City sealed it off." She traced the eastern path with her finger. "We take this route. Single file, ten feet apart. I lead, and Ethan brings up the rear. Sarah and Lily in the middle."

"Since when do you—" Marcus started.

"Since I spent fifteen years mapping these tunnels for SWAT operations." Marsh's voice carried the weight of command. Sarah exhaled, a faint look of relief flickering across her face as she fell into step behind Marsh. "Bennett, stay close to Lily. Your research might help us understand what that sigil's doing to her."

They moved through the darkness, Marsh's flashlight beam sweeping methodically across their path. She halted at a junction, holding up her fist. "Tripwire." She crouched, pointing out the nearly invisible line stretched across the passage. "Maintenance never puts these at ankle height. Someone rigged this recently."

She guided them around it, then past a section of collapsed ceiling that would have forced them into a bottleneck. Each obstacle she spotted seemed to validate her leadership, even Marcus falling quiet as she navigated them through the maze, his jaw clenched as he followed.

"Hold." Marsh's whisper carried back through the line. She knelt, examining something on the ground. Her eyes sharpened, catching the slight scuff of fresh tactical treads pressed into the dirt. "Boot prints, fresh. Multiple sets." She glanced at Marcus. "You said you came alone?"

His face remained neutral. "Lots of people use these tunnels."

"Not tonight." Marsh's hand rested on her holster. "And not with tactical treads."

Sarah hugged her notebook to her chest, her knuckles pale as she tried to steady her breathing. But each corner they rounded chipped away at her nerves, her professionalism crumbling with each unsettling step. A thick and cloying metallic scent filled the air, mingling with the damp chill that clung to the walls. Sarah stumbled, her ankle twisting on loose gravel. Lily caught her arm, steadying her.

"Thanks, I..." Sarah's words died in her throat.

The beam of Marsh's flashlight revealed a crumpled form ahead. Blood pooled beneath the body, still fresh enough to reflect the light. The victim's eyes stared unseeing at the ceiling, mouth frozen in a silent scream. A familiar silver-blue glow marked their arm—another chosen for The Night Watch.

Sarah pressed her face into Lily's shoulder, choking back a sob. Her professional detachment shattered. She'd reported on countless deaths, interviewed grieving families, and analyzed every cold fact—but seeing it firsthand, the raw violence of the curse broke something inside her. Her fingers dug into the edges of her notebook as if the familiar object could somehow protect her from the brutal reality before her.

"Deep breaths," Lily whispered, rubbing Sarah's back. "Focus on me, not..." She gestured vaguely at the scene before them, her hand steady on Sarah's shoulder, a gentle anchor in the chaos.

"I interviewed him yesterday." Sarah's voice cracked. "James Morrison, city planning office. He had two kids..." She clutched her notebook tighter, its familiar weight suddenly feeling hollow. "I should have warned him. The pattern in my notes—I knew the sigil was spreading through his department, but I thought I had more time to investigate..."

"This isn't your fault." Lily squeezed Sarah's trembling hands. "The curse chooses its victims. You couldn't have stopped it."

Sarah nodded weakly, but her shoulders remained hunched as they moved past the body. She stayed close to Lily, flinching at every echo, every shadow. The notepad that had once felt like armor now weighed her down, its pages powerless to guard her against the horrors of The Night Watch.

Ethan's muscles tensed as a howl echoed through the tunnel. Not human, not animal—something else. Sarah edged closer to Lily, her fingers digging into her own sleeves as she fought to steady her breathing. The sigil on Lily's arm pulsed brighter, casting weird shadows on the tunnel walls.

"We need to move faster." Marcus pushed past them, his face tight with barely contained rage. "That sound means we're being hunted."

A figure lurched from a side passage, its body twisted at impossible angles, limbs scraping against the stone as it dragged itself closer. Its jaw hung open, revealing rows of needle-sharp teeth, and the beam of Marsh's flashlight caught its face—what remained of it. Ethan recognized the hollow-eyed creature as one of the missing persons from his case files.

"Down!" Marsh's command cut through the air as she fired two shots. The creature jerked back, a sickening crunch accompanying each hit, but it didn't fall.

Sarah screamed, her voice breaking into a strangled sob. Ethan grabbed her arm, dragging her behind him as more shapes emerged from the darkness. The sigil's pull grew stronger, tugging Lily toward a narrow maintenance shaft.

"This way!" Lily pointed, her voice steady despite the terror in her eyes.

"It's a dead end," Marcus spat. "We should double back—"

"No time." Ethan shoved Sarah through the opening, trusting Lily's instincts. "Move!"

They squeezed through the tight space, the sounds of pursuit growing closer. The shaft opened into a larger chamber, ancient pipes lining the walls. Water dripped somewhere in the darkness, mixing with the sound of their ragged breathing.

The sigil's glow intensified, burning bright enough to illuminate their immediate surroundings. Lily gasped, clutching her arm. "It's getting stronger."

"Or whatever it's connected to is getting closer," Marcus muttered.

Ethan positioned himself between the group and the shaft they'd emerged from, his gun trained on the opening. Sarah's quiet sobs echoed off the walls as Lily held her, whispering reassurances that sounded hollow in the oppressive darkness.

The howls grew closer. Ethan's finger tightened on the trigger. Failure wasn't an option—not with Lily, not with Sarah. He would face down the curse itself before letting it take them.

CHAPTER NINE

ALLIES AND ADVERSARIES

A metallic clang echoed through the chamber, followed by rapid footsteps. Ethan spun toward the sound, gun raised. A small figure darted between the pipes, movements quick and erratic, half-hidden in shadow.

"Better safe in shadows than out in the open these days," the voice murmured, thin and jittery, from somewhere above them. A boy slipped down from a rusted pipe, hoodie oversized, hands tapping a restless rhythm on his thighs.

Ethan squinted, gun still raised. "Come out where we can see you."

The boy grinned, his chipped front tooth catching the light. "Tommy Collins. Streets call me Twitch." His gaze locked onto Lily's glowing arm, and his eyes narrowed. "Still fresh, that one. Got time before it peaks, but not much."

Marcus stepped forward, his posture tense. "How long have you been following us?"

"Long enough to know you're all lost," Twitch replied, his fingers drumming faster. "This tunnel?" He cocked his head. "Leads to them. Herding you like lambs to the pen, they are. All those lights and signs—it's just the bait."

Lily took a step closer, frowning. "You've seen this before?"

"Seen it, lived it, watched it chew people up and spit them out." Twitch's fingers stopped drumming, and his voice dropped to a whisper. "Dancing through the darkness, that's how you survive. Not stumbling."

Ethan studied Twitch, noting the twitchy movements and darting eyes that were oddly sharp, almost calculating. "You've survived encounters with them?"

Twitch shrugged. "Survived, hid, watched. They don't catch the ones who know their tricks." He took a step back, the grin gone from his face. "Your choice. Follow that cursed mark or follow someone who knows the real way out."

Sarah grabbed Ethan's arm, whispering, "How do we know he's not leading us into another trap?"

Ethan glanced at her, then back at Twitch, assessing. "We don't. But he's alive, and that counts for something." He lowered his gun slightly. "Lead us wrong, though, and you'll wish those creatures got you first."

Twitch tilted his head, his smile strange and mirthless. "I've wished that before. Time to move, though. They're getting closer, and those pipes won't keep them out much longer."

Marcus advanced a step, his voice tight with irritation, each word clipped and controlled. "Every new stray we pick up wants to lead us down a different path. We're wasting time we don't have."

"They're people, Marcus. Not strays." Ethan moved between Marcus and Twitch, his shoulders tense.

"They're liabilities. The mirror, the ritual—that's what matters. Not your crusade to save everyone we stumble across."

"My sister has the mark. Sarah has the information we need. And this kid—"

"Is another detour." Marcus's voice cut like steel. "Your sister's mark means we have a deadline. Every minute spent playing hero puts her at risk."

Ethan's fist clenched. "You suggesting we leave them behind?"

"I'm suggesting we focus on what keeps us alive."

Captain Marsh stepped between them, her presence commanding attention. "Both of you, stand down. Now."

"With all due respect, Captain—" Marcus started.

"That's an order." Her voice dropped low, brooking no argument. "I've watched good people tear each other apart in crisis. Not happening here."

Twitch bounced on his heels, though his gaze flickered downward for a split second. "Rules and orders ain't worth much down here, lady."

Marsh fixed him with a steady gaze. "Neither is dying because we couldn't work together." She turned to address the group, her tone unyielding. "We move as one. No splitting up, no leaving anyone behind. Clear?"

Sarah shifted uneasily, her fingers tightening on her notebook, while Lily exchanged a worried glance with Ethan.

Marcus opened his mouth to object, but Marsh's glare silenced him. "I said, are we clear?"

Ethan nodded first, followed by a reluctant Marcus. The tension eased, but didn't disappear entirely.

"Good." Marsh checked her weapon, her gaze sweeping over the group, softer now but resolute. "We stick together. That's how we survive. Now let's focus on staying alive long enough to argue about this later."

***

Ethan's gaze sharpened as a shadow separated from the darkness, slipping forward with fluid grace. He braced himself, every sense on high alert as the figure approached with open palms.

"Easy there, Ghost." A woman's voice, smooth as silk but sharp as a blade. "Heard you were back on the streets."

Ethan's voice held a razor edge. "Who are you?"

"Nina. Though some call me other things." She stepped closer, her dark eyes scanning the group, her presence seeming to draw shadows around her like a cloak. "Interesting collection you've got here."

Marcus straightened, his earlier hostility vanishing. "You know about the ritual?"

"I know many things." Nina's gaze lingered on Lily's mark. "The mirror you seek? It's not in the catacombs anymore. They moved it."

Marsh shifted slightly, her stance rigid and wary. "And how exactly do you know that?"

Nina's smile barely touched her lips. "Information is currency in this city. Always has been." Her fingers traced a pattern in the air, almost like a signature, as if marking her territory in shadows.

Ethan watched Marcus lean in, captivated by her every word. The same man who'd wanted to abandon Sarah and Twitch now seemed bewitched by Nina's knowledge.

"The ritual requires more than just the mirror," Nina continued, her voice almost a whisper. "There's a price. Always is in Eldoria."

"Why help us?" Ethan's posture stayed defensive, his eyes not leaving her. "What's your angle?"

Nina's gaze slid to Marcus. "Maybe I'm tired of watching this city devour itself. Or maybe I just want to back the winning horse. Your friend here understands." She smiled at Marcus, and the unspoken exchange between them made Ethan's skin crawl.

Marsh moved closer to Ethan, her voice barely a whisper. "Notice how our suspicious friend suddenly found his trust?"

Ethan watched Nina and Marcus, the way they moved in sync, like dancers in a choreographed performance. His eyes narrowed. "Yeah. The question is—why?"

Tommy's fingers tapped out an uneven rhythm, his gaze fixed on Marcus and Nina as he struggled to pick up fragments of their conversation. "You're buying this? She shows up out of nowhere, and you're ready to follow her lead?"

Marcus turned, his earlier warmth replaced by cold calculation. "Some of us know how this city works, kid. Nina's intel could save our lives."

"Or get us killed." Tommy's voice cracked. "I've seen her type before. They sell you out the moment someone offers a better price."

"Watch your mouth, street rat." Marcus stepped forward, looming over Tommy.

Nina's smile widened, her gaze shifting between Tommy and Marcus like a cat watching mice quarrel.

Marsh's boots scraped against the concrete as she positioned herself between them. "That's enough." Her voice sliced through the tension like a blade. "Here's how this works. We move as a unit: no lone wolves, no side deals. I take point, Ethan covers our rear. Any intel goes through me first."

Marcus opened his mouth to object, but Marsh's glare silenced him. "This isn't a debate. We've got civilians to protect and a mission to complete. Do you want to challenge that chain of command?" She jerked her head toward the tunnel's dark opening. "There's the exit."

Sarah edged closer to Lily, her notebook trembling in her hands. "I should have stayed in the office," she whispered.

Lily squeezed her arm. "Stay close. We'll get through this."

Marsh issued instructions with calm precision, assigning positions without hesitation. "Tommy, stay close, but keep your eyes forward. Lily, guard Sarah. We move fast and quiet."

Tommy fell into place, though his eyes never left Marcus and Nina. As they moved forward, the tunnel seemed to close in, the shadows stretching longer and swallowing up the light. Their fragile alliance was splintering, each footstep a reminder of the suspicion and fear tightening around them.

Nina's fingers traced patterns in the air as she walked, her voice dropping to a whisper that threaded through the tunnel like a chill. "The Eye's Offering isn't what you think. The mirror's just the beginning."

"What do you mean?" Ethan kept his distance, watching her every movement.

"Ancient rituals demand ancient prices." Nina's dark eyes lingered on Lily's mark. "Blood offerings aren't enough. The curse requires... deeper sacrifices."

Marcus stepped closer to Nina, his suspicion melting into something darker, more eager. "What kind of sacrifices?"

"The final kind." Nina's words hung in the air. "One life is freely given to save the rest."

Ethan felt a surge of revulsion. "That's not happening."

"Power has a price," Marcus cut in, his voice tense with excitement. "If one death could end this curse—"

"We're not sacrificing anyone." Ethan moved between Marcus and the others, his voice hard as steel.

Nina's laughter echoed off the tunnel walls. "Noble thoughts won't save you when the darkness comes. Sometimes survival means making impossible choices."

"There's always another way." Even as Ethan spoke, a sliver of doubt slipped into his voice.

Marcus leaned against the wall, eyes scanning the group with calculating interest. "Think about it. One life to save thousands. To end the curse forever."

"Listen to yourself." Ethan's voice rose, raw with disbelief. "We're talking about murder."

"Sacrifice," Marcus corrected, a hungry light in his eyes. "There's a difference."

Nina watched their exchange with quiet satisfaction, like a puppet master admiring her handiwork. "The ritual requires willing participation. The power lies in the choice."

Ethan caught how Marcus's gaze swept over the group, measuring them with a clinical detachment that made his blood run cold.

Tommy edged closer to Lily, gripping her sleeve tightly. His usual fidgeting stilled, and he looked up at her, eyes wide. "I don't like this."

Neither did Ethan. But he saw the seed Nina had planted taking root in Marcus's eyes—a dangerous, calculating glint that marked each of them as expendable.

***

Ethan caught another whispered exchange between Marcus and Nina—their third in the past few minutes. Nina's fingers brushed Marcus's arm as she leaned in, her lips barely moving. Marcus nodded, his expression darkening.

The tunnel's shadows stretched deeper, though not deep enough to hide their furtive glances. When Nina drifted toward the front of the group, Marcus's eyes followed her with an intensity that made Ethan's skin crawl.

A sound echoed through the tunnel—heavy footsteps shook loose dirt from the ceiling. The group froze.

Tommy pressed against the wall, his breath catching. "That's him. The Hammer."

"Viktor?" Sarah's voice quivered. "The enforcer?"

"Worse than that." Tommy's words tumbled out in a rush. "He's Novikov's shadow. Where Viktor goes, death follows."

The footsteps grew closer, each impact reverberating through the concrete. A low growl rolled through the darkness, too deep to be human.

"He's not like the others marked by the curse." Tommy's fingers traced invisible patterns on the wall. "Viktor chose it. Embraced it. Now he hunts anyone who tries to break free."

Sarah clutched her notebook tighter. "But why?"

"Because Novikov commands it." Tommy's eyes darted between the shadows. "The curse, the ritual, the hunt—all his game. And Viktor's his favorite piece on the board."

The growl morphed into something between a laugh and a roar. Metal scraped against stone, closer now.

Marsh's jaw tightened as she raised her fist, signalling silence. Her other hand hovered near her weapon, her stance solid, every muscle prepared for whatever came next. But Ethan saw Marcus and Nina exchange another look—this one filled with dark purpose. Nina's lips curved into a smile that didn't reach her eyes while Marcus's hand drifted to his jacket pocket.

The pieces clicked into place in Ethan's mind, and dread seeped into his bones. They weren't just conspiring—they were preparing. Whatever they planned had nothing to do with helping the group survive.

They were trapped between a monster in the shadows and traitors within—both forces ready to strike.

Sarah's legs trembled with each step, her muscles burning from the endless trek through the tunnels. Her notebook, usually a source of comfort, felt like lead in her hands. Sweat trickled down her neck despite the tunnel's chill.

"I can't—" She stumbled, catching herself against the damp wall. Her glasses slipped down her nose, fogged from her ragged breathing. "I need a minute."

Lily backtracked to her side, gripping Sarah's arm. "We have to keep moving."

"What's the point?" Sarah's voice cracked. "Even if we find this mirror, there's no guarantee—"

"There never is." Lily's fingers brushed the glowing sigil on her arm, its eerie light casting shadows. "But giving up means death. Not just for us, but for everyone marked in the future."

Sarah wiped her glasses with shaking hands. "I've covered so many stories about the Night Watch. Interviewed families left behind. But being here, being part of it—"

"I know." Lily squeezed her shoulder. "Before all this, my research was just academic. Now it's real. Too real."

Sarah's breath hitched. "How do you stay so focused?"

"Because the alternative is unthinkable." Lily helped Sarah straighten up. "Every person we save by breaking this curse is someone's brother, sister, parent. Someone's whole world."

Sarah nodded, steadying herself. The weight of her recorder pressed against her hip—filled with testimony she might never share. But Lily was right. This was bigger than any story she'd ever chased.

"Together, then?" Sarah asked.

"Together." Lily offered a tired smile. "One step at a time."

They matched their steps, moving forward into the darkness, each heartbeat steadying the others.

***

The tunnel opened into a vast chamber beneath the old quarter. Ethan's flashlight beam caught ancient stone walls, their surfaces marred by deep gouges. Not cuts or scrapes—these were claw marks, each groove wide enough to fit his hand.

Lily traced one of the marks, her fingers trembling. "These are fresh."

"Look at this." Sarah's voice quivered as she pointed her light at the ground. Massive footprints pressed into the stone floor, each one larger than a turkey platter. Whatever made them had enough weight to crack the ancient stone.

Nina crouched by one of the prints, her face grim. "We're not alone down here. Something's hunting us—something that's been doing this for a very long time."

"Predators in the dark," Twitch whispered, pressing a hand to the wall, eyes darting to every shadow. "Silent steps and steel claws, the hunter who never loses his prey."

"Viktor." Lily's voice dropped to a whisper. She pulled out Dr. Vane's research notes, pages crumpling in her grip. "Dr. Vane found references to him in texts dating back centuries. They called him 'The Hammer of Novikov.' He's not just an enforcer—he's a weapon, twisted by the curse into something inhuman."

"The Hammer falls heavy," Twitch murmured, voice tight with fear. "A man who became a beast. Who chose to drown in the curse, and now he swims in it."

"The stories say he volunteered for it." Nina's eyes darted between shadows. "Let Novikov experiment on him, corrupt him. Now, he hunts anyone who tries to break the curse. Guards the relics. Keeps the game going."

A low rumble echoed through the chamber, like distant thunder trapped underground. Dust sifted down from the ceiling.

"He's here." Twitch pressed against the wall, eyes wide. "He doesn't just take your life. He takes your mind, your name, everything. Leaves you hollow, like the empty halls he stalks."

The rumble grew closer, accompanied by the scrape of metal on stone—the sound of something massive moving through the tunnels with terrible purpose.

Lily clutched her arm where the sigil burned brighter. "The relic's close. We're almost there."

"So is he," Nina's voice hardened. "And he won't stop until we're all dead."

CHAPTER TEN

UNSEEN ENEMY

The passage narrowed, forcing them to walk single-file. Ethan's flashlight beam caught strange markings etched into the stone—spiralling patterns that made his eyes hurt.

"These symbols," Lily traced her fingers over the carvings. "They match the ones from Dr. Vane's journals. Warning signs, marking places where the curse runs deep."

Sarah pressed a hand to her chest. "The air—it's like it's pulling us. Anyone else feel that?"

They reached a cave-in, rubble blocking their path forward.

"We need to find another way around," Captain Marsh swept her light across the debris. "Split up, check these side passages. Stay within shouting distance."

Ethan took the leftmost tunnel, his boots crunching on loose stone. The beam of his flashlight caught more symbols; these carved deeper, more frantic.

"Help! Someone, please... God, it hurts..."

The voice froze him mid-step, blood turning to ice in his veins. He knew that voice down to his marrow, had heard it in his nightmares for the past three years.

"Andrea?" His throat went dry, tongue sticking to the roof of his mouth.

"Ethan? Is that you? I'm trapped, please... I can't feel my legs..."

He moved forward, heart pounding against his ribs like a trapped animal. Around the corner, a figure lay pinned beneath fallen rock, uniform caked with dust and darker stains. In the dim light, he saw Detective Andrea's face—his former partner, exactly as she'd looked that last night, down to the small cut above her eyebrow that had never gotten the chance to scar.

"Help me up, partner. Like old times. Remember that time in the Narrows? You dragged me out, kicking and swearing, but we got them. We were unstoppable, you and me... Until you left."

Ethan's hand reached out, trembling. Andrea's eyes caught the light wrong, too dark, too empty—like wells that went down forever. The skin around them was smooth, unmarked by the crow's feet she'd always complained about.

"You left me to die before. Please don't do it again. Three hours I waited, bleeding out in that basement..."

The words hit like a physical blow, driving the air from his lungs. Ethan's fingers curled into a fist. Andrea was dead. He'd identified her body himself and had traced the Y-incision with his eyes until the medical examiner pulled the sheet back up. This thing was wearing her face...

He backed away, forcing himself to turn, his boots scraping against the concrete floor. The voice called after him, shifting from Andrea's familiar tones to something else—something ancient and mocking, a sound like stones grinding against each other in the dark. The transformation made his skin crawl, and the hair on the back of his neck stood on end as that guttural, inhuman voice echoed off the walls. It was the sound of something that had never known warmth or mercy and had waited in shadow since before cities existed.

Ethan stumbled back to the group, cold sweat running down his spine and his hands trembling at his sides. The curse had reached into his memories, twisted them into something grotesque and wrong, weaponizing his past against him. His throat felt raw, as if he'd been screaming, though he couldn't remember doing so. How much more of what he saw could he trust? The thought burrowed into his mind like a splinter, making him question every shadow, every familiar face that might appear before him in this nightmare.

The curse didn't just haunt these streets—it had learned his darkest fears, and it knew how to wield them. He shuddered, forcing himself to breathe as the group's concerned faces flickered before him. What else would it tear from his past before this night ended?

Ethan's hands wouldn't stop shaking as he rejoined the group. The beam of his flashlight danced across the walls, betraying his unsteady grip. He kept glancing back toward the tunnel he'd fled, half-expecting Andrea's twisted form to emerge from the shadows.

Sarah crouched near a section of the wall, running her fingers over the etched symbols. "These markings... I've seen this pattern before. Back when I was investigating the disappearances at the old asylum."

Lily knelt beside her. "You recognize them?"

"They're part of a binding ritual. Ancient cultures used them to contain malevolent entities." Sarah traced the spiralling lines. "See how they overlap? Each layer represents a different aspect of containment - mind, body, spirit."

"That matches what I found in the archives." Lily pulled out her notebook, comparing her sketches to the wall. "If these were carved in desperation, they might be a message—one meant for anyone who found them. Like us."

Sarah nodded. "Like whoever made them was racing against time." She glanced at Ethan, noting his distant stare. "Hey, these symbols might be our key out of here. They're not just warnings - they're instructions."

Lily's sigil pulsed brighter as Sarah pointed out specific markings. "Look at the way these lines converge. It's not random. They're showing us something about the ritual's structure."

"The patterns repeat every seven symbols," Sarah said. "In my research, seven was significant in breaking curses. It represented completion, perfection."

Ethan barely registered their discussion, his mind still trapped in that tunnel with Andrea's voice. But Sarah's steady tone cut through his spiral.

"We're close to understanding this, Ethan. These walls are like a manual left behind by someone who fought this before."

Ethan forced himself to focus, the thought dawning that the curse wanted him distracted, lost in memories it twisted against him. The symbols were a lifeline, and he'd need every piece of it to survive.

***

The chamber's walls stretched up into darkness, every surface covered in interlocking symbols that seemed to shift in the beam of their flashlights. The air was thick and electric, charged with an energy that made the hairs on Ethan's arms stand up. Shadows flickered between the symbols, darting like figures hiding in the stone.

Sarah traced her fingers along a circular pattern, brow furrowed. "These markings... they match the doctor's sketches, but there's so much more here. It's like we're standing in the ritual itself."

Marcus leaned forward, his hand hovering over a symbol shaped like a blade. "That one represents sacrifice." He exchanged a quick, knowing look with Nina, who nodded.

Marsh's eyes narrowed. "You seem well-informed, Marcus. Care to share how?"

Marcus gave her a level stare. "Some things are better left unsaid, Captain."

Ethan, distracted by the memory of Andrea's voice, barely registered their exchange. He squinted at the symbols, the spirals twisting and blurring before him. Was the curse preying on his guilt, or was there a darker truth he'd failed to accept?

"Everyone stay where I can see you," Captain Marsh commanded, her stance widening as she positioned herself against the wall, one hand on her holster.

Lily stepped forward, pressing her hand against a symbol shaped like a twisted tree. The wall groaned, and dust rained down. A dart shot out, narrowly missing her. "Wrong one," she muttered, her hand jerking back.

"Every second counts!" Twitch's voice trembled, his eyes darting toward the dark tunnel. "Those things could find us any minute."

Sarah's fingers traced another line of symbols. "Look for patterns of three—survival, sacrifice, power. They're connected, layered like a code."

Nina stepped forward, her expression confident. "Start with the center. It represents the heart of power."

Marsh's voice cut through the tension. "And just how do you know that, Nina?"

Nina met her gaze without flinching. "I've been down these paths before, Captain. Trust me, or don't—but this isn't my first ritual."

Before Marsh could object, Sarah pressed the symbol. The wall hummed, and three more symbols began to glow faintly. A rumble echoed through the chamber, the floor shuddering beneath them.

Ethan's gaze drifted to Marcus and Nina, watching as their eyes met in silent understanding. His stomach twisted. They knew more than they were letting on. They were hiding something.

"Stay focused," Lily whispered to him, noting his distraction. "These walls are like a manual, written by someone who wanted to leave a way out."

The words grounded him. As Sarah and Lily worked, the symbols pulsed with life, each faint glow hinting at the power hidden in the stone. Ethan knew he had to stay present—no matter what tricks the curse had in store.

Marcus stepped forward, his boots crunching on scattered debris. "Stop." His hand shot out, gripping Sarah's wrist just before she touched another symbol. "See that slight discoloration around the edges? Pressure plate. Touch it wrong, and this whole section could collapse."

Ethan's shoulders tensed, his gaze sharp on Marcus, feeling a prickling doubt with every smooth, confident word. The conviction in his voice was too smooth, too practiced. Rehearsed, even.

"Here." Marcus pointed to a series of smaller markings. "These aren't ritual symbols; they're warnings. Ancient maintenance crews marked the weak points in the structural system."

Sarah nodded, her gaze shifting to where he indicated. "That actually makes sense. The builders would have needed a way to navigate safely."

Ethan edged closer to Lily, positioning himself protectively between her and Marcus. "And just how do you know all this?"

"Years of exploration. Trial and error," Marcus replied evenly, tracing his fingers along the wall with an unnerving calm. "You learn to read the signs or end up dead."

Ethan watched, uneasy, as Sarah mirrored Marcus's movements, avoiding the sections he'd identified. "He's right," she murmured, leaning closer. "Look at how the real markings are carved deeper, more deliberately."

"The traps are designed to keep the uninitiated out," Marcus said, tapping a spot on the wall. "But they left clues for those who knew where to look."

Lily's eyes lit up with realization. "Like a test. The worthy would know how to navigate safely."

Marcus's hand rested against the wall; his expression almost amused as he observed her understanding. Ethan noticed the slight nod Nina gave Marcus from her place in the shadows, and his unease deepened.

"This section's clear," Marcus announced, stepping back to let Sarah proceed. "Focus on the symbols arranged in triangular patterns. Those are the ones you want."

Ethan's gaze shifted to Sarah, watching as she continued without hesitation, her trust in Marcus unwavering. Every calculated gesture, every assured instruction from Marcus unsettled Ethan. The man was too familiar with this place, too comfortable in a chamber filled with death traps. And Sarah—intelligent, intuitive Sarah—seemed to trust him completely, moving through his directions without a second thought.

In the dim light, Ethan caught Lily's eye, sharing an unspoken concern. He'd seen manipulators before—those who controlled from behind veils of charm and assurance.

***

The stone door slammed shut behind them with a thunderous boom. Ethan spun around, his flashlight beam revealing ancient text carved into the chamber's far wall.

"Choose between the blood of one or the death of many," Sarah read, her voice steady. "A sacrifice freely given breaks chains, while survival breeds eternal darkness."

Twitch backed away from the wall, shaking his head. "This ain't right. Curses love blood. They make you think there are only two choices, and that's how they get you. There's always another way out—always."

"The text is clear." Marcus stepped forward, his finger tracing the carved words. "One death now saves countless lives. It's simple mathematics." His tone was calm, almost indifferent. "I've seen too many people try to take a third option that doesn't exist and end up paying the price."

Detective Andrea's face flashed through Ethan's mind—her final moments, her determination to save others at any cost. Would she have volunteered? The memory of her voice echoed in his thoughts, drowning out the heated debate around him.

"We're not murderers," Lily's voice cut through his haze. "The curse wants us to think violence is the answer. But there's always another solution."

Sarah moved closer to the wall, her fingers hovering over the intricate symbols etched beside the main text. The ancient markings seemed to pulse with a faint energy beneath her fingertips, though she knew it was probably just her imagination playing tricks in the dim light.

"Look at these markings. They're not just decorative—they're channelling symbols. What if we could redirect the curse's energy instead of feeding it? These symbols look like a containment grid... maybe we can weaken its hold." Her voice grew more excited as the possibilities crystallized in her mind, years of arcane research finally clicking into place as she traced the geometric patterns with a trembling finger.

Ethan barely registered her words, lost in memories of Andrea's last case. The weight of choice, the burden of consequence—

"Marlowe." Marsh's firm grip on his shoulder yanked him back to reality. "I've seen that look before. Had an officer once, good man, lost himself in 'what-ifs' when a crisis hit. He couldn't bring himself back in time." Her hand stayed firm on his shoulder. "We need you here, now."

Her words grounded him, pulling him from the spiral of memories that threatened to drag him under. The familiar weight of guilt loosened its grip on his chest as he drew in a steadying breath. She was right - he couldn't afford to lose himself now. Andrea was gone, her case filed away in a drawer he rarely opened, but these people needed him present, his mind sharp and focused on the intricate patterns before them.

Marcus's steps reverberated softly, each footfall sending faint vibrations through the chamber walls. "You know what I've learned from surviving the Night Watch? Alliances are fluid. When that sigil appears, all bets are off."

He paused near Sarah, who stood examining the symbols. His shadow fell across her notepad.

"Sometimes the strongest survive because they know when to cut their losses. When to recognize that someone else's death means your life." His voice carried a practiced casualness that made Sarah's skin crawl.

She fixed her eyes on her notes, pen moving across the paper in steady strokes. The subtle emphasis Marcus placed on certain words felt deliberate and calculated.

"The curse has its own justice, its own... priorities." He leaned closer, his eyes skimming her notebook as if her life were something he might casually erase. "Those who try to save everyone? They're usually the first to fall."

Sarah's pen paused mid-word. She'd interviewed enough killers to recognize the undertone in his voice—that mix of pride and warning wrapped in false concern. Her years of reading between the lines, of catching the subtle shifts in a subject's demeanor, were sending clear signals.

"Interesting perspective," she murmured, keeping her voice neutral as she documented the symbols. Her mind cataloged each red flag: his strategic positioning near exits, his eyes tracked everyone's movements, and his "helpful" suggestions always seemed to separate the group.

Marcus moved closer, examining her sketches. "Good eye for detail. Useful skill. It's a shame how many journalists become casualties during the Night Watch. Never knowing who to trust."

Sarah added another careful line to her drawing, suppressing a shiver. The threat wasn't even veiled anymore, but she wouldn't give him the satisfaction of a reaction. Instead, she shifted her position slightly, ensuring she remained in Marsh's line of sight.

Ethan watched Marcus guide Sarah through another set of symbols, his stomach churning at the predatory grace in the man's movements. Every gesture seemed calculated, and each word was carefully chosen.

"These markings indicate a weak point." Marcus's hand brushed Sarah's shoulder as he leaned in. "Like you, Sarah. Exhaustion makes people... vulnerable. Slows their reactions."

Sarah's pen stilled for a fraction of a second. Ethan caught the slight tremor in her hand, the way she angled herself away from Marcus.

"We should rest soon," Marcus continued. "Some of us might not have the strength to continue. Difficult choices ahead."

The words hit too close to Andrea's final moments. Ethan had heard similar manipulation then—subtle suggestions that led to fatal decisions. He shifted closer to Sarah, positioning himself between her and Marcus.

"Nobody's staying behind." Ethan's voice carried a steel edge. "We move as a group."

Marcus's smile didn't reach his eyes. "Noble sentiment. But nobility gets people killed in the Night Watch. Ask your partner."

The casual mention of Andrea sparked something in Ethan. The curse had used her image to manipulate him earlier. Now Marcus wielded her memory like a weapon. The parallel wasn't lost on him. Lily caught his eye, her expression mirroring his concern. He wouldn't let history repeat itself. Not with Sarah, not with his sister, not with anyone. The curse had already claimed too many lives through manipulation and false choices.

"The only one making threats here is you, Marcus." Ethan kept his voice low and steady. "I'm starting to wonder whose game you're playing."

Marcus's facade cracked instantly, revealing something cold and calculating beneath. It reminded Ethan of Alexei's handiwork—the same practiced manipulation and push toward inevitable violence.

"I'm trying to keep us alive," Marcus said, but Ethan saw through it now. Every suggestion and helpful observation had been steering them toward sacrifice and Alexei's twisted version of survival.

CHAPTER ELEVEN

BLOOD AND LIGHT

The chamber opened before them, its high ceiling disappearing into darkness. In the center, atop a stone pedestal, sat an object that made Ethan's eyes water when he tried to focus on it. Ancient symbols carved into the floor formed concentric circles around the pedestal, their edges worn smooth by time.

Lily's breath hitched her grip on her arm, tightening as if the sigil was burning from within. Her gaze remained locked on the relic, unable to look away. "This is it. We found it."

The relic seemed to respond to her sigil's glow, pulsing with its own inner radiance. Its surface shifted between solid and translucent, like smoke trapped in glass.

Sarah moved forward, her notebook already in hand. Her fingers traced the air above the carved symbols. "These match Dr. Vane's sketches, but there's more here. Much more."

"The outer ring represents binding," Marcus said from the chamber entrance. His eyes darted between the shadows, assessing angles and corners before he stepped inside. "Those curved marks? They're meant to contain power."

Sarah's pen flew across the page. "And these inner symbols... they're different from the others we've seen. More complex."

Marcus approached the pedestal, his movements measured. "These aren't just containment runes. They're channelling marks." He pointed to a series of interlocking glyphs. "Someone went to a lot of trouble to direct energy through specific paths."

"The Ritual of Severance," Sarah muttered, comparing her notes to the floor markings. "These symbols match fragments from the old texts, but they're complete here. They show how the energy should flow."

Ethan watched Marcus approach the relic, noting how the man's casual stance betrayed his intense focus on the object. As the relic pulsed, the symbols on the floor seemed to shiver in response, casting shadows that stretched and twisted around the group. For a fleeting moment, Ethan felt as if they were being watched, the weight of unseen eyes pressing in from the dark edges of the chamber. The relic's light flickered, and the shadows crept closer, shifting with their own life.

Sarah traced her finger along the ancient text; her brow furrowed in concentration. "These markings... they're connected. Each symbol feeds into a larger pattern of—" She stopped, face paling. "Oh god."

"What is it?" Ethan moved closer, careful to stay in his exact spot.

"The whole chamber's rigged. Look at how these lines intersect." Sarah pointed to where the floor symbols created intricate geometric patterns. "Each connection point marks a trigger. One wrong step and..." She swallowed hard.

Nina slid forward like a shadow, her eyes scanning the ground. "Classic Novikov. He's always loved his little games." She stepped carefully between two symbols, demonstrating a safe path. "See how the worn spots avoid certain areas? That's your tell."

Marcus nodded, pulling out a small flashlight and shining it at a low angle across the floor. The beam revealed subtle variations in the stone's surface. "Pressure plates. It's old school but effective. The magic's just window dressing for good old-fashioned engineering."

"No." Sarah shook her head, comparing the floor to her notes. "The magic is what makes them lethal. These symbols... they're channelling the relic's power. Alexei's twisted the original protections, turning them into weapons."

Nina mapped another section of safe ground, her movements precise. "Then we plot every trigger point. Create a safe route." She pulled chalk from her pocket and marked an X. "Starting here."

"The magic's not stable, though," Sarah insisted, her pen flying across her notebook. "These power flows, they're shifting. What's safe now might not be in five minutes."

Marcus crouched near the edge of the symbol ring, studying the patterns. "Then we move fast. Map what we can while we can." He marked another safe spot with Nina's chalk. "Better than standing here waiting to die."

A faint tremor rippled beneath their feet, almost imperceptible but enough to make the relic's glow falter. Sarah's eyes widened. "We're running out of time."

Marcus stepped toward the relic. "We can't afford dead weight. Anyone who can't keep up stays behind."

Ethan's teeth clenched. "That's not happening. We move together or not at all."

Marcus's gaze narrowed, his hand hovering close to his belt. "One weak link can bring down the whole chain," he said, his tone as cold as the stone underfoot. Ethan held his ground, feeling the weight of each life around him. "Not today."

"Enough." Captain Marsh's voice cut through the tension like a blade. She moved between them, her stance commanding attention. "This isn't a democracy or a debate. We're dealing with automated defences and unstable magic. That requires strategy, not ego."

She pointed to the chamber's left side. "Sarah, you and Nina map the symbol patterns. Your eye for detail is what we need." She turned to Marcus. "Your experience with traps makes you our point man. Take Twitch - his size gives him the best chance of avoiding pressure plates."

Marcus opened his mouth to object, but Marsh cut him off. "This isn't negotiable. Ethan, you and Lily focus on that relic. Your sister's connection to it might be our best shot at understanding what we're dealing with."

The authority in her voice left no room for argument. Even Marcus straightened slightly, responding to the familiar tone of command.

"We work in pairs. We watch each other's backs. And we move carefully." Marsh checked her watch. "Ten minutes to map our route. Then we execute. Questions?"

The silence that followed spoke volumes. Marsh had taken control not through force or manipulation but through tactical competence. Even Marcus gave a grudging nod before moving to his assigned position.

Ethan watched as the group split according to Marsh's instructions, their movements becoming more coordinated and more purposeful. The captain had done what he couldn't - turned their scattered band into something resembling a team.

Lily stumbled, her hand clutching her forearm where the sigil pulsed. Ethan caught her before she hit the ground, steadying her against his shoulder.

"Something's wrong." Sweat beaded on her forehead. "The relic, it's... pulling at me."

The sigil's glow matched the rhythm of the relic's light, creating a visual echo that made Ethan's stomach turn. Lily's eyes glazed over, her body tensing.

"I can see..." She blinked rapidly. "Shadows. People. They're trapped, Ethan. So many of them, crying out—" Her voice cracked as she doubled over.

Ethan moved to lift her. "That's it. We're getting you out of here."

"No." Sarah grabbed his arm. "The connection between her and the relic is part of the ritual. Breaking it now could be catastrophic."

"Look at her!" Ethan's voice echoed off the chamber walls. "This is killing her."

Lily gripped his sleeve. "I see what they did. How they bound it." Her words came in gasps. "The sacrifice wasn't just blood. It was... consciousness. Memory. They fed the relic with pieces of themselves."

Sarah flipped through her notes frantically. "The texts mentioned a vessel, someone to channel the power. Lily, your sigil—it chose you for this."

Ethan watched helplessly as another wave of pain hit his sister. Her fingers dug into his arm as the relic's light intensified, casting strange shadows across her face. The sigil seemed to writhe beneath her skin.

"I won't let you become a sacrifice," Ethan said.

"It's not your choice." Lily's voice was stronger now despite her obvious pain. "I have to do this. For everyone who's been lost. For Andrea."

Sarah placed a hand on Ethan's shoulder. "The ritual requires a conduit. Someone strong enough to channel its power. Fighting it will only make things worse."

Ethan felt the weight of each heartbeat as he watched his sister suffer, torn between his instinct to protect her and the knowledge that she had to endure this trial.

Twitch's breaths came in shallow gasps, his wide eyes darting between the shadows.

"They're here. All of them. Watching us." Twitch pressed himself against the wall, eyes darting between dark corners. "Can't you feel them? Like fingers on the back of your neck?"

Sarah clutched her notebook to her chest, edging closer to Lily. Her usual professional demeanor cracked, revealing raw fear beneath. "The symbols, they're... moving. Changing." Her voice quivered. "Lily, you see it, don't you? Please tell me you see it too."

Nina stood apart from the group, examining her nails with an almost bored expression. "Fascinating how it affects everyone differently." Her lips curved into a knowing smile. "Some minds are more... susceptible than others."

"What do you mean by that?" Ethan demanded.

Nina's smile deepened, something predatory flashing in her eyes. "Oh, I don't expect you to understand," she murmured. "But the relic only feeds if you offer it something. And you—" she glanced around the group, "—have plenty to give."

Ethan bristled at her tone. "If you know something, now's the time to share."

Marcus paced the chamber's edge, his movements growing more predatory. His hand kept straying to his weapon, fingers flexing. His eyes never left the relic, calculating, measuring the distance.

"Everyone maintains position," Captain Marsh commanded, her voice cutting through the growing tension. "Focus on your assigned tasks. Don't let it in your head."

But Ethan noticed the way her fingers tightened around her weapon, a subtle shift in her usually composed stance. Even she wasn't immune to the relic's influence.

"Time's running short," Nina whispered, just loud enough for Ethan to hear. "The question is, who will break first?" Her smile held no warmth. "The relic always knows."

Ethan stared at the intricate pattern of symbols stretching across the chamber floor. The markings seemed to pulse and shift, forming new configurations with each passing moment. His stomach tightened as he realized what they meant.

"The paths are mirrored," Sarah said, consulting her notes. "Two people must cross together - one seeing, one blind. The symbols suggest it's about balance, about..." She hesitated. "Trust."

Marcus stepped forward, a calculating gleam in his eyes. "Simple enough. Ethan, you'll wear the blindfold. I'll guide you through."

"Like hell," Ethan growled, but Lily caught his arm.

"The sigils are clear," she said, tracing the patterns with her finger. "Each pair must represent opposing forces - sight and blindness, knowledge and faith." She looked up at Sarah. "We need perfect synchronization, or the traps will trigger."

Captain Marsh studied the floor, her expression grim. "The patterns are changing. We'll need to move fast once we start."

"I've handled worse," Marcus said. "Ethan needs to trust someone who knows what they're doing."

Sarah stepped between them, her notebook clutched tight. "There's another way. Lily should go with Captain Marsh - they both understand the sigils. And Ethan..." She met his eyes. "You go with Marcus."

Ethan's heart sank in his chest. The thought of putting his life in Marcus's hands made his skin crawl. Every instinct screamed to refuse, to find another way. But as the symbols twisted into new shapes, he knew that logic was winning over instinct.

"Fine," he said through gritted teeth. "But if this is a trick-"

"Save the threats," Marcus cut him off, pulling a strip of cloth from his pocket. "Finally, you're learning to follow directions," he said, a challenge in his voice.

Lily squeezed Ethan's hand, her eyes calm and resolute. "The process is what matters, Ethan," she whispered. "Marcus can't break the ritual, no matter what he tries."

Ethan took a deep breath as Marcus tied the blindfold, darkness enveloping him. Every sound, every shift in the air felt amplified. He was trusting Marcus with his life—and every second filled him with dread.

Twitch's ragged breathing echoed through the chamber, his eyes darting between shadows that seemed to reach for him. Captain Marsh noticed the boy's trembling hands and how he kept shifting his weight from foot to foot.

"They're everywhere," Twitch whispered, backing away from his position. "In the walls, under the floor. Can't you hear them scratching?"

"Stay where you are," Marsh commanded, but her voice seemed distant to the terrified boy.

Twitch shook his head violently. "No, no, they're coming closer. I can feel them!" He stumbled backward, his foot catching on an uneven stone.

"Don't move!" Sarah shouted, but it was too late.

A sharp click echoed through the chamber. Twitch's eyes widened as the floor beneath him shifted. The chamber echoed with the brutal scrape of metal against stone, followed by the sickening thud of spikes piercing flesh.

"Twitch!" Marsh lunged forward, reaching for him.

"They're here! They're—" Twitch's final scream cut off abruptly, replaced by a gurgling that sent a shiver through the group.

Marsh's fingers grazed the fabric of his jacket, her hand closing on empty air as he was pulled further from her grasp. She stood frozen, her hand outstretched, a single drop of blood rolling down her finger.

When the mechanism finally stilled, silence fell over the chamber. Marsh stood frozen, her outstretched hand still reaching for where Twitch had been. Blood dripped from her fingers.

Ethan ripped off the blindfold and watched the colour drain from Sarah's face as she stared at the bloody spikes where the boy had stood moments before. Nina turned away, her usual composure cracking. Even Marcus seemed shaken; his mouth open wide.

Lily's sigil pulsed with renewed intensity. The relic's light seemed to flicker in response to the death, casting dancing shadows across Twitch's remains.

Sarah collapsed against the chamber wall, her shoulders shaking with silent sobs. Her notebook fell from her trembling hands, pages splaying across the stone floor. Blood from Twitch's death had spattered across her notes, turning careful observations into crimson-stained accusations.

"He was just a kid," she whispered, her voice cracking. "Just a scared kid."

Captain Marsh placed a steady hand on Sarah's shoulder, but the gesture seemed hollow in the wake of such violence. The authority that had commanded their respect minutes ago now wavered under the weight of responsibility.

"This is what happens when we carry dead weight." Marcus's voice cut through the heavy silence. "The boy was a liability from the start. Better to learn that lesson now than later when it costs more lives."

"Shut your mouth," Ethan growled, but Marcus continued, his tone clinical and detached.

"You all wanted to play hero, to save everyone. But that's not how survival works. I tried to tell you - we need to think about ourselves first."

Nina nodded slightly, shifting closer to Marcus's position. The chamber felt colder, divided by more than just the ancient symbols on the floor.

"We need to keep moving," Marsh said, her voice fighting for control. "Sarah, I'm sorry, but we can't-"

"Sorry?" Marcus sneered. "Your leadership just got a child killed. Maybe it's time someone else took charge."

Ethan grabbed the blindfold, tying it back around his eyes with sharp, angry movements. "Let's finish this, Marcus. Show us how it's done."

Marcus's hand closed around Ethan's arm, his grip unnecessarily tight. "Finally, some sense. Step where I tell you, exactly when I tell you."

"Just remember," Ethan said through clenched teeth, "I might be blind right now, but I won't always be."

They moved across the chamber floor, each step a dangerous dance between trust and suspicion. Marcus's commands came in clipped tones, professional but tinged with something darker. "Right. Now forward, slow. Stop. Left, three inches."

Ethan followed every muscle tense, knowing that his life rested in the hands of a man who'd just dismissed a child's death as a necessary sacrifice. The air in the chamber felt thicker with every step, the relic's pulsing light casting warped shadows across the ancient symbols.

"Almost there," Marcus said, his tone as detached as ever. But there was something else beneath it—a flicker of satisfaction, as though guiding Ethan was less about survival and more about control.

Ethan stumbled slightly, his boot scuffing against a raised edge. Marcus's hand tightened on his arm like a vice. "Careful," he hissed. "One more mistake like that, and it's over for both of us."

"Just keep talking," Ethan gruffed. "I'll get us through this."

Finally, Marcus's tone shifted to a clipped sharpness, giving way to something almost triumphant. "One more step, and we're clear."

Ethan took the final step forward, the uneven stone beneath his feet giving way to a smooth floor. He ripped off the blindfold, blinking against the chamber's dim light. His breath came in sharp bursts, his chest tight with adrenaline.

"We made it," Marcus said, releasing Ethan's arm with a smug grin. "Guess you can follow orders after all."

Ethan turned to face him, his jaw tight. "Don't mistake necessity for trust," he said, his voice low. "You may have gotten me across, but I'll never forget how you talk about sacrifice like it's just a calculation."

Marcus smirked, unbothered. "You're still alive, aren't you?"

Ethan glanced back at the chamber's deadly floor, then toward Lily and the others. "For now," he said, brushing past Marcus and toward his sister. "But that doesn't mean I owe you anything."

The moment hung heavy between them, a tenuous truce forged in survival but destined to break under the weight of their opposing ideals.

Ethan turned his focus to the relic, already glowing brighter in anticipation of their next move.

Sarah wiped her tears with trembling hands and forced herself to focus on the chamber walls. Her fingers traced the intricate patterns, stopping at an unusual variation in the ancient text.

"Wait..." She pulled out her notebook, flipping to earlier sketches. "These symbols, they're different. Modified." Her voice steadied as she slipped into analytical mode. "Look at the serifs, the extra marks. They're recent additions."

Ethan moved closer, studying where she pointed. "Recent, how?"

"Someone's been altering the original curse." Sarah's hand skimmed across the wall. "See these flourishes? They're precise and calculated. This isn't decay or damage - it's deliberate enhancement."

"Alexei Novikov." Lily's voice was barely a whisper. "Dr. Vane mentioned him in her research. An occultist obsessed with manipulating ancient power."

Sarah nodded vigorously. "Yes! These modifications match his documented style perfectly. The way he twists protective symbols into traps, how he corrupts binding runes..." She gestured to where Twitch had fallen. "That wasn't just an ancient defence mechanism. It was designed to feed on fear, to target the most vulnerable."

"The traps, the way some people seem to lose themselves to the curse ..." Marsh examined the walls with new understanding. "You're saying Novikov's controlling it all?"

"Not just controlling - enhancing. He's turned the original curse into his own twisted game." Sarah's hands shook as she documented the modifications. "The Night Watch isn't just some ancient ritual anymore. It's his playground, and we're all just pieces on his board."

Nina shifted uncomfortably, avoiding everyone's gaze. Marcus's face hardened into an unreadable mask.

"So breaking the curse isn't enough," Ethan said, watching his sister's sigil pulse. "We're up against someone actively manipulating everything we do."

"Someone who's probably watching us right now," Sarah added, her voice dropping to a whisper as she stared at the altered symbols surrounding them.

Ethan watched Marcus pace along the chamber's edge. Each step seemed calculated, precise - like a predator sizing up its territory.

"We're wasting time analyzing symbols," Marcus said, gesturing at Sarah's furious note-taking. "What matters is getting out alive. The rest is academic."

"Everything matters," Marsh countered, her hand resting on her holster. "Understanding how Novikov modified the curse could be the key to surviving it."

Marcus's laugh held no warmth. "Surviving it? Look what happened to the kid. Knowledge didn't save him. Action does. Movement. Making the hard choices when they need to be made."

"Choices like what?" Ethan stepped between Marcus and his sister, noting how the mercenary's eyes darted to Lily's sigil.

"Like accepting that not everyone makes it out." Marcus spread his hands. "Some of us are stronger, more capable. Natural selection at its finest."

"That's not how this works," Marsh said, her voice sharp. "We move as a unit."

"A chain is only as strong as its weakest link, Captain." Marcus's smile didn't reach his eyes. "And right now, we're dragging around quite a few weak links."

Nina nodded slightly at Marcus's words, edging closer to him. The movement wasn't lost on Ethan - another piece clicking into place.

"Funny how you're suddenly a survival expert," Ethan said, observing Marcus's reaction. "Almost like you knew what we'd find down here."

"I adapt. I learn. Unlike some, I don't let sentiment cloud my judgment." Marcus's gaze swept over Sarah's tear-stained face and Lily's pained expression. "The curse wants victims? Fine. Better them than us."

Marsh's hand tightened on her weapon. "Choose your next words carefully."

"Or what, Captain? You'll shoot me?" Marcus's smile widened. "Then who'll guide you through the next set of traps? Who'll make the calls you're too weak to make?"

***

Lily lunged forward, snatching the relic from its pedestal. The chamber shuddered, ancient dust raining from above. Ethan's heart stopped, but no deadly traps sprung.

"Move," Marsh barked, taking point. "Sarah, keep tracking those symbols. Marcus, rear guard."

They picked their way through the remaining chamber, following Sarah's directions past pressure plates and trigger points. Lily clutched the relic to her chest, its pulsing light casting strange shadows on the walls. Ethan stayed close to his sister, watching her face contort with each throb of her sigil.

The chamber's exit opened into a wider tunnel junction. Marsh raised her fist, signalling a halt. Her eyes swept the space, checking sight lines and defensive positions.

"We rest here." She pointed to a recessed alcove. "Ten minutes to catch our breath, check supplies."

Ethan helped Lily sit against the wall. She slumped forward, exhausted, the relic dim in her lap. Dark circles shadowed her eyes, and her hands trembled.

"Here." He offered his water bottle, but she shook her head.

"Save it," she whispered.

Marsh positioned herself at the junction's edge, weapon ready. "Ethan, help me secure the perimeter."

He joined her, checking the opposite approach. His muscles ached, and his mind felt fuzzy from the constant tension. The weight of keeping everyone alive - keeping Lily alive - pressed down on his shoulders.

"You're doing good," Marsh said quietly. "Keeping your head when others aren't."

Ethan watched Marcus and Nina whisper in the shadows. "Someone has to."

"We'll get them through this." Marsh's voice held the steady authority that had kept the group together. "But I need you sharp."

He nodded, understanding the responsibility they shared. The curse might be draining them, but they couldn't afford to break. Not with Lily's life hanging in the balance.

Sarah pulled a worn notebook from her jacket, flipping through pages of cramped handwriting. Her hands shook as she showed them a sketch of interlocking symbols - the same ones they'd seen in the chamber.

"These symbols have haunted my research," Sarah said, her voice barely above a whisper. "They've shown up in ancient manuscripts, carved into ruins across the city, and even in accounts from survivors of past Night Watches. Every path we've taken follows their design."

Ethan's stomach twisted. He'd seen those same markings scattered throughout their journey, like breadcrumbs leading them deeper into the maze.

"He's been orchestrating this," Sarah continued. "The traps, the sigils—they're not just remnants of the curse. They're part of something larger. Alexei's handprints are all over this."

"How do you know it's him?" Marsh asked, her eyes scanning the tunnel entrance as if expecting him to emerge.

Sarah flipped to another page, revealing a crude yet unmistakable sketch of a face—a symbol intertwined with the markings. "This emblem is tied to Alexei Novikov. It's been traced back centuries, appearing wherever the curse surfaces. Every survivor who described it said the same thing: they felt like they were being watched."

Lily's sigil pulsed brighter, as if responding to Sarah's words. She clutched the relic tighter, her knuckles white.

"I've spent years connecting the dots," Sarah said, her voice shaking. "The curse isn't just some ancient relic of Eldoria's past. Alexei took it, modified it, and turned it into this... labyrinth. He feeds off the fear, the deaths. Each victim makes him stronger."

"And now?" Ethan asked, his voice tense.

Sarah's gaze shifted to Lily's glowing sigil. "Now he's waiting for someone like her. Someone with the connection to complete his ritual."

The relic pulsed in sync with Lily's mark, casting sickly shadows across the tunnel walls. Ethan moved closer to his sister, his protective instinct flaring.

"We're playing his game," Sarah whispered. "Have been since the beginning. Every step, every death—it's all been by design."

Nina shifted uncomfortably in the shadows. Even Marcus's usual confidence seemed shaken by Sarah's revelations.

Chapter Twelve

SHATTERED BONDS

Lily's hands shook as she traced the relic's surface. The image of Twitch's body, broken and lifeless, refused to leave her mind. His last scream echoed in the chamber's silence.

"He was just a kid," she whispered. The sigil on her arm pulsed, each throb a reminder of their precarious situation.

Marcus leaned against the wall nearby, cleaning his knife with methodical precision. "Sometimes survival means making hard choices. The ritual..." He paused, steel glinting in the dim light. "Well, is it worth dying for?"

"That's enough," Marsh cut in, but the words had already taken root.

Ethan watched his sister's face fall, her usual determination cracking. The relic's glow dimmed, matching her wavering resolve.

"Maybe he's right." Lily's voice cracked. "We don't even know if this will work. The symbols, the ritual - what if we're following breadcrumbs to our deaths?"

"We stick to the plan," Marsh said, her tone brooking no argument. She moved to the group's center, commanding attention through presence alone. "That boy's death won't be for nothing. We finish what we started."

But Lily clutched the relic closer, doubt clouding her eyes. "I thought I understood it all. The patterns, the curse's rules. But now..." She looked at her glowing sigil. "What if I'm leading everyone to their deaths?"

"That's what the curse wants," Sarah interjected. "It feeds on doubt, on fear."

Marcus shrugged. "Or maybe it's trying to warn us."

"I said enough." Marsh's voice carried steel, but Ethan saw how Lily's shoulders slumped further.

The chamber felt smaller suddenly, the weight of their choices pressing in. Lily's earlier confidence had crumbled, replaced by the heavy mantle of responsibility. Each pulse of her sigil seemed to ask: how many more would die before the night ended?

Lily's fingers trembled against the relic's cold surface. Twitch's face, young and terrified in those final moments, burned behind her eyes. The weight of his death crushed her chest, making each breath a struggle.

"I did this," she whispered. "I led him here."

Ethan moved closer, his presence solid and warm beside her. "This isn't your fault."

But the words felt hollow. The sigil pulsed on her arm, each throb a reminder of the power she'd foolishly thought she could control. Dr. Vane's teachings about the ritual, once so clear and promising, now seemed like a desperate grasping at straws.

A smooth and compelling voice whispered in her mind—Alexei's voice. *The ritual is a lie. Only the strong survive.*

"What if we're wrong?" Her voice cracked. "What if there is no way to break it?"

"Remember what Dr. Vane told you," Ethan said, his hand steady on her shoulder.

Lily closed her eyes. She saw Dr. Vane's office, papers scattered across her desk, determination burning in her eyes. *"The curse feeds on doubt,"* she had said. *"It will try to break your resolve when you're closest to the truth. That's when hope matters most."*

But hope felt distant now, slipping through her fingers like smoke. The sigil burned brighter, its power seeping into her bones. Alexei's whispers grew stronger, promising safety and survival—if only she'd let go of this foolish quest.

"I don't know if I'm strong enough," Lily admitted, her voice barely audible. The relic's glow pulsed in sync with her sigil, a dance of power she no longer trusted herself to lead.

The whispers grew stronger in Lily's mind, each one carrying Alexei's smooth, compelling voice. *The ritual will destroy you all. Survival requires strength. Let go of this foolish quest.*

Her fingers trembled against the relic's cold surface. The sigil pulsed faster, matching her racing heart.

"Something's wrong." Sarah's voice cut through the silence. She pointed her flashlight at the ground, revealing fresh marks in the dirt. Deep gouges ran parallel as massive claws had torn through the earth.

Marsh crouched to examine them. "These are fresh."

A heavy presence pressed against Lily's consciousness, different from Alexei's whispers but somehow connected. Raw, primal, hungry. The relic grew colder in her hands.

Viktor comes for you, Alexei's voice purred in her mind. *My hammer falls without mercy.*

"He's here," Lily whispered, her throat tight. "Viktor. I can feel him."

Ethan's hand went to his gun. "What do you mean, feel him?"

The pressure in her mind increased. Through it, she caught glimpses - tunnel walls seen through different eyes, the scent of prey, the thrill of the hunt. The connection to Alexei's enforcer felt like ice in her veins.

"The curse," she managed. "It's not just marking us. It's connecting us. Viktor's... changed. He's part of it now."

More claw marks appeared on the chamber walls, higher up, as if something massive had climbed past. The relic's glow dimmed, responding to her growing terror.

Accept the truth, Alexei whispered. *The weak perish. The strong survive.*

A distant scrape echoed through the tunnel like a stone being torn apart. The whispers in Lily's mind swelled, drowning out her thoughts with Alexei's chilling certainty. "He's coming."

***

Nina traced her fingers along the chamber wall, stopping at a series of interconnected symbols. "These markings... they're not just decorative. They're a map."

Ethan moved closer, studying the etched lines that spread like a web across the stone. The relic in Lily's hands pulsed in response to Nina's touch.

"There are five points." Nina's voice dropped. "Each represents a relic of power. What you're holding? That's just the first."

Marcus stepped forward, his expression hard. "We don't have time to chase trinkets across the city."

"The Eye's Offering is the key." Nina's gaze fixed on Lily. "That's the one that matters most. The others... they stabilize the ritual, make it safer. But they're not essential."

Captain Marsh's hand settled on her weapon. "You seem to know an awful lot about this."

"Knowledge is survival in Eldoria." Nina shrugged. "But missing pieces make the ritual unstable. More dangerous. The Eye's Offering alone could tear reality apart."

"We're not gambling with people's lives," Ethan said. "We do this right."

Marcus laughed, the sound sharp and cold. "Right? Look what 'right' got us so far. Twitch is dead. Viktor's hunting us. We grab the Eye and end this."

"And risk the whole ritual backfiring?" Marsh stepped between Marcus and Nina. "Not happening."

"Time isn't on our side," Marcus pressed. "Every minute we waste chasing relics—"

"Is better than rushing in half-prepared," Ethan cut him off.

Nina's fingers danced across more symbols. "The choice is yours. But remember - the curse adapts. It learns. The longer we take, the stronger it grows."

The group split apart, tension crackling between them. Marcus and Nina clustered near the tunnel entrance, while Marsh and Ethan stood firm by Lily, who clutched the first relic tighter.

The sigil on Lily's arm pulsed, casting shadows that made the chamber's markings writhe like living things.

Marcus prowled the chamber, his restless energy radiating tension with every measured step. The mercenary's eyes kept darting to the tunnel entrance, then back to Nina.

"We're wasting time with these relics." Each step Marcus took landed with a muted thud, his movement cutting through the uneasy silence. "The curse is picking us off one by one. How many more Twitches before we accept reality?"

"The ritual is our best shot," Marsh said, her posture tense and unyielding.

Marcus spread his arms. "Best shot? Look around. We're rats in a maze, following breadcrumbs left by dead men. Nina's right - the Eye's Offering is all that matters."

Lily's fingers trembled around the relic. "But if we skip steps, the backlash could—"

"Could what?" Nina cut in. "Kill us? We're already dead if we stay this course."

Ethan stepped closer to his sister. "The ritual's not negotiable. We finish what we started."

"Such noble intentions." Marcus's smile didn't reach his eyes. "How's that working out for you, Marlowe? For any of us?"

Sarah hunched over her notes, avoiding the conflict. Nina drifted toward Marcus, their shoulders almost touching.

"Enough." Marsh's voice cracked like a whip. "We stick to the plan. Anyone who doesn't like it can leave. Now."

Marcus held up his hands in mock surrender. "Just trying to keep us alive, Captain. Some of us remember what happened to the last group that attempted this ritual."

Lily's breath caught. The relic's pulse quickened with her heartbeat.

"We need to move," Marsh said. "Together or not at all."

The group formed two distinct clusters - Marcus and Nina by the entrance, the others around Lily. The chamber's shadows deepened between them, a physical manifestation of their divide.

Ethan recognized the look in Marcus's eyes. He'd seen it before in cornered predators, waiting for the perfect moment to strike.

Ethan stepped between the divided groups, his shoulders squared. "This isn't about just making it through tonight. We're trying to break a curse that's killed hundreds."

"Pretty speeches won't save us," Marcus sneered.

"Neither will shortcuts." Ethan turned to face the others. "Dr. Vane spent years researching this ritual. Every component matters. The relics balance each other."

Nina crossed her arms. "And how many died following her research?"

"Which is exactly why we can't rush this." Ethan's voice carried the weight of every victim he'd failed to save. "Andrea died because we didn't understand what we were dealing with. Because we tried to face this curse without proper preparation."

Marsh nodded. "Marlowe's right. We do this by the book."

"The ritual isn't just about power," Ethan continued, meeting each person's gaze. "It's about choice. About standing together against something that's torn this city apart for generations." He placed a hand on Lily's shoulder. "My sister's been marked, but she's not just another victim. She's our chance to end this."

Sarah looked up from her notes. "The symbols support what he's saying. Each relic represents a different aspect of the binding."

"This isn't a democracy," Marcus commented.

"No, it's not." Ethan stepped closer to the mercenary. "But neither is it your personal mission. We're not sacrificing anyone. We're not taking shortcuts. Either help us do this right, or leave."

The chamber fell silent except for the soft pulse of the relic. Marcus stood ready to pounce, but something in Ethan's stance made him back down.

"Fine." Marcus raised his hands. "Your funeral."

"Our success," Marsh corrected. "Together."

Sarah slumped against the chamber wall. "I can't stop seeing it. The way Twitch just—" Her voice cracked. "He was so young."

Lily knelt beside her, the relic's pulse casting a soft glow across their faces. Her sigil throbbed, a constant reminder of what was at stake. "I know. I keep thinking if I'd been faster if I'd warned him—"

"What if the ritual demands more?" Sarah's fingers dug into the notebook's pages. "What if that's what it's designed for? To take us one by one until—" She drew a shuddering breath. "Dr. Vane's notes mentioned sacrifices. Blood magic."

"This isn't like that," Lily said, but uncertainty crept into her voice. She touched the sigil on her arm. "It can't be."

"You don't sound convinced." Sarah met Lily's gaze. "I've covered stories about occult rituals before. They always end the same way - with bodies and grief and—"

"Stop." Lily's hand trembled as she gripped the relic tighter. "I've studied this for years. The ritual is about breaking bonds, not creating them through death."

But Sarah's words had struck a nerve. Lily felt the weight of doubt pressing down, mixing with her guilt over Twitch. The sigil pulsed harder, responding to her uncertainty.

"Then why did Twitch die?" Sarah's voice dropped to a whisper. "Why does it feel like we're being hunted, picked off? Like we're part of some bigger sacrifice?"

Lily opened her mouth to respond, but the words stuck in her throat. She'd believed so strongly in her research, in the path she'd chosen. But now, with Twitch's death fresh in her mind and Sarah voicing the fears she'd been fighting to ignore, her conviction wavered.

"I don't know," Lily admitted, the words tasting bitter. "I thought I understood it all. But now—" She stared at the relic in her hands, its light seeming dimmer than before.

Marcus crouched beside Sarah, his voice dropping to a gentle murmur. "You're right to question this. How many more deaths will it take before we admit this ritual is just another trap?"

Ethan's brows lowered, but Marcus continued before he could interrupt.

"Think about it. Five relics scattered across a cursed city? That's not a path to salvation - it's a killing field." Marcus gestured at the relic in Lily's hands. "But the Eye's Offering? One focused sacrifice to end it all. Clean. Simple."

Sarah's fingers twisted in her notebook pages. "But Dr. Vane's research—"

"Got people killed." Marcus leaned closer. "You've seen the bodies, written the stories. How many more obituaries do you want to pen?"

Lily's grip on the relic loosened slightly. "The ritual's supposed to break bonds, not create them through death."

"Is that what you believe?" Marcus's eyes fixed on her sigil. "Or what you need to believe? Because right now, that mark is drawing death to us like moths to flame."

"We agreed to stick together," Marsh warned.

Marcus spread his hands. "I'm just being realistic. Every minute we waste hunting trinkets puts us all at risk." He turned back to Lily. "Your research is admirable, but sometimes the simplest solution is the right one. The Eye's Offering could end this tonight."

Nina nodded from her position by the tunnel. "He's not wrong. The longer we take, the stronger the curse grows. Sometimes survival means making hard choices."

Lily's confidence visibly wavered as she looked between the relic and her glowing sigil. Sarah shifted closer to Marcus, her earlier resolve cracking under the weight of his words.

"The ritual..." Lily's voice faltered. "There has to be another way."

"There is," Marcus said softly. "But you have to be willing to see it."

Marsh stepped into the center of the chamber. "Everyone, eyes on me." Her voice carried the weight of decades of command, cutting through the whispers of doubt Marcus had planted.

Ethan watched as she squared her shoulders, her hand resting on her holstered weapon. The gesture wasn't threatening - it was grounding, a reminder of order in chaos.

"I've spent twenty years watching this curse tear families apart. Seen good people twisted by fear into monsters." Marsh's gaze swept across their faces. "Every time someone tried to fight it alone, they died. Every time someone looked for an easy way out, they failed."

The relic's pulse seemed to quiet as if listening.

"This ritual?" She gestured to Lily's research. "It's not just about survival. It's about ending a cycle of death that's poisoned our city for generations. Dr. Vane didn't piece this together overnight. She built on the work of others who died trying to break this curse."

Sarah lowered her notebook. Nina shifted, unable to meet Marsh's steady gaze.

"You want to talk about sacrifice?" Marsh's voice hardened. "Look around. Every marking on these walls, every piece of research - they're messages from people who died trying to show us the right way. We owe it to them to finish what they started."

Lily's grip on the relic steadied.

"So yes, this is dangerous. Yes, we might die. But if we abandon the ritual now, if we let fear drive us to shortcuts, then Twitch died for nothing." Marsh stood straighter. "I won't let that happen. We do this right, or we don't do it at all."

The chamber fell silent. Even Marcus's usual smirk faltered under the weight of her words.

"Now," Marsh said, "are we ready to move forward? Together?"

One by one, heads nodded. The group drew closer, their earlier division healing under Marsh's steady leadership.

Lily's hands trembled around the relic as a familiar chill crept through her thoughts. The chamber's shadows deepened, and beneath the steady pulse of the artifact, she heard it - Alexei's voice, closer than before, sliding through her mind like ice water.

"You feel it, don't you?" The whisper caressed her consciousness. "The power growing inside you. The sigil isn't just a mark - it's a key. Your key."

She pressed her back against the cold stone wall, trying to ground herself in its solidity. The relic's light flickered in response to her racing heart.

"The others don't understand what you're becoming." Alexei's voice wound through her thoughts like smoke. "They see the ritual as their salvation, but you... you're so much more than a simple component."

Lily's fingers traced the sigil on her arm. Its glow had intensified, pulsing in time with Alexei's words. Each beat sent waves of awareness through her as if the curse itself recognized something in her blood.

"Breaking bonds requires more than relics and symbols," the voice continued. "It demands transformation. Are you prepared for what that truly means?"

She opened her mouth to scream, to warn the others, but the sound died before it could form. The chamber's ancient markings seemed to writhe in her vision, rearranging themselves into patterns that whispered of prices yet to be paid.

"The curse flows through your veins now," Alexei's voice grew stronger, more insistent. "When the time comes, you'll understand the true cost of freedom. The question is - are you willing to pay it?"

The relic flared in her hands, its light casting her shadow against the wall - a shadow that seemed to move independently, reaching toward something unseen. The sigil burned brighter, and Lily felt a surge of power that both terrified and thrilled her.

CHAPTER THIRTEEN

TETHERED TO FATE

Ethan watched Marcus pace the chamber like a caged animal. "Five relics, five different locations. Do the math - together, we waste precious time."

"And separated, we're easy prey." Marsh planted herself between Marcus and the rest of the group. "Viktor's still out there. Not to mention whatever else this curse has waiting for us."

Nina slid closer to Marcus, her eyes darting between him and the others. "He's got a point. More ground covered means better chances. We've all survived this long on our own."

"Survived, yes. But that's not enough anymore." Ethan stepped forward, keeping his voice steady. "This isn't about individual survival. The ritual requires all five relics to work together."

Marcus's laugh echoed off the walls. "Always the idealist, Marlowe. Tell me, how many people have died following your noble causes?"

"Enough." Marsh's hand slammed against the wall. "This isn't a debate. We move as one unit."

"Or what, Captain?" Marcus squared his shoulders. "You'll arrest me? Your badge means nothing down here. The only law that matters is survival."

Nina nodded. "The chosen ones always die in groups. Safety in numbers is just an illusion."

"The curse wants us divided." Ethan moved between Marcus and Marsh. "Every symbol, every trap - they're designed to split us apart. Make us easier targets."

"Then some of us become targets." Marcus's eyes hardened. "Better than all of us dying because we're too slow."

Sarah clutched her notebook tighter. "The research suggests the relics need to be gathered in a specific sequence. If we split up and get them in the wrong order-"

"More theories and maybes." Marcus cut her off. "While we stand here debating, that sigil is burning through Lily's arm. Time isn't on our side."

The chamber filled with the sound of arguing voices, each person taking sides. Ethan watched as the group he'd fought so hard to protect began fracturing under fear and desperation.

Sarah's hands trembled as she flipped through her notebook, her shoulders pressed against the cold stone wall. Her eyes darted between Marcus and Nina, who huddled in whispered conversation across the chamber.

"I can't shake this feeling." Sarah's voice cracked as she leaned closer to Ethan and Lily. "The way they look at us like we're just pieces in their game."

Ethan followed her gaze. Marcus caught his eye and smiled - all teeth, no warmth.

"We need to stay focused." Lily winced as her sigil pulsed. "The ritual-"

"The ritual requires trust." Sarah's pen scratched frantically across the paper. "Look what happened to Twitch. One wrong move and..." She stopped writing, her hand frozen mid-sentence.

Ethan remembered Father Gabriel's words in the church. 'In darkness, we must stand together. It's not about what we believe, but who we stand with.'

"I thought I could document this, find the truth." Sarah's voice dropped to a whisper. "But the truth is we're falling apart. Marcus and Nina are waiting for their moment. And when it comes-"

"We won't let it." Ethan kept his voice low but firm.

Sarah shook her head. "You don't understand. I've seen this before - reporting on gang wars and corrupt officials. Groups fracture from within. One betrayal, that's all it takes." She clutched her notebook to her chest. "We won't make it. Not together. Not with them."

The chamber's shadows seemed to deepen around them, matching the growing doubt in Sarah's eyes. The low murmur of their voices seemed to ripple through the chamber, feeding the unease that gnawed at Sarah's resolve.

***

Lily pressed her palm against the damp chamber wall, steadying herself. The weight of their journey pressed down on her shoulders as she closed her eyes, seeking a moment's respite. The darkness behind her eyelids shifted and morphed.

Her eyes snapped open to a different scene. Bodies littered the streets of Eldoria, twisted and broken under a blood-red sky. The stench of decay filled her nostrils as she stumbled forward.

Sarah's corpse sprawled across broken concrete, her precious notebook clutched in skeletal fingers. Marcus and Nina lay tangled together, their flesh grey and sunken. Captain Marsh's uniform hung in tatters from her decomposing frame.

Her breath caught in her throat. Ethan's body slumped against a wall, his leather jacket torn, his face - that familiar face she'd known all her life - now a grotesque mask of death. His empty eye sockets stared at nothing.

"This path leads only to destruction." Alexei's voice cut through the horror. He materialized before her, pristine in his dark suit, untouched by the decay surrounding them. "But it doesn't have to end this way."

He extended his hand. "Follow me, and spare them this fate. The choice is yours alone."

The vision shattered. Lily gasped, her back hitting the chamber wall. The sigil on her arm burned fiercer than before. Her companions stood around her, alive, whole - but for how long? The image of Ethan's corpse lingered in her mind, impossible to shake.

She glanced at the symbols on the wall that had seemed so clear before. Now they whispered of doubt, of paths that led only to death. The ritual she'd believed in so strongly felt like sand slipping through her fingers.

Alexei's words echoed in her thoughts. A choice. Her choice. The weight of it pressed against her chest, making it hard to breathe.

***

Marcus traced a path on their makeshift map, his finger landing on an old factory district. "The next relic's here. We split into two teams; move faster."

"Teams stay within visual range." Captain Marsh's voice cut through the chamber. "No one goes dark; maintain radio contact."

"That defeats the purpose of splitting up." Marcus crossed his arms. "Time isn't on our side."

Ethan watched the power play unfold. The way Marcus positioned himself, how he'd caught Sarah and Nina's attention - it wasn't random.

Every move was calculated, every suggestion wrapped in logic that pulled at their desperation.

"We move as I direct." Marsh stepped closer to Marcus, her badge catching the dim light. "Your experience is noted, but this is my operation."

Marcus's lip curled. "Your operation? Look around, Captain. We're beyond police jurisdiction."

"He has a point," Sarah whispered, earning a sharp look from Marsh.

"Two teams." Marcus addressed the group, ignoring Marsh. "Sarah and Nina with me. We'll-"

"Sarah stays with my team." Marsh's hand rested on her holster. "Non-negotiable."

The tension crackled. Ethan shifted his weight, ready to move if needed. He'd seen that look in Marcus's eyes before - in suspects who were about to do something stupid.

But Marcus smiled instead, raising his hands in mock surrender. "Whatever you say, Captain."

They formed up - Marsh took point, and Marcus was on the rear guard. But Ethan noticed how the others glanced at Marcus now, seeking his subtle nod of approval. Marcus's influence had taken root even as they followed Marsh's hand signals.

Ethan kept close to Lily, one eye always on Marcus. The man was building something - an alliance, a following, or worse. And Marsh, for all her authority, was losing ground with every step.

Marcus pulled Nina aside as the group navigated the dark corridor, his voice low enough that only she could hear. "Something's wrong. I feel it - like hooks in my mind, pulling me forward."

Nina's eyes narrowed. She'd seen this before in others who'd delved too deep into Eldoria's mysteries. "Not the sigil?"

"Different. Stronger." Marcus pressed his palm against the cold wall, steadying himself. "Like someone's whispering directions straight into my thoughts."

Nina glanced ahead at the others, making sure they were out of earshot. "The old texts speak of puppet strings - threads of power that reach beyond the mark." She traced a pattern in the air, mimicking the ancient symbols. "We might not be the ones choosing our path."

Sarah hung back from the leading group, Dr. Vane's warnings echoing in her mind. The doctor had been adamant about Alexei's reach - how he could twist the curse, bend it to his will. She'd shown Sarah her research notes, pages filled with accounts of marked victims who'd acted against their own interests, guided by an unseen hand.

"The curse isn't just about the hunt," Dr. Vane had told her. "It's his instrument, his way of conducting a darker symphony."

Marcus stumbled, catching himself against the wall. Nina steadied him, her fingers digging into his arm. "You feel it too, don't you?" he asked.

"We're being herded," Nina whispered. "Like cattle to slaughter."

Sarah watched their exchange, her reporter's instincts screaming that something was terribly wrong. Dr. Vane's theories were proving true - Alexei's influence extended far beyond the glowing marks on their skin.

Marcus pulled Nina deeper into the shadows, letting the group move ahead until their voices faded to whispers. His fingers pressed into her arm, not a gesture of comfort but of control.

"The others will slow us down." His eyes darted to where Marsh's flashlight beam cut through the darkness. "They're dead weight."

Nina studied his face, noting the hardness that hadn't been there before. The confident mercenary mask had cracked, revealing something raw and primal underneath. "What about Sarah? She's useful."

"Sarah's loyal to Marsh." He spat the captain's name like poison. "And Ethan?" A cold laugh. "Still playing hero while his sister bleeds them dry with her crusade."

The distant echo of footsteps grew fainter. Marcus's shoulders tensed, his body angling away from the group's direction. Nina recognized the shift - she'd survived long enough in Eldoria's under- world to know when someone was cutting ties.

"We need to be ready." Marcus checked his weapons with mechanical precision. "When things go bad - and they will - we can't hesitate."

"The ritual-" Nina started.

"Is a death trap." Marcus's voice dropped lower, edges sharp with certainty. "You've seen how they operate. Marsh with her rules, Ethan with his morals. They'll get us killed trying to save everyone."

He straightened, adjusting his tactical vest. The others were barely visible now, their lights like dying stars in the tunnel's throat. Marcus didn't move to follow.

"We didn't survive this long by playing team sports." His hand rested on his holster, a habit that seemed more threatening than reassuring now. "Remember that when the time comes."

***

Pain shot through Lily's arm like liquid fire. The sigil blazed, its silver-blue light casting harsh shadows across the tunnel walls. Her knees buckled.

"Lily!" Ethan caught her before she hit the ground. Her skin burned beneath his touch.

Her eyes rolled back, unfocused. The chamber spun away, replaced by fractured images - blood seeping through ancient stones, the obsidian mirror reflecting countless faces twisted in agony. Above it all loomed the watchtower, its silhouette stark against a blood-red sky, radiating a dark energy that seemed to anchor the curse itself. At the center of it all, a pulsing heart of darkness called to her.

"The tower," she gasped, her voice thin. "It's... feeding on them. All of them."

Ethan cradled her head, his throat tight. She'd grown so pale, dark circles deepening under her eyes with each vision. Each step toward the relic seemed to drain more life from her.

Sarah crouched beside them, pressing a water bottle to Lily's lips. "The sigil's connection is getting stronger. It's using her as a conduit. The watchtower... it's the source, isn't it?" Her voice trembled, eyes flickering to her notes.

Lily's hand clutched Ethan's jacket. "It's the anchor... the heart of the curse." She struggled to sit up, her arms shaking with the effort. "We have to keep moving."

"You can barely stand," Ethan's voice cracked. He'd sworn to protect her, but watching the ritual slowly consume her...

"I'm the only one who can complete it." Lily's words came between ragged breaths. "The sigil chose me for a reason. The tower—" She stopped, swallowing hard. "It's where everything ends."

Sarah pulled out her worn notebook, fingers trembling as she flipped through the pages. "These symbols, they're not just ancient markings. They're his signature." Her voice dropped to a whisper. "Alexei's been leaving breadcrumbs, watching us piece them together."

Ethan shifted his grip on Lily, who still struggled to catch her breath. "What do you mean?"

"Look here." Sarah traced the curved lines etched into the chamber walls. "These match patterns from unsolved murders dating back decades—cases where victims were found with similar markings." She showed them a series of photographs, crime scene shots of bodies marked with intricate designs. "He's been perfecting this ritual, testing different combinations."

Marsh moved closer, her flashlight beam steady on Sarah's evidence. "You've been tracking him."

"For years. But I never understood the full scope until now." Sarah's hands shook as she revealed more photos. "Each victim, each marking - variations of what we see here. He's been refining the curse, learning its limits."

Nina pressed against the wall, her face pale. "So we're what - his latest experiment?"

"More than that." Sarah's eyes met Lily's. "He's orchestrating every step, watching how we handle each challenge. The symbols change slightly with each group that's tried this ritual. He's testing different variables, different combinations of people."

Ethan's jaw dropped. "Like some sick game."

"A game he's mastered." Sarah tucked her notebook away. "But understanding his patterns might be our only advantage. These symbols - they're not just directing us through the tunnels. They're telling us how previous groups failed."

Marsh nodded slowly. "Knowledge we can use."

"If we survive long enough to use it," Marcus muttered.

Sarah straightened, her reporter's instincts cutting through her fear. "That's exactly what he wants - for us to doubt, to turn on each other. But we have something previous groups didn't." She gestured to her research. "We can see his hand in this. We can anticipate his moves."

***

The relic pulsed with an ethereal green glow, suspended in a crystalline case at the chamber's center. As they approached, shadows writhed across the walls, taking forms that made Ethan's skin crawl.

"There it is." Lily's voice wavered. "The Heart of Dawn."

The floor shifted beneath their feet. Ancient gears ground to life, and sections of the floor began to sink and rise in an ever-changing pattern. The air reeked with an acidic smell that burned Ethan's lungs.

"Gas." Marcus backed away, covering his nose with his sleeve.

The gas burned their throats with every breath, its sharp tang filling their airways. Sarah doubled over, coughing violently, while Lily pressed a trembling hand to her nose, her eyes tearing from the fumes. Even Marcus, usually unfazed, had his sleeve pulled tight over his face, his gaze darting between the relic and the shifting floor. Marsh's voice came through hoarse and strained. 'Keep moving! Don't let it overwhelm you!' But the gas seemed to shrink their lungs with each inhale, each step heavier than the last.

"This whole chamber's rigged. We need to clear out," yelled Marcus.

"Not without the relic." Marsh stepped forward, her flashlight beam cutting through the growing haze. "We've come too far."

Marcus grabbed her arm. "You want to die for a piece of rock? Those floor plates are pressure-sensitive. One wrong step and—"

"And what?" Marsh yanked free. "We let another group of chosen ones die? Watch more bodies pile up in our morgue?"

"Better them than us." Marcus's eyes hardened. "Sometimes survival means making hard choices."

"That's not a choice." Marsh's voice cut like steel. "That's cowardice."

Sarah hesitated, her eyes darting between the relic and the growing chasm below. "Marsh, he's not wrong about the gas. We don't even know if we can reach it in time."

The chamber rumbled. More floor sections dropped away, revealing a bottomless darkness below.

"Two minutes." Marcus checked his watch. "That's how long we have before this gas knocks us out. You want to risk everyone's lives for your noble crusade, Captain?"

"This isn't about nobility." Marsh pulled out a length of rope. "It's about doing what's necessary. Even if that means risking everything."

The gas burned stronger. Through streaming eyes, Ethan watched the deadly dance of rising and falling floor plates, the relic's glow beckoning them forward like a siren's call.

Lily's hands trembled as she reached for the Heart of Dawn. The relic's pulsing light matched the rhythm of her sigil, creating a disorienting synchronicity that made her head swim.

Choose wisely, dear Lily. Alexei's voice slithered through her mind, clear as crystal despite the chaos around them. *The power to save them all lies within you.*

Her fingers brushed the crystalline surface. The sigil on her arm flared white-hot, drawing a gasp from her lips.

They'll never understand the sacrifice required. But you will. You already do.

"Lily?" Ethan's voice seemed distant, muffled by the thundering in her ears.

The relic slid into her grasp, deceptively light, yet its power bore down on her as if the weight of the entire city had been placed in her hands. Images exploded behind her eyes—streets flooded with blood, the watchtower shattering into jagged pieces, and Alexei standing at its crumbling peak, his laughter rolling through the chaos like thunder. His hands, raised high, seemed to control the destruction as easily as a conductor leads an orchestra.

The ritual demands transformation. You're the key, the vessel, the chosen one who will reshape this city's destiny.

"Got it!" She clutched the relic to her chest, but the victory felt hollow. The whispers lingered, wrapping around her thoughts like thorny vines.

Soon, you'll face a choice that will determine their fate. Their lives hang by a thread, and you hold the scissors.

The group rushed to secure their exit, but Lily remained rooted, staring into the relic's depths. She saw reflections of possible futures in its shifting light – each more terrible than the last. Alexei's presence grew stronger, his influence seeping into her bones like ice water.

The time approaches, dear Lily. Will you be ready to pay the price?

CHAPTER FOURTEEN

DESCENT INTO DARKNESS

Sarah matched Nina's brisk pace through the shadowed streets, her notepad glossy cover slick in her sweating palm. Above them, the jagged spire of the distant clock tower carved through the sky was an ominous reminder of Eldoria's cursed history.

"The curse started with the founding families," Nina said, her voice light but precise, her boots finding smooth paths across the cracked pavement. "They built the watchtower as a focal point for their rituals."

Sarah's pen flew across her notepad, each scratch a small act of defiance against her mounting unease. "That lines up with the archives I reviewed. But the timing doesn't quite add up. The first recorded incidents—"

"Those came later. Much later." Nina's casual wave dismissed centuries of documented research. "The real power gathered during the industrial boom—when the workers flooded in. So much suffering, so many lives lost. Perfect fuel for dark magic."

The certainty in Nina's tone made Sarah pause mid-scribble. The timeline didn't match. Eldoria's earliest cursed incidents had been meticulously documented long before the industrial expansion.

"What about the Merchant's Guild records?" Sarah asked, forcing her voice to remain steady. "They show—"

Nina's sharp laugh cut her off. "Those dusty old ledgers? Hardly gospel. The truth runs deeper than any of that."

Sarah's pen hovered. Her eyes flicked to Nina, then to Marcus, walking ahead with Ethan. Nina's glance toward him was fleeting, but the subtle nod was unmistakable.

"You seem unusually well-informed about the city's history," Sarah ventured, her tone carefully neutral even as her pulse quickened.

"I listen." Nina's reply was clipped. "In the underground, secrets don't stay buried for long. The curse thrives on them."

Her gaze shifted again, darting to Marcus, whose fingers twitched in response—an unspoken signal. Sarah's unease deepened.

Nina's version of events contradicted documented history, her narrative weaving new threads into a story Sarah thought she understood. But it wasn't just the inconsistencies. It was the silent exchanges with Marcus, their synchronization too deliberate to be a coincidence.

Sarah slowed her pace, letting Nina drift ahead. Her mind raced, cataloging the inconsistencies, the subtle gestures, and the deliberate way Nina deflected questions while offering just enough detail to keep Sarah intrigued.

Nina moved with the confidence of someone accustomed to shadows—accustomed to wielding secrets like weapons. But Sarah's instincts screamed that these weren't Nina's secrets to keep. The question was, why share them now, and to what end?

Ethan's flashlight beam caught the sheen of frost creeping across the tunnel walls, an impossible sight in the underground passages. The temperature plummeted with each step, clouding his breath.

Lily stumbled, clutching her marked arm. The sigil's glow flared brighter, its sickly blue light staining the rough walls and throwing jagged shadows.

"You okay?" He steadied her, noting how she trembled beneath his grip.

"It's burning." She pressed her palm over the mark. "Like it's trying to tell me something."

The shadows moved. Not the expected flicker of light, but a writhing, reaching motion that defied natural behavior. Fingers of darkness curled toward their feet, making Ethan's skin prickle with cold dread. Ethan's skin crawled as darkness pooled in impossible angles, defying the laws of light and shadow. He shifted closer to Lily, positioning himself between her and the unnatural movements.

Ancient sigils carved into the tunnel walls seemed to squirm and reshape themselves, their edges blurring and reforming into new configurations. The symbols pulsed with a deep crimson light that made his eyes water.

Captain Marsh crouched by the wall, her gloved hand tracing fresh gouges etched deep into the stone. Four parallel lines, deep enough to score the rock. Her jaw tightened as she measured the spacing with her hand.

"Viktor's been through here," she murmured, eyes scanning ahead. "Recently."

The city pressed in around them, its malevolence a physical weight. The air grew thick and stale, carrying whispers just below the hearing threshold. Every surface felt wrong - too cold, smooth, and alive beneath their touch.

Ethan's hand found his gun, though he knew bullets would do little against whatever force animated these tunnels. His sister's labored breathing beside him only heightened his anxiety. The sigil's light painted her face ghoulishly as she fought against its burning influence.

Marsh's gaze scanned ahead, unrelenting. "Stay sharp. This isn't just Viktor." She stood, her hand hovering near her holster. "The city's watching us."

***

Ethan's instincts screamed danger the moment they crossed into the chamber. The grinding of ancient gears filled the air, followed by the whisper of steel against stone.

"Down!" Marsh's command cut through the darkness.

Blades burst from the walls in gleaming arcs. The group dropped and rolled, metal singing through the spaces they'd occupied seconds before.

Lily stood frozen, her eyes glazed. The sigil on her arm blazed with intensity, casting wild shadows across her face.

"Lily, move!" Ethan lunged toward his sister.

Marcus's eyes flicked to Lily, then to the exit. His hands twitched, indecision carving deep lines into his face. Survival meant leaving others behind—that had always been his rule. But as the blade sliced through Lily's arm, the weight of his choice settled like a stone in his gut. Blood bloomed across her sleeve.

"You bastard!" Ethan slammed Marcus against the wall. "You were right there! You could have pulled her back!"

"I'm not her keeper." Marcus shoved back. "Everyone's responsible for themselves."

"She was counting on you to watch her back!" Ethan's fist clenched. "Like we've all been watching yours."

"Enough!" Marsh's voice cut through the air like steel. She stepped between them, her eyes cold and unyielding. "We don't have time for this. Keep moving, or none of us survive."

Blood dripped from Lily's wound, each drop echoing in the chamber. The mechanical whir of hidden gears filled the silence between their ragged breaths.

"He's right." Marcus straightened his jacket. "We can't afford to babysit each other. The weak don't survive this game."

"There's a difference between weakness and trust," Ethan spat. "But I guess you wouldn't know anything about that."

Marsh's hand pressed firmly against Ethan's chest, holding him back. "Save it. We need to keep moving."

Tension crackled between them as they regrouped, and the trust that had tentatively bound them was now fraying at the edges.

Ethan crouched beside Lily as Sarah pressed a cloth against the wound. Blood seeped through the fabric, but the sigil's pulsing glow intensified with each drop spilled.

"Hold still," Sarah whispered, cleaning around the edges of the cut.

Lily's eyes rolled back, her voice dropping to a hollow rasp. "The tower burns black... streets filled with ash..." Her fingers clutched at empty air. "He says... says only blood will break the chains."

"Who says?" Ethan gripped her hand. "Lily, stay with me."

"The tower feeds," Lily whispered, her voice a thread between worlds. "It burns with the lives it's consumed, drawing strength from their fear. H e... Alexei... waits at its heart, tethered by chains of blood. He promises... promises we can end it. Just need the right sacrifice."

The sigil flared brighter, casting harsh shadows across her pale face. Sarah's hands stilled over the wound.

"This isn't just blood loss," Sarah said. "The sigil's responding to her pain, drawing power from it."

Ethan's heart fell to the pit of his stomach. Every instinct screamed to grab Lily and run, to get her as far from this nightmare as possible. But the way the sigil pulsed in time with her words, how the air seemed to bend around her...

"We need to keep moving," Marsh said from her position by the door.

"Give her a minute," Ethan snapped.

"The captain's right," Sarah said quietly. "Whatever connection Lily has to the curse - it's growing stronger. We might need that."

Ethan stared at his sister's face, twisted in pain yet somehow peaceful, as though the visions offered answers they desperately needed. The thought of using her connection to the curse turned his stomach, but they were running out of options.

"The tower calls," Lily whispered. "It hungers."

"We don't have time for this," Marsh snapped, her eyes darting toward the tunnel ahead. "If she's the key, we use her. You want to save her? Then break the damn curse before it breaks all of us."

***

The group stumbled into a crumbling alcove, their breaths echoing off ancient stone. Ethan slumped against the wall, his muscles screaming from the constant tension. Sweat dripped down his neck despite the chill air.

Marsh raised her fist - the universal signal to halt. "Everyone take five. Check your gear." Her voice carried the weight of authority earned through years on the force.

Marsh was barely able to contain her frustration. She'd led officers through riots and firefights, but this—herding a group of broken people through a cursed city—was like trying to hold sand in her hands. "Listen up. What happened back there - that's how people die. We're facing something bigger than any of us. The only way through this is together."

Ethan watched Sarah press close to Lily, both women trembling. Sarah's reporter's notebook lay forgotten at her feet, her usual professional demeanor cracked by fear.

"I've seen good officers fall because they forgot basic training," Marsh continued. "Discipline keeps you alive. Unity keeps you strong. We stick to the formation; we watch each other's backs, we make it through."

Her words rang hollow against Marcus and Nina's withdrawn forms. Marcus's low voice carried just enough to set Ethan's nerves on edge. He couldn't catch the words, but the way Nina's eyes flicked toward Marsh before darting away made it clear they weren't discussing survival tactics.

Marsh's eyes showed frustration as she tracked their movements. She squared her shoulders, but Ethan caught the flicker of doubt. The captain was losing her grip on the group, and she knew it.

"Five minutes," she barked, though her voice carried less conviction than before. "Then we move."

***

The footsteps came first—heavy, measured, each impact sending vibrations through the stone floor. Ethan's breath caught in his throat. The sound carried purpose, the slow stride of a predator who knew its prey was cornered.

Marsh's hand shot up, fingers spread in warning. Her other hand found her weapon, thumb clicking off the safety. The group froze, every breath held as though it might be their last.

The air changed, thickening with an oppressive weight that pressed against their lungs. Ethan's skin prickled with an ancient, instinctive fear—the kind buried deep in humanity's bones from when they were prey, not predators.

A low growl rolled through the tunnel, too deep to be human. It wasn't just sound but pressure, vibrating through the stone and scraping against Ethan's nerves like steel on glass.

Fresh gouges appeared in the wall beside them, deep furrows carved by claws that could tear through rock. Ethan's eyes darted to the marks, his stomach twisting at their size and precision.

Viktor's presence filled the space like a physical weight, though he remained hidden. The curse had twisted Alexei's enforcer into something darker, more primal. The air reeked of blood and metal, sharp enough to sting Ethan's nostrils.

Ethan thought he saw a flicker of motion from the corner of his eye—a shadow, impossibly large, sliding through the blackness. A glint of red—eyes?—flashed briefly before vanishing.

Sarah's fingers dug into Ethan's arm. She was trembling, her wide eyes staring into the darkness behind them. Even Marcus, for all his bravado, pressed himself flat against the wall, his face pale.

Marsh's fingers tightened on her weapon. Her ears perked as another growl echoed, closer now. It wasn't just a sound—it was a promise. They weren't being followed anymore. They were being hunted.

Sarah caught Marsh's sleeve, pulling her back as the others crept forward. Her heart hammered, but she kept her voice steady, barely above a whisper.

"Something's not right with Nina. Watch how she moves through here—like she knows exactly where to step."

Marsh's eyes narrowed, scanning the group ahead. Nina navigated the treacherous path with fluid grace, each movement precise and calculated.

"She hasn't shown a hint of fear," Sarah continued. "Even when Viktor—" She swallowed hard, the memory of that inhuman growl still fresh. "Everyone else is terrified. But Nina? She's acting like this is just another day."

Marsh's jaw tightened. "Could be a survival instinct. Streets teach you to hide fear."

"It's more than that." Sarah glanced ahead, making sure they weren't overheard. "The way she described those old tunnels earlier—details that aren't in any public record. I've researched this city for years, Captain. She knows things she shouldn't."

"We're all on edge," Marsh said, but Sarah caught the subtle shift in her stance, the way her hand drifted closer to her weapon. "Making accusations now could tear us apart. We need to stay focused."

"I'm not suggesting we confront her. Just... watch her. Please."

Marsh gave a slight nod. "Keep your observations to yourself for now. Document everything you notice, but be discrete. The last thing we need is panic spreading through the group."

Sarah fell back in line, her reporter's instincts buzzing. She'd built her career on noticing details others missed. Now, those same instincts screamed that Nina was playing a deeper game—one that could get them all killed.

The whispers slithered through Lily's mind, each syllable dripping with honeyed poison. Alexei's voice felt closer now, as if he stood right behind her, his breath ghosting across her neck.

"They watch you stumble, little dove. See how they whisper? They know you're weak. A liability."

Lily's fingers curled into fists, knuckles white. The sigil pulsed on her arm, its glow seeping through her sleeve. Each throb sent waves of heat through her body, making her dizzy.

"Your brother pretends to care, but he's already failed you once. Remember Andrea? He couldn't save her either."

She bit her lip, tasting copper. Ahead, Marcus and Nina picked their way through the rubble, their movements synchronized and practiced. Sarah trailed behind them, scribbling in her notebook. Captain Marsh's boots scraped against pebbles as she swept her flashlight across the walls.

"Only you understand what must be done. The power runs through your veins now. Why fight it?"

The tunnel walls seemed to breathe, expanding and contracting with each pulse of her sigil. Lily stumbled, catching herself against the rough stone. Her palm came away sticky with something dark.

Ethan's hand steadied her shoulder. "You okay?"

She nodded, not trusting her voice. Her brother's concern felt distant, muffled, as if she heard it through water.

"You're shaking." Ethan's grip tightened. His eyes searched her face, seeing past her forced smile.

"Just tired," she managed.

Alexei's laughter echoed in her skull. "Lie to him like he lies to you. The curse chose you for a reason, Lily. You're stronger than all of them combined."

The sigil flared, and Lily swallowed a scream. Colors bled at the edges of her vision. The tunnel ahead stretched impossibly long, twisting like a serpent.

Ethan's hand hadn't left her shoulder. She felt his worry radiating off him in waves, saw it in the way his eyes kept darting between her and the shadows ahead. He knew something was wrong. But how could she tell him about the voice when she wasn't even sure what was real anymore?

***

Ethan's boots crunched on the scattered debris of the collapsed bridge, his heart still racing from their near miss. Behind him, Sarah helped Lily catch her breath while Marcus dusted off his jacket with calculated nonchalance.

"That's it." Marsh's voice cut through the darkness. "Marcus, you're done leading us through these tunnels."

Marcus's head snapped up. "Excuse me?"

"You saw those stress fractures. You knew that bridge wouldn't hold all of us, yet you pushed forward anyway."

"We made it, didn't we?" Marcus spread his arms wide. "Sometimes you have to take risks to survive."

"Risks?" Marsh stepped closer, her face inches from his. "You're gambling with our lives. This isn't about survival—it's about control."

Nina pushed between them. "Back off. Marcus is the only reason we've made it this far. Where were you when those blades came down in the last chamber? He pulled Sarah clear."

"After he triggered the mechanism," Ethan said, moving to stand beside Marsh. "Captain's right. Your stunts are going to get someone killed."

Marcus's laugh echoed off the tunnel walls. "That's rich coming from you, detective. Still trying to protect everyone? How'd that work out with Andrea?"

Ethan's fists clenched behind his back. Marsh's arm shot out, holding him back.

"We're not leaving anyone behind," Sarah called out. "But we need to work together."

"Together?" Nina sneered. "You mean following the Captain's orders until we're all dead? At least Marcus understands what it takes to survive down here."

Marsh's fingers drummed against her holster. "One more incident like that bridge, and you're out. Both of you. I won't let your power play kill this group."

"You won't let?" Marcus's voice dropped low. "You're not in charge here, Captain. None of us are. The only authority that matters is survival."

They stood in tense silence, the group physically split between those backing Marsh and those standing with Marcus. The unity they'd maintained since entering the tunnels had cracked, revealing the deep fault lines of mistrust beneath.

Nina traced her finger along the tunnel wall, her nail catching on an ancient symbol. "You know, Captain, these relics we're collecting—they're not just magical trinkets. Each one carries a piece of Eldoria's soul."

Ethan caught the slight tilt of her head toward Marcus, who leaned against the opposite wall with practiced indifference.

"The Heart of Dawn showed us visions," Nina continued. "But what if we're reading them wrong? What if your way of doing things is exactly what the curse wants?"

Sarah's pen scratched against her notebook, her eyes darting between Nina and Marcus. The reporter's shoulders tensed with each calculated word from Nina's lips.

"The curse doesn't want anything," Marsh said. "It's not sentient."

Nina's laugh carried a sharp edge. "That's where you're wrong. Every ritual has a consciousness behind it. Sometimes following the rules gets more people killed than breaking them."

Marcus nodded, the motion so subtle Ethan almost missed it. Sarah didn't. Her pen stopped moving, and she shifted closer to where Nina stood.

"Interesting theory," Sarah said. "Where exactly did you learn about these rituals, Nina?"

Nina's fingers drummed against her thigh. "Around. You pick things up when you've survived on these streets as long as I have."

"Really?" Sarah's voice hardened. "Because your version contradicts every historical record I've found."

Marcus pushed off the wall, positioning himself between Nina and Sarah. "Maybe your records are wrong. Nina's kept us alive this far."

Ethan watched Nina's hand brush Marcus's arm—a gesture that lasted less than a second but spoke volumes. Sarah caught his eye, giving him a slight nod. They'd both seen it.

"The relics respond to intent," Nina said. "Maybe that's why they react so strongly to Lily. She's not afraid to embrace their power, unlike some of us."

The group pressed forward through the tunnel, their footsteps echoing off the damp walls. Lily's legs buckled as a wave of dizziness struck her. The tunnel dissolved into shadow, and Alexei's form materialized before her, tall and imposing in his dark suit.

"You feel it, don't you?" His voice slithered through her mind. "The power growing inside you with each relic we collect."

Lily tried to look away, but his presence filled her consciousness. The sigil on her arm pulsed in response to his nearness.

"They'll turn on you, you know." He gestured to the shadowy forms of her companions. "Marcus and Nina already plot against you. But they're not the only ones. Even your brother will choose his own survival over yours when the moment comes."

"You're lying," Lily whispered, her voice trembling as the sigil on her arm flared white-hot, the pain twisting through her like the doubt creeping into her heart.

"Am I? Look closer at the relics' reaction to you. You're not just another player in this game - you're its heart. The curse flows through your veins now. They'll sacrifice you to end it, just as others have been sacrificed before."

The vision shattered like glass, leaving Lily gasping as the tunnel snapped back into focus. The walls seemed closer now, pressing in with a suffocating weight, the air heavy with damp and shadows that felt alive. She steadied herself against the wall, praying no one had noticed her faltering step.

But Ethan watched her from the corner of his eye. He saw how she wiped the sweat from her forehead, how her hands trembled as she pushed away from the wall. The confidence she'd shown earlier had cracked, replaced by something darker. Her eyes darted between their companions, lingering longest on Marcus and Nina.

Ethan recognized that look - the same hollow, haunted gaze Andrea wore in her final days. His chest tightened as he realized Lily wasn't just slipping away; she was vanishing into a battle none of them could see, and he didn't know if he could pull her back this time. But every time he tried to catch her gaze, she looked away, keeping whatever tormented her locked inside.

CHAPTER FIFTEEN

HUNTER'S PROWL

A deep thud echoed through the tunnel, followed by another. And another. The rhythmic footfalls carried the weight of inevitability.

Ethan's blood ran cold. He knew those steps. The way they fell, measured and purposeful, like an executioner's march.

The shadows along the walls writhed and stretched, reaching toward them with ghostly fingers. The air grew thick, pressing against Ethan's chest until each breath burned.

"Viktor," Sarah whispered, her face draining of color.

The name hit the group like a physical blow. Nina's hand gripped Marcus's arm tightly. Lily's sigil flared bright enough to paint the walls in harsh relief.

"Move!" Marsh commanded, her voice sharp and unwavering.

They ran, their footsteps a frantic rhythm against stone, a chaotic drumbeat compared to Viktor's steady approach. The tunnel twisted left, then right. Ethan's lungs screamed for air as he pushed forward, Sarah just behind him.

Lily faltered, the sigil's light dimming as she stumbled. Ethan reached back, gripping her arm and pulling her forward. "Stay close!"

A wave of malevolent energy swept over them, making the air colder and heavier. The darkness behind them shifted, taking on substance. A massive shadow stretched across the wall—broad-shouldered, head shaved, moving with terrible purpose.

"This way!" Marcus yelled, pointing to a side passage.

Marsh's voice cut through the rising panic. "No! We stick together. Follow my lead!"

Ethan hesitated, his instincts warring with Marcus's desperate suggestion. But the determination in Marsh's voice won out. He tightened his grip on Lily and nodded to Sarah.

The group surged forward, Marcus and Nina reluctantly falling in line. Marsh led them into the next stretch of tunnel, her flashlight bouncing against the walls. The sound of Viktor's steps grew fainter, but the oppressive energy remained, a constant reminder that he was still hunting them.

For now, they were together. But the cracks in their unity had grown wider. Ethan could feel it with every uneasy glance and hurried step.

The group huddled in a small alcove, catching their breath. Water dripped somewhere in the darkness, each drop echoing like a tiny heartbeat. Ethan kept his eyes on the tunnel behind them while the others rested.

Nina cleared her throat. "We need to talk."

Something in her voice made Ethan turn. She stood apart from the group, her face hard in the dim light.

"The Ritual of Severance is a lie," Nina said, her voice calm but edged with a certainty that made Ethan's stomach drop. It was the same calm she'd shown in the tunnels, the same confidence in the face of every trap and threat—a calm born from knowing the endgame before any of them had. "It's always been a lie."

Sarah straightened. "What are you talking about?"

"There's only one way out." Nina's hand slipped into her jacket. "The Eye's Offering. A life is freely given to break the curse."

Marsh stepped forward, but Nina pulled out a curved blade, its edge gleaming. "Don't."

"You're insane," Ethan growled, moving to shield Lily.

Nina's laugh was hollow. "Insane? I've watched this curse destroy everything for years. The Eye's Offering is real. One life to save countless others." Her gaze fixed on Lily. "And your sister's already marked. The sigil makes her perfect."

"Over my dead body," Ethan snarled.

"If that's what it takes." Nina's grip tightened on the blade. "I won't rot in this cursed city forever. Someone has to die, and the sigil's chosen her. Why fight it?"

"Drop the knife, Nina," Marsh ordered, her voice cutting through the tension like steel through the air. Her hand hovered near her holster, steady despite the chaos unfolding around her. "Whatever you think you're achieving, this isn't the way. You'll only destroy yourself—and the rest of us."

"You don't understand. None of you do." Nina's eyes were fever-bright. "This is the only way. And I'll do whatever it takes."

The betrayal hit Ethan like a physical blow. Every word she'd whispered, every glance exchanged with Marcus, every carefully timed suggestion—it all clicked into place now. Nina hadn't just been surviving the curse. She'd been steering them, shaping their path to align with her twisted goal.

Marcus shifted his weight, the knife in Nina's hand catching what little light remained in the tunnel. Her words from moments ago still rang in his ears, a seductive whisper of survival at any cost.

"Think about it," Nina murmured, her voice low enough that only he could hear. "How many times have you seen rituals fail? How many bodies have you stepped over? The Ritual of Severance is just another dead end."

His mind raced, flashing back to the faces of those he'd left behind in the last three Night Watches. Their desperate belief in ancient texts and forgotten rituals had led them to brutal, inevitable deaths. He'd told himself it was their faith that killed them, not his refusal to stay. Each time, the curse had claimed them anyway.

"Marsh clings to her rules because she's afraid to face the truth," Nina whispered, her words curling around Marcus like smoke. "Her way is chaos. Her way is death. The Eye's Offering is order—one sacrifice to save the rest. You've seen how this story ends when they cling to hope. Do you want to be another name lost in the dark?"

Marcus's eyes flicked to the others. Ethan stood guard over Lily, his face set with a determination Marcus couldn't fathom. Sarah hovered near Marsh, her notebook forgotten, her fingers gripping her pen like a weapon. Marsh's stance radiated control, but her eyes betrayed the exhaustion beneath her authority. These people had fought harder than anyone he'd known, but fighting wasn't enough. Survival demanded something colder. They were good people, maybe too good for what needed to be done. But something in him hesitated, remembering how they'd worked together, how they'd survived Viktor's pursuit.

"We could walk away from this city," Nina pressed. "Free. Alive. All it takes is one choice."

His training screamed at him to side with Nina—to grab the clean, simple solution and ensure his own survival. It was instinct, as natural to him as breathing. But something else clawed at him—a quiet, insistent voice reminding him of Sarah's trust, of Ethan's unwavering loyalty to his sister, of the way Marsh had put herself between him and danger without hesitation. Could he really turn his back on them now?

Watching Lily's sigil pulse in the darkness, seeing the trust in Sarah's eyes when she'd followed his guidance through the trapped chamber - it felt different this time.

Nina's fingers brushed his arm. "Time to choose, Marcus. Are you a survivor or a sacrifice?"

The question hung between them, heavy with promise and threat. Marcus felt the familiar pull of self-preservation warring with something unfamiliar - something that felt dangerously like loyalty.

***

Heavy footsteps thundered through the tunnel, cutting off their stand-off. Viktor's massive frame emerged from the darkness, his eyes glowing with an unnatural light. The curse had twisted him further—veins of shadow coursed through his skin like cracks in obsidian marble.

"Move!" Marsh's command shattered the group's paralysis. She shoved Sarah forward, her voice as sharp as the blade in Viktor's massive hand.

Viktor lunged, his fist slamming into the stone wall just inches from Ethan's head. The impact sent shards of rock cascading onto the group. The tunnel groaned under the force.

"Left tunnel!" Marsh barked, shoving Sarah toward the nearest passage. "Lily, stay with Ethan. Marcus, rear guard!"

The group stumbled forward, their footsteps clattering on the uneven ground. Viktor's measured pace followed the heavy impacts of his boots echoing like an executioner's drum. He didn't run—he didn't need to. Every stride closed the gap, his shadow stretching over them like the hand of death.

Steam hissed from a ruptured pipe above, filling the air with scalding mist. Marsh yanked Sarah out of its path, the heat singing their skin. "Through here!" She pointed to a maintenance hatch.

Viktor's primal and guttural growl reverberated through the tunnel, freezing them in place. A clawed hand darted through the mist, catching Nina by the arm. She screamed as Viktor lifted her, his grip unrelenting.

"Drop her!" Ethan yelled, emptying his pistol into Viktor's chest. The bullets barely staggered him, their force dissipating against his shadow-wreathed form. With a snarl, Viktor hurled Nina against the tunnel wall, her body crumpling as she hit the ground.

The sigil on Lily's arm flared bright enough to cast Viktor's monstrous outline on the walls, but its light seemed to enrage him further.

"Keep moving!" Marsh barked, slamming a maintenance gate shut behind them. The metal buckled under Viktor's next swing, groaning with the strain. "This won't hold long."

The group scrambled through the labyrinthine passages, Marsh's commands the only thing keeping them moving. "Right! Down the ladder! Watch your step—the third rung's gone!"

Ethan helped Lily descend, her sigil pulsing wildly in the flickering light. Below, the tunnels widened into a flooded chamber. Dark water rippled across the floor, the reflections distorting like writhing shadows.

Behind them, Viktor's roar shattered the momentary silence. The gate gave way with a deafening crash, the twisted metal clanging against the stone.

"We need a distraction!" Ethan shouted.

Marsh's gaze darted to a crumbling support column in the center of the chamber. "That'll have to do." She pointed to Marcus. "Rig it to collapse!"

Marcus hesitated. "You're kidding."

"Move!" Marsh roared.

Marcus sprinted toward the column, grabbing a rusted pipe to wedge into the crumbling stone. "This better work!" he muttered.

Viktor's silhouette appeared in the tunnel, his form towering and almost angelic, shadow twisting unnaturally around him. He stepped into the water, its surface rippling outward like the heartbeat of the curse itself.

"Now, Marcus!" Marsh shouted.

The column groaned, cracks spidering across its surface as Marcus twisted the pipe with all his strength. Finally, the structure gave way, the chamber quaking as the ceiling above began to collapse. Rocks tumbled, crashing into the water as dust and debris filled the air.

"Go, go, go!" Marsh ordered, shoving the group toward a narrow exit as the chamber collapsed behind them. Viktor lunged forward, his clawed hand reaching through the falling rubble. Ethan felt the chill of his grasp brush his back as he hauled Lily through the opening.

The tunnel behind them caved in with a deafening roar, sealing Viktor beneath tons of rock. The echoes of his growls faded as silence reclaimed the passage.

The group collapsed against the walls, coughing and gasping for air. Dust coated their faces, and their limbs trembled with exhaustion.

"That was too close," Sarah whispered, clutching her notebook like a lifeline.

Marsh wiped the sweat and grime from her forehead, her voice steady despite the chaos they'd just survived. "He's not gone. That'll only slow him down. We need to keep moving."

Ethan glanced back at the rubble, the faint vibrations of Viktor's presence still lingering. "How do you stop something that can't die?"

Marsh met his gaze, her expression grim. "You don't. You outlast it."

The group exchanged weary glances before forcing themselves to their feet. Their unity was threadbare, but for now, they were alive.

***

Sarah's hands shook as she pulled Dr. Vane's journal from her bag. The pages crackled, worn and dog-eared from countless readings. Ethan watched her flip through the pages, her fingers tracing the doctor's frantic scrawl, her breath uneven.

"The Eye's Offering isn't salvation," Sarah said, her voice barely above a whisper. "It's a trap. Dr. Vane found evidence in the city archives—records of previous attempts."

She turned the journal toward them. Sketches of twisted bodies and corrupted sigils filled the margins, dark ink smudged from years of handling. "Each time someone attempted the offering, the curse grew stronger. Alexei doesn't want to end it. He wants to bind himself to it permanently."

Ethan's stomach churned. "The whole city would become his playground."

"Worse." Sarah pointed to a passage. "The suffering would feed him. Every death, every moment of terror—it would all flow into him. Eldoria would become a perpetual engine of pain. There'd be no escape, no way to stop him."

The sigil on Lily's arm pulsed, a low thrum of light breaking through her sleeve. She wrapped her hand around it, fingers trembling as she tried to steady herself. The glow seemed to grow hotter, sharper, with each word Sarah spoke.

"You're certain?" Lily asked, her voice thin and strained, her eyes flickering between the journal and Sarah.

"Dr. Vane tracked the pattern through centuries of records." Sarah's finger traced a timeline in the journal. "Every 'successful' offering made the curse more powerful, more permanent. The victims stopped being random. The torture became... calculated."

Ethan's jaw clenched as the pieces fell into place—the game, the rules, the deliberate targeting. It wasn't just about death. It was about suffering, about breaking people before they died.

You see now, don't you? Alexei's voice slithered through Lily's mind, cold and insidious. The power it could bring. The control.

Lily squeezed her eyes shut, her breath catching. But she couldn't block him out. The whispers coiled tighter, their promises seeping into the cracks of her resolve.

Ethan noticed her trembling and moved closer, his voice low. "Lily, what's wrong?"

She didn't answer. She couldn't. The sigil flared again, and the pain that accompanied it felt like a blade twisting in her arm. Ethan's hand hovered near her shoulder, but the distance between them felt insurmountable.

Marsh broke the silence, her voice steady despite the weight of the revelation. "If what Sarah's saying is true, we need to shut this down fast. No shortcuts. No risks. We can't let Alexei get what he wants."

Lily barely heard her. The tunnel felt suffocating now, the walls pressing in as Alexei's voice grew stronger. You don't have to fight this, Lily. It's your destiny.

Nina stepped closer to the group, her movements fluid and deliberate, like a predator closing in on uncertain prey. "How many more have to die before we accept that following these old texts is madness?" Her voice carried a quiet strength, slicing through the oppressive atmosphere of the tunnel.

Ethan watched her gesture toward Sarah's journal, her lips curling into a knowing smile. "Look at us—running through these tunnels like rats, chasing fairy tales while Viktor hunts us down. And for what? Another failed ritual?"

Marsh stepped forward, her shoulders squared despite the exhaustion pulling at her frame. "We have a plan," she said, her tone firm but frayed at the edges.

"A plan?" Nina's laugh was soft, mocking, echoing off the stone walls. "How's that working out for you? Twitch is dead. Lily's suffering. And we're no closer to ending this nightmare than when we started."

Marcus shifted his weight, his eyes darting toward Nina. The tension in his posture betrayed the doubt bubbling beneath his surface resolve.

"There's a simpler way," Nina said, her voice dropping to a conspiratorial whisper. Her eyes swept over the group, lingering on Marcus. "One that doesn't require us to decode ancient symbols or follow rules written by dead men. One that actually works."

Sarah clutched the journal tighter as if its worn pages could shield her from Nina's words. But Ethan could see the seeds of doubt Nina had sown taking root. He caught Marcus taking a half-step closer to Nina, away from Marsh and Ethan.

"The Eye's Offering isn't just about sacrifice," Nina continued, her eyes gleaming in the dim light. "It's about power. Control. The ability to shape this curse instead of being shaped by it. Isn't that worth more than blind faith in dusty pages?"

Marcus's hesitation gave way to something harder, more resolute. His hand drifted to his weapon—not quite a threat, but a clear declaration of his shifting loyalties.

"You're talking about murder," Ethan said, his voice low and sharp.

"I'm talking about survival," Nina countered smoothly. "About ending this curse once and for all. Sometimes the simplest solution is the right one." Her smile at Marcus was faint but unmistakable, a private acknowledgment passing between them like a spark in the dark.

Marsh stepped between them, her voice cutting through the charged air. "You think we're just going to let you hijack this group with your twisted logic? Think again."

Nina didn't flinch. "You're out of time, Captain. And out of options. It's just a matter of who sees the truth first."

The whispers swelled in Lily's mind, drowning out the heated clash of voices between Nina and Marsh. Alexei's presence coiled around her thoughts, his words a velvet trap lined with steel.

They fear your power, Lily. Do you see how they argue over who will be the sacrifice? Who is weak? Who is expendable?

Her trembling fingers pressed against the sigil, its pulsing light spilling between them like liquid fire. Pain lanced up her arm, sharp and unrelenting, but beneath it pulsed a darker rhythm—a tempting, raw energy that hummed in tune with Alexei's voice.

Look at your brother, Alexei whispered, his tone soft with feigned pity. He always shields you and keeps you in the dark. But why? Because he thinks you're weak. A liability. A foolish girl chasing fairy tales.

Lily's gaze flicked to Ethan. He stood as a barrier between her and Nina, his shoulders rigid with tension, his every move calibrated to protect. The thought twisted uncomfortably in her mind—was it protection, or was it control? Did he truly trust her, or was she just another burden for him to carry?

The sigil flared again, the light searing her palm. She stifled a gasp as Alexei's words seemed to etch themselves into her very bones. You could end this, Lily. No more fear. No more running. No more being their tool. I alone see the truth of what you are—and what you could become.

She pressed her back against the cold stone wall, desperate for its solidity. But the world around her blurred, the tunnel's damp chill fading into insignificance next to Alexei's intoxicating presence. The power coursing through her veins felt more real than the ground beneath her feet.

I understand your gift. They will drain you, use you, and discard you when you're no longer useful. To them, you're just another piece of their ritual, nothing more.

Lily's hands trembled as she tugged her sleeve down, hiding the sigil's unearthly glow. Sarah's concerned glance brushed over her. Marsh's calculating gaze lingered, but Lily avoided their eyes. The distance between her and the group felt insurmountable, each of Alexei's whispers widening the gap.

Together, we could reshape this city. No more victims. No more games. Just power—yours to wield, pure and unbreakable.

The sigil pulsed in agreement, its light a steady beacon beneath her sleeve. A part of her recoiled, but another—a deeper, darker part—wanted to believe him. To reach for the certainty he promised, the freedom from doubt and fear. Her throat tightened as the thought settled: what if Alexei was right? What if the fragile hope of the ritual wasn't enough?

Ethan stepped away from Lily, his shoulders squared against the weight of the moment. The tunnel's shadows deepened the lines of exhaustion on his face, but his eyes burned with conviction.

"You talk about survival," he said, his voice cutting through the tense air. "But what kind of survival is worth becoming the very thing we're fighting against?"

Nina's smile faltered, her confidence dimming as Ethan moved closer, his words gaining strength with every step.

"Look around you. Twitch died believing in something bigger than himself. Andrea gave her life trying to expose the truth. They didn't die, so we could take shortcuts or make deals with devils."

Sarah shifted beside him. "And that truth wasn't simple. Dr. Vane unravelled the lies over the years, piece by piece, so we wouldn't repeat the same mistakes. The curse isn't just about death—it's about control. If we give in now, we hand Eldoria to Alexei on a silver platter."

Marsh's gaze swept across the group, her hand falling from her holster. She nodded, her voice firm. "Ethan's right. We've lost too many good people to throw it all away now."

Nina's expression flickered—uncertainty, frustration, and defiance colliding beneath her carefully maintained mask. Marcus glanced between her and Marsh, his fingers twitching near his weapon, the air heavy with unspoken tension.

Ethan raised his voice, drawing their focus back. "The curse feeds on fear and desperation. That's what Alexei wants—to push us until we sacrifice everything we believe in. But the moment we do that, he's already won."

The sigil on Lily's arm flared, casting flickering light over the group. Ethan stepped closer to her, his tone softening. "This ends here—with us. Together. And we're going to finish it the right way."

The group stilled, the only sound the distant drip of water and the faint hum of the sigil. Ethan held Nina's gaze, his resolve unyielding, but the shadows around her seemed to grow sharper, her defiance simmering just beneath the surface.

Marsh's voice broke the silence. "We move forward as a team. No more fractures."

The quiet agreement hung in the air, but unease lingered. Nina's eyes tore over to Marcus.

Marcus's hand settled on his weapon, his stance shifting as he moved to stand beside Nina. "We're done playing by your rules," he said, his voice hard and resolute. "The Eye's Offering is the only way."

"You're both insane," Marsh spat, drawing her gun in one fluid motion.

The tension snapped taut, each side poised for violence. The metallic scrape of weapons being drawn echoed off the tunnel walls. Ethan stepped in front of Lily, his eyes darting between Marcus and Nina.

Nina's smirk widened, her voice dripping with contempt. "You really think—"

A bone-rattling roar tore through the air, drowning out her words. The tunnel shook violently as debris rained down from above. Viktor's monstrous form slammed into the ground, not from the tunnel entrance but through the ceiling itself. He rose slowly, his massive frame illuminated by the faint glow of Lily's sigil. His cursed flesh glistened like molten rock, pulsing with raw malice.

Ethan's heart leapt into his throat. "Go! Now!"

Viktor's claws lashed out, narrowly missing Nina and Marcus as they dove to either side. The ground cracked beneath the impact, sending shockwaves through the group. Marsh fired two shots at Viktor's exposed chest. The bullets sparked uselessly against his skin, angering him further.

"Left passage!" Marsh barked, shoving Sarah toward the narrow escape route.

Viktor's eyes fixed on Lily. His guttural growl sent shivers through the group. The sigil on her arm flared bright.

"Get her out of here!" Ethan shouted, yanking Lily toward the side passage as Viktor surged forward.

But before Viktor could charge, the sigil's glow shifted unnaturally, its light darkening to a sickly red. The air turned cold, and an eerie stillness swept over the tunnel.

"Ah, my enforcer," Alexei's voice purred, silky and chilling, filling the space without a clear source.

Everyone froze. Even Viktor hesitated, his claws twitching mid-swing. Shadows and fog coalesced behind the group, twisting into Alexei's form as though the tunnel itself birthed him. He stepped forward, calm and composed in his dark suit, his presence commanding even Viktor's rage.

"Did I interrupt something?" Alexei asked, his voice smooth but laced with menace. His cold eyes swept over the group, lingering on Lily.

Nina's bravado wavered, her earlier confidence melting into visible unease. Marcus's hand dropped slightly from his weapon, the enormity of Alexei's presence rendering the standoff insignificant.

"You see," Alexei continued, addressing Lily as though the others didn't exist, "they all fear what they cannot control. But you and I, little one, we know better, don't we? The sigil, the power—it belongs to you. Not them."

Lily trembled, her hand instinctively covering the pulsing mark on her arm.

"Get out of our way," Marsh demanded, her voice steady despite the visible strain in her stance.

Alexei smiled, slow and predatory. "This is no longer your fight, Captain. It never was."

Without another word, Viktor roared, his rage reigniting at Alexei's subtle nod. The beast lunged, Alexei dissolved into the night, and chaos erupted once more.

Marsh shoved Sarah toward the passage, shouting directions as the group scrambled. "Move! Don't stop!"

The group barely managed to evade Viktor's relentless pursuit. But Alexei's haunting presence lingered in their minds long after they escaped, his voice echoing through Lily's thoughts as the sigil pulsed faintly beneath her skin.

***

The chaos of Viktor's attack had given Nina the perfect chance to slip away. Her fingers brushed the ritual dagger hidden in her coat pocket—a jagged, ancient blade she'd acquired from a whispering contact in Eldoria's underworld. They had warned her of the Eye's Offering and the power it promised to those bold enough to wield it.

Blood trickled from a fresh cut along her cheek where debris had struck her during the escape. She wiped it away with her sleeve, a bitter smile twisting her lips. The others clung to their lofty ideals, blind to the simple truth: survival had no room for sentiment.

"You had your chance," she muttered under her breath, pulling out a leather-bound notebook. Its brittle pages held the fruits of her obsession—decades of half-whispered rituals, cryptic notes, and the failures of those who had tried before her.

The ritual demanded more than blood; it required betrayal. Sacrifice. The deliberate severing of trust and unity. Bonds had to break for the curse to take hold and transform, granting power to its wielder.

Nina's fingers trembled as she flipped to a page covered in dark, jagged symbols. The sigil burned into Lily's arm was the final piece of the puzzle. It was a beacon, a sign that the curse had chosen her. Viktor's pursuit and the relics' alignment—all of it pointed toward this moment.

Nina crouched and pulled a piece of chalk from her coat. The sharp scrape against the stone echoed faintly, her practiced hands marking the floor with precision. Each symbol pulsed faintly in the dim light as if feeding off the lingering energy of Alexei's twisted influence.

"One life to save thousands," she whispered, the words tasting hollow. She knew the truth: one life to save herself. She had survived too long, sacrificed too much, to let the curse claim her now.

The final symbol glowed faintly as she completed the circle. Her breath caught, her heart racing with equal parts fear and exhilaration. The markings seemed alive, writhing faintly as the ritual space began to hum with unnatural energy.

She checked her watch. Time was short. They'd be searching for her, especially Marcus. He'd been useful—an ally, for a time—but his hesitation had made him weak. She couldn't afford weakness now.

Nina stood, her eyes lingering on the ritual space she had prepared. It pulsed with dark promise, waiting for her to act. For Lily to arrive.

"This ends here," she murmured, tightening her grip on the dagger. "For me."

***

The ancient stone walls blurred around Lily as pain lanced through her skull. Her knees buckled, and the cold floor rushed up to meet her. The sigil on her arm flared white-hot, its light carving jagged shapes into the surrounding shadows.

Alexei's presence enveloped her, his voice a silk-wrapped blade. "Look, child. See what paths stretch before you."

The chamber dissolved. She stood in front of the clock tower, where shadows roamed unchecked, tearing through panicked crowds. Fires raged, painting the sky an apocalyptic orange. Her friends lay strewn like broken dolls—Sarah's lifeless fingers still clutching her notebook, Marsh's badge glinting on a uniform soaked with blood, Ethan's glassy eyes locked in a final look of betrayal. The city's soul bled out, feeding an insatiable hunger.

The scene twisted. She saw herself standing tall at the heart of a ritual, ancient symbols spiralling around her as raw power surged through her veins. The curse bent to her will, twisting into a weapon she wielded with unrelenting precision. Eldoria bowed before her, not in ruin but in submission.

"You stand at a crossroads," Alexei whispered, his words a seductive promise. "Your brother's path leads only to destruction. Your friends' fear chains them to failure. But you—you could be so much more."

Fresh visions tore through her mind. In one, she recoiled from the sigil's power, and the curse consumed all she held dear. Ethan's cries of anguish echoed as he was torn from her grasp. In another, she embraced it fully, becoming a figure of terrible majesty. Her friends looked on with awe and fear as she remade the city in her image.

"The curse chose you for a reason." Alexei's form materialized before her, sharp features illuminated by the pulsing sigil on her arm. "You are its vessel, not its victim. Your choice approaches. Will you cower in weakness or rise to claim your destiny?"

Reality snapped back with a gasp. Lily clutched her burning arm, her throat raw from an unspoken scream. Ethan's face swam into focus, his hands steadying her shoulders. "Lily! What happened? Talk to me."

The sigil throbbed in time with her hammering heart, each pulse a brutal reminder of Alexei's words. She pushed herself to her feet, her legs trembling beneath her. Her brother's concern felt distant, drowned beneath the crushing weight of Alexei's whispers.

The fate of Eldoria and her friends is balanced on a knife's edge. Every step, every decision, felt impossibly charged. And as she met Ethan's worried gaze, she knew—no one else could make this choice.

Chapter Sixteen

THE TOWER BECKONS

Heavy footfalls rattled loose dirt from the tunnel ceiling. Ethan's hand clenched tighter around his flashlight as a guttural growl reverberated through the passage. The sound bounced off the stone walls, making it impossible to tell how close Viktor was—or from which direction he'd strike.

"Keep moving," Marsh whispered, her voice low and firm. She took the lead, her sharp gaze cutting through the shifting shadows. Her weathered face betrayed no fear, but her eyes flicked to every crevice as though expecting Viktor to materialize at any moment.

The group shuffled through the narrow corridor, their steps uneven against the damp, jagged floor. Lily's sigil pulsed with an unnatural glow, casting fleeting, grotesque patterns on the walls. The air thickened with every step, heavy with decay and the metallic tang of blood.

Sarah crouched near the wall, her fingers brushing glowing symbols etched into the ancient stone. "These markings... they're intensifying." She flipped open Dr. Vane's journal, skimming its pages by the sigil's light. "We need to take the left fork. The symbols—"

A deafening crash cut her off. Behind them, the screech of metal tearing against stone announced Viktor's relentless advance. The beast was closing in, his movements turning the tunnels into a cacophony of impending death.

"Move!" Marsh snapped, yanking Sarah forward by the arm. "Save the questions for later."

Marcus shoved his way to the front, his expression grim. "We're sitting ducks in here. One wrong turn, and he'll pin us like rats in a trap."

"Stay together!" Marsh's voice rose, sharp and commanding. "That's what he's counting on—to split us up."

The growls deepened, vibrating the very air around them. Viktor's presence seeped into the passage like a toxin, and the group's hurried breathing mingled with the relentless echo of their footsteps. The oppressive stench of blood and corruption seemed to cling to them, making it harder to draw a full breath.

Sarah's hands trembled as she flipped through the journal on the move. "The symbols—they're forming a trail. A guide. If we follow—"

Another crash silenced her as the tunnel walls trembled violently. Chunks of stone rained down, forcing them to shield their faces. The ground beneath their feet seemed to shift as though the tunnels themselves were alive.

"Less reading, more running," Marsh barked, her voice razor-sharp. She pushed them forward, herding them like soldiers on a battlefield. "Eyes on the person in front of you. Do not lose sight of each other."

Ethan reached for Lily, keeping her steady as her sigil's pulsing light faltered, dimming briefly before reigniting with a vengeful glow. Behind them, Viktor's growls built into a feral roar that rolled through the tunnels, making their hearts pound in terror. Each step forward felt like a race against the inevitable.

***

The tunnel yawned open into a vast chamber that stole Ethan's breath. Blood-red light spilled across ancient stone walls that seemed to stretch endlessly upward, their jagged surfaces alive with pulsing symbols. At the chamber's heart, a crystalline shard floated, suspended by crackling tendrils of dark energy. Its presence made Ethan's skin crawl, the air humming with a malevolence that seemed to sink into his bones.

Lily stumbled, clutching her arm as her knees buckled beneath her. The sigil burned like molten iron, its light synchronizing with the relic's erratic pulses. Each flare sent visible waves of pain rippling through her body.

"The final relic," Sarah whispered, her voice trembling with awe and dread.

"Hold." Marsh's raised hand froze them in place. Her flashlight swept the chamber, revealing the faint glint of metallic edges hidden in the floor and walls. Pressure plates, pendulums, and razor-sharp blades lay dormant but waiting—hungry. The maze of death promised a single misstep would cost them dearly.

"You've come so far, little Lily." Alexei's voice oozed through the chamber, filling every corner and crevice. It carried a mockery wrapped in silken temptation. "Why fight what you already know to be inevitable? Accept my gift. Embrace the power that is rightfully yours."

Lily clung to Ethan's arm, her fingers digging deep as if to anchor herself to reality. The relic pulsed brighter. Lily's sigil blazed in response, the light beneath her skin illuminating her veins as though they carried fire instead of blood.

"The things I could show you," Alexei whispered, his tone dripping with honeyed deceit. "The freedom I offer. No more pain. No more fear. Why suffer needlessly when salvation is within your grasp?"

The symbols on the chamber walls twisted and writhed, their glow intensifying in time with Alexei's words. The air seemed to thrum with an unspoken promise, every beat pulling Lily closer to the relic's influence.

"Lily," Ethan's voice broke through the haze, pulling her attention to his face. His grip on her shoulder was firm, his eyes burning with determination. "He's lying. Don't listen to him."

But Alexei's whispers coiled tighter around her mind. His promises were intoxicating, his words a balm against the relentless pain. And as the relic's glow reached out to her like an outstretched hand, Lily's resolve wavered.

Nina stepped forward, her eyes locked on the floating relic. "We're running out of time. The Eye's Offering is the only way - one sacrifice to save thousands."

"She's right," Marcus backed away from the group, positioning himself closer to Nina. "Your ritual is a fantasy. How many more have to die while we chase fairy tales?"

Marsh's hand dropped to her holster. "Stand down. Both of you."

"Look around!" Nina gestured at the writhing symbols. "This chamber, these markings - they're calling for blood. The curse demands it."

Ethan moved between them and Lily. "We're not sacrificing anyone. The ritual will work."

"Will it?" Nina's voice softened as she addressed Lily directly. "You feel it, don't you? The power calling to you? The ritual will fail, just like all the others. But the Eye's Offering - that's real power. That's freedom."

Lily's breath caught in her throat. The sigil pulsed harder; each beat sending waves of conflict through her mind. Nina's words rang with a terrible logic that cut through her pain.

"Lily, don't listen to them." Ethan's voice cracked with desperation. "Remember what Sarah found in Dr. Vane's journal. The Eye's Offering is a trap."

"A trap?" Marcus laughed coldly. "Look at us. We're already trapped. At least this way, we choose our fate."

"Choice?" Marsh's voice cut like steel. "Murder is never an option!"

"I'm talking about survival." Nina took another step toward Lily. "You know I'm right. You can feel it in your blood, can't you? The ritual will destroy you. But the Offering - that's salvation."

Lily's hands trembled as the opposing forces tore at her resolve. The relic's light seemed to reach for her, promising release from the pain that wracked her body. Ethan's presence anchored her to hope, but Nina's words wormed their way deeper, feeding the doubts that had taken root in her heart.

Viktor's hulking form filled the chamber entrance, his cursed energy rippling in waves that mirrored the relic's pulsating glow. Ethan's heart hammered against his ribs as Viktor's inhuman eyes locked on Lily, blazing with an unnatural fire that spoke of Alexei's will.

"Choose, or I will choose for you." Viktor's voice rumbled like distant thunder, each word heavy with malice.

The chamber groaned as ancient mechanisms roared to life. Hidden blades screeched out of the walls, while the floor beneath them shifted, sections rotating and sliding apart to reveal yawning pits. The air grew oppressive, heavy with the metallic tang of death.

Lily screamed, the sigil on her arm flaring blindingly bright. The relic answered, releasing a wave of dark energy that sent Sarah tumbling toward an open pit.

Marsh lunged, catching Sarah's wrist just in time. "Move! Now!"

Nina darted left as Marcus rolled right, narrowly dodging a blade that hissed through the air. Ethan grabbed Lily, pulling her behind a rotating column as a spike shot up where she had stood.

"Keep moving!" Marsh's voice cut through the chaos, her free hand drawing her weapon.

Viktor advanced, unfazed by the traps. His claws crushed a spinning blade with ease, shattering it into useless fragments. His shadow grew as he approached, absorbing the chamber's crimson light. "The master grows impatient," he snarled.

"The Eye's Offering!" Nina's shout carried over the grinding stone. "It's the only way!"

The relic's pulsing quickened, its light growing blinding. Lily doubled over, clutching her arm as pain wracked her body. The sigil burned hotter, searing her skin. Her tears blurred the impossible choices before her.

Ethan's voice cracked with desperation. "We stick to the plan! The ritual is the only way!"

"The ritual will kill us all!" Marcus countered, his voice sharp and cutting. "Choose the Offering!"

The relic flared again, sending cracks spidering across the chamber floor. Viktor's roar shook the air as he stepped closer. "Decide, or I will end this myself."

Lily swayed under the weight of the moment, her resolve buckling. Her eyes flicked between the relic's beckoning light, Viktor's unstoppable form, and Ethan's desperate face. Every choice felt like a death sentence.

Ethan lunged at Marcus, his fist connecting with his jawbone. The impact sent Marcus stumbling back toward a rotating platform. "You knew about this! You've been working with Nina the whole time!"

Marcus spat blood and charged, driving his shoulder into Ethan's chest. They crashed against a stone column. "I'm trying to save us all, you self-righteous bastard!" His knee drove up, but Ethan twisted away.

"By sacrificing my sister?" Ethan's elbow cracked against Marcus's temple. The mercenary staggered but maintained his footing.

"One life for many." Marcus swept Ethan's legs, sending him crashing to the floor. "That's how survival works."

The chamber trembled as Viktor's footsteps drew closer. Ethan rolled away from Marcus's boot, springing up to slam him against the wall. "You're nothing but a coward hiding behind excuses."

Marcus headbutted Ethan, blood streaming from his split eyebrow. "At least I'm not hiding behind false hope!"

Their grappling brought them dangerously close to a pit's edge. Marcus's eyes gleamed with desperate fury as he tried to force Ethan over. "The ritual will fail. You know it. Everyone dies anyway."

"Not while I'm breathing." Ethan drove his knee into Marcus's stomach.

Viktor surveyed the room, and his eyes locked onto Lily.

Ethan shoved Marcus aside, abandoning their fight. "Lily, move!" He sprinted toward his sister as Viktor charged forward.

Marcus scrambled back, his face twisted with shame as the group closed ranks without him. He watched them retreat together while he stood alone, the weight of his choices crashing down on him.

Marcus stumbled backward, his breath ragged as he sought refuge behind a fallen pillar. His heart pounded, each beat echoing the thrum of the cursed relic at the chamber's core. Every decision he'd made leading to this moment raced through his mind—Nina's whispers, the survival instincts he'd allowed to guide him, and the betrayal that had shattered the fragile bonds of the group.

"You idiot," Nina's voice cut through the cacophony, sharp and venomous. She strode toward the relic, her arms raised, lips forming ancient, guttural words. The sigils lining the chamber walls flared violently, their crimson light warping to a malevolent purple. "The Eye demands sacrifice. Lily's blood will break the curse and set us free!"

Marcus pressed his back against the cold stone, Ethan's furious accusation flashing in his mind. The contempt in Marsh's glare, the heartbreak in Sarah's eyes—all of it burned into him. He'd told himself he was making the hard decisions no one else could, but Nina's fevered chants turned that lie to ash. Her promises had been a trap, a twisted distortion of his fears and desires.

The relic pulsed in sync with Nina's chant, waves of dark energy rippling outward and saturating the air with oppressive power. Marcus's skin prickled as he realized the truth: Nina didn't seek salvation. She craved domination, the power to reshape the curse to her will.

"Her blood will unlock the Eye!" Nina's voice reached a crescendo, her words vibrating with the force of the curse. "The curse ends with her!"

Viktor's shadow stretched across the chamber, swallowing all light in its path. Marcus craned his neck to see the hulking enforcer, his cursed form radiating a palpable hunger. Marcus raised his weapon, his hands trembling against the weight of his own failure. He knew it was futile; Viktor's glowing, inhuman eyes were fixed on him, promising annihilation.

Sarah's hands trembled as she clutched Dr. Vane's journal, its weathered pages crackling beneath her fingers. Nina's dark chant filled the chamber, each syllable twisting the air into writhing shadows. The reporter's heart thundered, but her mind remained sharp, racing through the ancient texts she'd studied.

"You're wrong, Nina." Sarah's voice cut through the chaos, steady despite her fear. She stepped forward, positioning herself between Nina and the group. The journal fell open to a page covered in flowing script, symbols matching those that pulsed along the chamber walls.

Nina's chant faltered for a moment, her eyes narrowing. "You can't stop this, Sarah. You're just a journalist playing a scholar."

Sarah's fingers traced the symbols in the journal as she began to speak, her words flowing in a counter-rhythm to Nina's dark magic. Light bloomed where her voice touched the air, pushing back against the shadows that writhed around Nina.

The chamber shuddered as the opposing energies clashed. Cracks spider-webbed across the ceiling, ancient dust raining down. The relic's pulsing grew erratic, its glow fluctuating between deep crimson and brilliant white as Sarah's counter-chant strengthened.

"Impossible," Nina snarled, her own chant growing more desperate. "You can't know these words!"

But Sarah did know them. Every night spent poring over forbidden texts, every hour analyzing Dr. Vane's research - it all crystallized in this moment. Her voice grew stronger, each word precise and purposeful, weaving light through the darkness Nina had summoned.

The sigils on the walls flickered violently, caught between the two opposing forces. Sarah's counter-chant rose in volume, matching Nina's dark energy with equal force. Sweat beaded on her forehead as she maintained the complex rhythm of ancient words, refusing to back down even as the chamber's very foundations seemed to shake apart around them.

The three relics tore free from their moorings, drawn together by an invisible force. They collided in a burst of blinding light, fusing into a single crystalline mass that pulsed with raw power. The merged relic cast waves of energy through the chamber that made Lily's teeth ache and her bones vibrate.

Her sigil erupted in white-hot agony. Lily screamed, dropping to her knees as liquid fire seemed to pour through her veins. The chamber around her blurred and faded, replaced by devastating visions.

She saw herself seated on a throne of obsidian and bone, power radiating from her form like a dark sun. Cities bowed before her will. The very fabric of reality bent to her whims. In this vision, she was no longer human - she had become something greater, terrible and beautiful. The pain that had plagued her was gone, replaced by raw strength that could reshape the world.

But as that vision faded, another took its place. She saw Eldoria in ruins, its people trapped in an endless cycle of terror and death. Children wept in the streets while shadows stalked the night. The curse spread like a cancer, feeding on suffering and despair. Her refusal to embrace the power had doomed them all to this fate.

"Choose," Alexei's voice whispered in her mind, smooth as silk and sharp as steel. "Accept your destiny as my vessel. Take the power that was always meant to be yours. Or watch as everything you love crumbles to dust."

The visions pulled her deeper, reality growing more distant with each passing moment. She barely felt her body slump to the ground, and she barely heard Ethan calling her name. The merged relic's light seemed to reach for her, promising either salvation or damnation.

Viktor's heavy footsteps approached her vulnerable form, but they seemed to come from very far away. She was lost in the storm of possibilities, drowning in the weight of an impossible choice.

"Ethan, get your sister out of here!" Marsh's voice cracked through the chaos. She yanked her service weapon free, levelling it at Viktor's advancing form. "Sarah, keep reading. Whatever you're doing, it's working."

Ethan scooped up Lily's limp form, her skin burning hot against his chest. Her eyes had rolled back, showing only whites, and her lips moved in silent conversation with something he couldn't see.

Marsh fired three rapid shots. The bullets struck Viktor's massive chest, but he didn't slow. She dove left, but not fast enough; his claws raked through the air, grazing her thigh and tearing through the fabric as she stumbled. "Move! Now!"

Sarah's voice grew stronger, and her counterchant matched Nina's rhythm. Light bloomed wherever her words touched the air, pushing back the writhing darkness.

Marsh rolled to her feet, but her left leg buckled. Blood soaked her uniform where Viktor's attack had caught her. She stumbled, catching herself against a pillar. Her breath came in sharp gasps, but her gun remained steady.

"Captain!" Ethan shifted Lily's weight, wanting to help.

"Stay back!" Marsh's order held no room for argument. She fired again, aiming for Viktor's knees. The bullets sparked off his cursed flesh. "Focus on Lily. Sarah needs time."

Viktor's massive hand shot out, catching Marsh's shoulder. He slammed her against the wall with bone-crushing force. Her weapon clattered to the ground, but she drove her knee up into his gut, buying herself space to slip free.

Blood trickled from the corner of Marsh's mouth as she put herself between Viktor and the group. Her tactical vest was shredded, and her movements had lost their precision. But her eyes remained sharp, calculating each step as she drew Viktor's attention away from the others.

"That all you got?" Marsh spat blood and shifted her stance. Her right arm hung limp, but her left fist raised in challenge. "Come on, you bastard. Let's finish this."

The sigils along the chamber walls writhed and shifted, their ancient forms melding together. Ethan watched in horror as they traced words into the fog that burned with an eerie light: "The vessel must choose."

Alexei's voice filled the chamber, seeming to come from everywhere and nowhere at once. "You feel it, don't you, Lily? The power that could be yours. The strength to reshape this broken world."

In Ethan's arms, Lily's body convulsed. Her eyes snapped open, but they weren't her own - they blazed with an inner fire that matched the pulsing of the merged relic.

"The ritual will destroy you," Alexei's voice caressed like silk over steel. "But embrace my gift, and you'll transcend your mortal limitations. You'll have the power to protect everyone you love."

The relic's energy surged, sending waves of force through the chamber. Its light seemed to reach for Lily, drawing her toward it like a moth to flame.

"Don't listen to him!" Sarah's voice cracked with desperation as she pushed an imaginary force towards Nina. "The ritual can work. We can break the curse together!"

Lily struggled in Ethan's grip, her skin burning hot against his arms. Her expression twisted with inner turmoil as Alexei's influence bore down on her.

"Choose," Alexei commanded. "Accept your destiny as my vessel, or watch everything you love turn to ash."

The relic's power built to a deafening crescendo. Lily's back arched as energy coursed through her, her scream mixing with the chamber's resonant hum. The sigil on her arm blazed like a star, marking her as the focal point of forces beyond mortal understanding.

Ethan's grip tightened, desperation etched into his every move. "Lily!" he shouted, his voice breaking. "Stay with me! We've come too far—*you've* come too far!"

But Lily's body trembled with the weight of impossible choices, her consciousness teetering on the edge. The relic's light wrapped around her, a siren song promising salvation and ruin all at once.

And as Alexei's voice whispered again—soft, persuasive, unyielding—everything hung in the balance. The fate of Eldoria, the survival of her friends, her very soul. It all hinged on one choice.

CHAPTER SEVENTEEN

ASCENSION OR OBLIVION

The relic's crystal pulsed faster, each surge sending tremors through the chamber. Dark energy arced across the room like lightning, cracking ancient stone and unravelling the sigils etched into the walls. The air buzzed with raw, unrelenting power, a storm fueled by Lily's indecision.

The floor buckled beneath them, gears grinding to life. Serrated blades shot from hidden slots, their metallic shriek slicing through the chaos. Sarah dove forward, the blade missing her by inches as it buried itself into the stone.

"Move!" Marsh barked, shoving Ethan aside just as part of the ceiling collapsed, raining debris. Dust clouded the air, choking their shouts as they scrambled for cover.

Viktor loomed larger with every step, his cursed flesh glowing faintly as it absorbed the chamber's energy. Each heavy footfall left cracks in the stone, glowing with the same ominous light as the relic. The air rippled around him, distorting reality itself.

A sharp mechanical click preceded another trap—poison darts whistling from wall fixtures. Ethan yanked Lily behind a crumbling column, shielding her as darts peppered the space they'd just vacated. Her skin burned against his, her body locked in a violent tremor as the sigil on her arm flared brighter.

The relic's unstable energy lashed out in powerful waves, shaking loose more chunks of stone from the ceiling. Sarah abandoned her position, her counterchant faltering as she scrambled for safety. The symbols on the walls flickered, their glow fading as Nina's dark incantation grew louder, twisting the air with malevolent purpose.

Viktor's claws sliced through a falling boulder, shattering it into harmless fragments. The pieces crashed to the ground on either side of Marsh, who limped backward, blood streaking her leg. Her pistol was raised, her aim steady despite the wound, but Viktor's glowing eyes locked onto her with unwavering intent.

Blades whirred from the walls, pits yawned open beneath their feet, and jets of flame erupted from hidden vents. The chamber closed in on them, chaos stripping away any semblance of safety. Each pulse of the relic shrank the space between survival and death, tightening the noose around the group.

Through the chaos of the chamber, Nina's eyes gleamed with a feverish light. Her fingers traced symbols in the air, drawing power from the relic's unstable energy. Dark tendrils coiled around her arms, responding to her will as she positioned herself behind a fallen column.

"The Eye demands blood," Nina's voice carried over the grinding of ancient gears. Her hands moved faster, weaving complex patterns that pulsed with evil purpose.

Sarah's counterchant faltered as Nina gathered the chamber's power. The air crackled with tension, reality warping around Nina's form as she directed the dark energy. With a snarl of triumph, she unleashed a blast of corrupted magic straight at Sarah.

"Down!" Marsh's voice cut through the chaos. She shoved Sarah aside, taking the full force of Nina's attack. The dark energy slammed into her chest, lifting her off her feet. She hit the ground hard, her body smoking from the impact.

Ethan's blood ran cold at the sight of Marsh's crumpled form. He lunged forward, tackling Nina before she could channel another blast. His shoulder crashed into her midsection, breaking her concentration. The dark energy dispersed in a shower of sparks as they hit the ground.

Nina writhed free of his grip; her face twisted with rage. She scrambled backward, disappearing behind a curtain of falling debris as another section of ceiling collapsed.

"Captain!" Sarah crawled to Marsh's side, checking for signs of life. Relief flooded her face as Marsh's chest rose with shallow breaths.

***

The relic's light flared blindingly bright, forcing Ethan to shield his eyes. When he lowered his arm, his heart stopped. Alexei Novikov stood in the center of the chamber; his form wreathed in shadows that seemed to drink in the surrounding light. The temperature plummeted, frost spreading across the stone floor from where he stood.

"Your struggles amuse me." Alexei's voice filled the chamber, each word carrying the weight of centuries. His dark eyes fixed on Lily, ignoring the others as if they were insects beneath his notice. "The curse is woven into the fabric of this city. Into me."

The shadows around him writhed and twisted, reaching out like hungry tendrils. Viktor dropped to one knee, bowing his head before his master. Nina's face lit up with reverent fear as she pressed herself against the wall.

"You feel it, don't you?" Alexei stepped toward Lily; his movements were fluid and predatory. "The power coursing through your veins. The potential. Why fight what you could embrace?"

Lily's sigil pulsed in response to his presence, drawing a gasp of pain from her lips. Ethan moved to stand between them, but an invisible force locked his muscles in place.

"I offer you everything." Alexei raised his hand, dark energy swirling around his fingers. "Submit to me. Accept your role in this grand design, and I will show you power beyond imagination. Continue to resist..."

His smile revealed teeth too sharp to be human. "Well, you've seen what happens to those who defy me."

The chamber's very stones seemed to vibrate with his power, ancient sigils flaring to life in response to his presence. The air grew thick with malevolent energy, making it difficult to breathe.

Ethan watched as Sarah's trembling hands lifted Dr. Vane's journal. Her voice cracked at first but gained strength with each ancient syllable she spoke. The words seemed to ripple through the chamber, distorting the air like heat waves rising from summer pavement.

Nina's grip on the Eye's Offering faltered. The dark energy surrounding her fingers flickered and sputtered like a dying flame. "No," she snarled, her features twisting with rage. "You don't understand what you're doing."

But Sarah pressed on, her voice steady and clear. The journal's pages glowed with a soft blue light that pushed back against the shadows. Alexei's form wavered, his perfect composure cracking for the first time.

"Impossible," he hissed, taking a step back. "Those words were lost centuries ago."

The sigils etched into the chamber walls pulsed erratically, their usual menacing glow disrupted by Sarah's incantation. Each word seemed to strike at the very foundations of Alexei's power, forcing him to maintain his grip on reality.

Nina lunged toward Sarah, but her movements were sluggish as if she were fighting against an invisible current. The Eye's Offering dimmed in her grasp, its power retreating from her touch.

"Keep reading," Ethan called out, finding he could move again as Alexei's hold weakened. He positioned himself between Nina and Sarah, protecting the journalist as she continued the chant.

The chamber walls vibrated with competing energies - Alexei's ancient curse clashing with the protective power of Sarah's words. The sigils' light danced across the stone, their pattern disrupted for the first time in centuries.

Ethan felt the group drawing closer together, united by Sarah's voice. Even Lily's sigil seemed less painful, its glow steadying to match the rhythm of the incantation. The knowledge hidden in Dr. Vane's journal was proving to be their strongest weapon against the darkness that had held Eldoria in its grip for so long.

Through the chaos of the chamber, Lily's head throbbed as Alexei's whispers slithered through her thoughts like ice-cold serpents. His promises of power echoed in her mind, each word a hook trying to drag her deeper into darkness.

"Remember Andrea," Ethan's voice cut through the din. "Remember why we started this."

Lily's gaze swept across the chamber. Ethan stood firm despite the blood trickling from a cut above his eye. Sarah's hands shook, but her grip on the journal never wavered. Marsh, though injured, kept her weapon trained on Nina with unwavering focus.

The sigil burned on Lily's arm, but the pain felt different now. She saw the truth with sudden clarity through the haze of Alexei's influence. Every promise of power, every vision of strength and control - they were chains disguised as wings meant to bind her to his will.

"You could reshape this city," Alexei's voice purred in her mind. "Rule beside me. Save everyone you love."

But Lily saw through the lie. The curse that plagued Eldoria wasn't meant to be controlled or harnessed. It needed to be broken, and her role as the vessel wasn't about wielding power but channelling it away from the city's heart.

Her fingers curled into fists as she pushed back against Alexei's influence. The sigil's glow steadied, matching the rhythm of her heartbeat rather than the pulse of his dark energy. She wasn't meant to submit to the curse's power. She was meant to be its undoing.

Lily's muscles screamed in protest as she pushed through Alexei's invisible barrier. Each step felt like wading through wet concrete, but she forced herself forward. The sigil on her arm blazed brighter with every inch gained, cutting through the darkness that filled the chamber.

The relic pulsed in sync with her heartbeat, its crystalline surface reflecting fragments of light across the ancient walls. Energy crackled through the air, making her hair stand on end. She felt the weight of Alexei's gaze, heavy with centuries of malice and control.

Her legs threatened to buckle, but she locked her knees and lifted her chin. The whispers in her mind grew to screams, promising power, threatening pain, offering everything she'd ever wanted. But she saw them now for what they were - desperate lies from a creature who feared losing his grip on the city he'd enslaved.

Behind her, she heard Sarah's steady chanting, felt Ethan's unwavering presence, sensed Marsh's tactical positioning. They weren't just fighting alongside her - they were anchoring her, giving her the strength to face down the architect of Eldoria's suffering.

The relic's energy built to a fever pitch, sending waves of force rippling through the chamber. Ancient sigils flared and dimmed in chaotic patterns, their usual order disrupted by the competing powers.

Lily met Alexei's dark gaze, refusing to flinch from the influence in his eyes. Her voice cut through the chamber's chaos, steady and clear: "You won't control me. This ends here."

The sigil on her arm flared like a newborn star, its light slicing through Alexei's carefully constructed shadows. The group tensed around her, readying themselves as the relic's power reached its peak.

Chapter Eighteen

BEAST'S RECKONING

Alexei's laughter filled the chamber, a sound that twisted like a blade through Ethan's chest. Tendrils of dark energy coiled around the ancient pillars, casting writhing shadows that seemed to move of their own accord.

"You think a few words from a dead woman's journal can undo what I've built?" Alexei's voice carried the weight of centuries. His towering form stretched impossibly upward, darkness pooling at his feet like an endless void. "I have shaped this city's soul longer than your bloodlines have existed."

The temperature plummeted. Frost crackled across the chamber walls, spreading in jagged patterns that mirrored the cursed sigils. Ethan's breath emerged in white puffs, each inhale heavier than the last as Alexei's oppressive force pressed down on them.

"Your sister's defiance is touching, Detective." Alexei's gaze locked onto Ethan, his dark eyes blazing with ancient malice. "But I've broken stronger vessels—better men than you have crumbled into dust at my feet. Even your precious Dr. Vane dared to defy me. Would you like to know her final moments?'

Ethan's knuckles whitened as his grip tightened around Lily. Alexei's taunt bit deep, but his resolve held. *Not this time,* he thought. *Not again.*

Sarah's chant faltered as Alexei raised a clawed hand. The journal in her grasp began to blacken at the edges, smoke curling from the ancient paper. The relic's light dimmed, its glow swallowed by the growing shadow around Alexei's form.

"Generations of Eldoria's children have fed my power," Alexei continued, his voice a silken snarl. "Their fear, despair, futile resistance—all of it strengthens the bonds woven into this city's foundations. Do you think you are different? You are not the first to try breaking my curse, and you will not be the last to fail."

The chamber groaned, cracks spider-webbing across the ceiling as Alexei's power built to a crescendo. Dust and debris rained down, and Marsh threw herself over Sarah to shield her from the falling stone. Viktor, standing like a sentry in the corner, seemed to grow even more prominent as the relic's destabilizing energy poured into him.

Alexei's smile bared too many teeth as he raised his arms. "The Night Watch is my game," he declared, his voice resonating like a bell of doom. "You are merely pawns who forgot their place."

Viktor's form twisted and contorted, his muscles bulging grotesquely as Alexei's power coursed through him. He launched forward with inhuman speed, his massive frame cutting through the darkness like a freight train.

"Left! Move left!" Marsh's command cracked through the air. She positioned herself between Viktor and the others, her stance wide and ready.

Ethan pulled Lily behind fallen debris as Viktor's fist shattered the stone where they'd stood moments before. The impact sent shockwaves through the chamber floor, forcing Sarah to stumble backward.

The relic pulsed with violent energy, its crystalline surface crackling with wild arcs of power. Each pulse synchronized with Lily's sigil, sending waves of pain through her body. Ethan felt her grip tighten on his arm as another surge hit.

"Keep moving!" Marsh shouted, ducking under Viktor's swing. "Don't let him pin us down!"

The chamber's walls groaned under the relic's unstable emissions. Chunks of ceiling crashed, forcing the group to dodge debris and Viktor's relentless assault. Each blast from the relic carved new channels in the stone, creating an ever-shifting battlefield of rubble and shadow.

Viktor's eyes blazed with supernatural fire as he charged again, this time aiming straight for Lily. Ethan threw himself in front of her, bracing for impact. Marsh appeared from the side, ramming her shoulder into Viktor's knee. The blow barely slowed him, but it forced him off course.

"The relic!" Sarah's warning came as another energy surge exploded outward. The blast caught Viktor mid-stride, sending him crashing into a pillar. But it also forced everyone to scramble for new cover as the chamber's floor began to crack and buckle.

Lily's sigil flared brighter with each pulse, its glow matching the relic's chaotic rhythm. Ethan felt the heat of it through his jacket as he kept her close, moving from shadow to shadow as Viktor recovered and resumed his pursuit.

Through the chaos of falling debris and Viktor's rampage, Ethan caught a flash of movement. Nina darted from behind a fallen column; her face twisted with desperate determination as she sprinted toward the floating relic.

"The Eye demands sacrifice!" Nina's voice cracked with fervor. Her hands clutched the ritual dagger, its blade gleaming with an unnatural sheen. "Don't you see? This is the only way!"

Before Ethan could move, a familiar figure materialized between Nina and the relic. Marcus stood there, translucent and ethereal, his form rippling like smoke in the chamber's unstable light.

"What—" Nina stumbled backward, the dagger trembling in her grip. "You're dead. I saw you die!"

Marcus's apparition reached out, his ghostly hand passing through Nina's shoulder. She shuddered violently, her eyes widening in terror. Ethan seized the opportunity, tackling her from the side. The dagger clattered across the stone floor as they hit the ground.

"Let go!" Nina thrashed against Ethan's hold. "Marcus understands! Tell them!"

But Marcus's spectral form shook his head, his features sorrowful yet determined. Sarah gasped, pressing against the wall as the apparition drifted past her. Marsh's hand instinctively went to her weapon, though she knew it would be useless against a ghost.

Nina's struggles weakened as Marcus's form loomed over them—a cold wave washed through the chamber, different from Alexei's oppressive chill. The apparition's presence seemed to drain Nina's strength, and she slumped into Ethan's grip, unconscious but breathing.

"Marcus?" Lily's voice quivered as the ghostly figure turned toward her. But the apparition was already fading, dissolving like mist in the morning light, leaving them all questioning what they'd witnessed.

Ethan secured Nina's limp form, his mind racing. Had Marcus's spirit intervened? Or had the relic's wild energy merely conjured a shared hallucination? The questions hung in the air, unanswered, as the chamber continued to crumble around them.

Through the chaos, Ethan caught Marsh's subtle hand signal. Her sharp eyes flicked between Viktor's hulking form and the unstable relic, her meaning unmistakable: *Use the relic's energy against him.*

"The relic's destabilizing him," Sarah shouted urgently from her cover behind a crumbling pillar. "It's disrupting the curse, but not enough to stop him outright. We have to amplify it!"

Viktor let out a roar, his monstrous frame absorbing another surge from the relic. The energy rippled across his cursed flesh, forcing him to stagger, but his strength remained terrifyingly intact. His clawed hand lashed out, slicing through the air inches from Marsh as she dodged to the side.

Ethan nodded at Sarah, then at Marsh. "We hit him from all sides. Focus the energy where it hurts most."

Sarah began chanting, her voice steady despite the chaos. She timed each word with the relic's pulsing light, and the sigils carved into the chamber walls flared brighter, intensifying the relic's unstable glow. Waves of power lashed out, forcing Viktor to snarl in pain as shadows peeled away from his cursed form.

Marsh took the lead, and her movements were calculated. She darted into Viktor's line of sight, taunting him with sharp whistles and feints. "Come on, big guy!" she yelled, her voice cutting through the air like a whip. "Show me what you've got!"

Viktor roared and charged, his massive form smashing through debris as Marsh backpedalled, drawing him closer to the relic's most potent emissions. His claw raked the floor, leaving gouges in the stone as another energy surge forced him to stumble.

"Ethan, now!" Marsh barked.

Ethan sprinted in from the side, swinging a jagged piece of fallen stone with all his strength. The makeshift weapon connected with Viktor's shoulder, cracking against the cursed armor-like flesh. Viktor barely flinched, swatting Ethan aside with a backhanded blow that sent him tumbling.

Sarah's chant reached a crescendo, and the relic's energy erupted in a blinding flash. The chamber trembled as cracks spider-webbed through the walls. Viktor reeled, clutching at his head as the relic's light bored into his monstrous form.

"Lily!" Sarah shouted, her voice strained. "The sigil—she's the key to amplifying it!"

Lily, trembling but resolute, stepped forward. Her sigil burned like molten silver, its light syncing with the relic's pulses. Each step she took toward Viktor sent a wave of energy cascading through the chamber, forcing him to his knees.

Viktor's claws lashed out in desperation, but Marsh was already moving. She leaped onto his back, wrapping her arm around his neck in a chokehold. "Ethan!" she called, her voice strained as Viktor thrashed beneath her.

Ethan recovered and lunged forward, driving a shard of jagged stone into a vulnerable spot where the relic's light had stripped away Viktor's cursed armor. Viktor bellowed, his voice shaking the chamber as the shadows enveloping him began to unravel.

The relic surged one final time, its light piercing Viktor's chest. His massive frame froze, the cursed energy boiling away like mist in sunlight. His claws fell limp, and he collapsed to his knees.

For a moment, silence reigned. Viktor's monstrous form began to shrink, the darkness peeling away to reveal the broken man beneath. His eyes, no longer blazing with Alexei's fire, locked on Lily. For the first time, they held not rage but a flicker of gratitude.

"Free them," Viktor rasped, his voice barely a whisper, before slumping forward, unconscious.

***

Sarah's hand gripped Lily's shoulder, steadying her as they faced the floating relic. Its wild energy had settled into a steady pulse, like a beating heart suspended in mid-air.

"Remember what Dr. Vane wrote," Sarah's voice cut through the chamber's oppressive silence. "The symbols must be activated in sequence. Start with the one representing dawn."

Lily's fingers traced the air, following the ancient markings that circled the chamber. Her sigil flared in response, sending waves of silver light cascading across the walls. Each symbol she touched blazed to life, their radiance pushing back the shadows that clung to the corners.

"That's it," Sarah guided, her eyes darting between Dr. Vane's journal and the illuminated patterns. "Now, the binding runes!"

The chamber's temperature plummeted. Frost crystallized across the stone floor as Alexei's presence manifested, his power pressing down like a physical weight. Lily's breath came out in white clouds as she continued the ritual, her hands shaking but determined.

"You dare challenge my work?" Alexei's voice echoed from everywhere and nowhere. The shadows between the glowing symbols writhed and twisted, taking on serpentine forms. "You know nothing of true power, child."

Lily's sigil burned brighter, matching the intensity of the relic. The chamber's symbols responded, their light forming a web of energy that connected to the floating crystal. Each connection strengthened the ritual's power, and Alexei's attention zeroed in on her like a physical force.

"The next sequence," Sarah urged her voice tight with tension. "Don't let him break your concentration."

Dark tendrils of energy lashed out from the shadows, only to dissolve against the ritual's growing light. Alexei's presence loomed closer, his power focusing entirely on Lily as she threatened the very foundation of his curse.

"I gave you a choice," Alexei's voice carried an edge of steel. "Now, you force my hand."

The darkness erupted from Alexei like a tidal wave, smothering the chamber's light. Ethan's heart hammered as he watched black mist snake across the floor, reaching for his sister with lethal intent.

"Keep going!" He lunged forward, swinging a broken piece of masonry through the nearest tendril. It dissipated like smoke, only to reform seconds later.

Marsh fired her service weapon into the mass of shadows surrounding Alexei. The muzzle flashes illuminated his gaunt face, twisted with rage. The bullets passed through him harmlessly, but the light made him recoil.

"The flares!" Sarah dug through her pack, tossing emergency flares to Marsh and Ethan. "Light breaks his hold!"

Lily's voice rose above the chaos, chanting the ritual words as her fingers traced symbol after symbol. Her sigil blazed against the oppressive dark, a beacon of silver-blue light.

Alexei's power manifested as a wall of pure darkness, pressing down on them with crushing force. Ethan ignited his flare, the harsh red light carving a path through the shadows. Marsh followed suit, positioning herself between Lily and the writhing tendrils.

"Insignificant insects," Alexei's voice boomed. The chamber trembled as waves of cursed energy pulsed outward. "You cannot hope to undo centuries of power."

Sarah's voice joined Lily's, the counter-chant strengthening the ritual's protective barrier. Ethan slashed through another tendril as it whipped toward Lily's throat. The darkness pressed closer, threatening to snuff out their meagre lights.

"I won't let you touch her!" Ethan's voice cracked as he fought against the overwhelming pressure. Marsh stood shoulder-to-shoulder with him, her flare held high as more tendrils lashed out.

The relic pulsed in sync with Lily's chant, each beat pushing back against Alexei's assault. But the darkness kept coming, an endless tide of cursed energy bearing down on them with murderous intent.

The chamber's shadows coalesced into scenes around Lily - visions of impossible power. She saw herself standing atop Eldoria's highest tower, the city remade in her image. Streets gleamed with golden light, free from darkness and fear. The curse's victims rose and were restored to life, including Andrea. Her brother smiled, proud and whole again.

"All this could be yours," Alexei's voice caressed her mind. "The power to heal. To protect. To ensure no one else dies needlessly."

The relic's energy surged through Lily's body, offering a taste of that promised strength. Her sigil burned with potential, each pulse revealing new possibilities.

"Think of Ethan," Alexei pressed. "You could erase his pain, his guilt. Give him back everything he's lost."

Lily's hands trembled as she gripped the relic tighter. The power sang through her veins, sweet and seductive. One word, one choice, and she could remake the world.

But beneath the golden visions, she caught glimpses of truth - the twisted nature of Alexei's gifts, the price of such power. She saw the darkness hiding behind his promises and felt the corruption that would consume her soul.

"No." Lily's voice cracked, then strengthened. She forced the power outward, channeling it into the ritual symbols. "You can't tempt me with lies."

The relic's energy responded to her rejection, its light shifting from seductive gold to pure silver. The sigil on her arm aligned with the ritual's purpose, burning away Alexei's influence.

"Then you choose death," Alexei snarled.

Lily ignored his threat, pouring herself into the Ritual of Severance. The relic's power flowed through her, igniting symbol after symbol in a cascade of cleansing light. Each activation weakened Alexei's hold, pushing back the corrupted shadows of his influence.

The chamber's energy reached a fever pitch as Lily completed the final sequence. The relic's light merged with her sigil, creating a blinding column that shot toward the ceiling. Ancient symbols blazed across every surface, their power harmonizing with the ritual.

Alexei's form flickered, his connection to the curse wavering. "What have you done?" His voice cracked with something new - fear.

The sigil on Lily's arm burned white-hot, lifting her off the ground. Power coursed through her body, different from Alexei's corrupted offerings. This energy felt clean and pure, drawing strength from centuries of resistance against the curse.

"No!" Alexei's shadows whipped frantically around him, trying to maintain their hold. "I am eternal! I am the night itself!"

Lily thrust her marked arm forward. The sigil's light struck Alexei like a physical blow, cutting through his defences. Where it touched, his darkness crumbled away, revealing the hollow shell beneath.

"This is impossible," he rasped, his form unravelling at the edges. Shadows peeled away from him in strips, dissolving into motes of light.

The sigil's power poured through Lily, channelling the combined strength of the ritual and relic. Alexei's screams echoed off the chamber walls as his body began to disintegrate. Layer by layer, his carefully constructed power crumbled.

"You cannot... I will not..." His final words dissolved into an inhuman howl of rage and despair. The chamber shook with the force of his destruction, centuries of cursed energy unravelling in seconds.

Alexei's form exploded into a shower of shadow and light, the fragments scattering like ash in a wind that wasn't there. The curse's hold over Eldoria snapped like a cut thread, sending a shockwave of power rippling through the city's streets.

The oppressive weight that had haunted Eldoria for generations lifted. The perpetual darkness that had clung to every corner began to fade, replaced by the first genuine light the city had seen in centuries.

The chamber's walls groaned, ancient stone protesting as the relic's power faded. Chunks of ceiling crashed down around them, forcing Ethan to dodge as he scooped up his unconscious sister.

"Run!" Marsh's command cut through the chaos. She grabbed Sarah's arm, yanking her away from a falling column. "This whole place is coming down!"

Lily hung limp in Ethan's arms, her skin cold but her pulse steady. The sigil on her arm had faded to a pale silver outline, barely visible against her skin. He clutched her closer as another section of the ceiling collapsed.

Sarah stumbled ahead of them, Dr. Vane's journal clutched to her chest. "The tunnel entrance - there!" She pointed to a narrow opening, partially hidden behind crumbling stonework.

The floor buckled beneath their feet. Marsh steadied Ethan as he struggled to maneuver through the debris with Lily's dead weight. The air filled with dust and the screech of stone grinding against stone.

"Watch it!" Marsh shoved Ethan forward as a massive slab crashed down where he'd stood moments before. The impact sent shockwaves through the floor, opening fissures in the ancient stone.

They reached the tunnel entrance as the chamber's support columns began to snap. Each crack echoed like gunshots, followed by the thunderous collapse of centuries-old architecture.

"Through here!" Sarah squeezed into the passage first, reaching back to help guide Lily's unconscious form through the narrow space. Ethan pushed his sister forward, trying to protect her head from the low ceiling.

Marsh brought up the rear, her flashlight beam cutting through clouds of debris. The tunnel shook violently, threatening to seal them inside. They scrambled forward as the passage started to cave in behind them.

With a final burst of speed, they cleared the collapsing section. The roar of destruction followed them, growing fainter as the ancient chamber crumbled into history. They emerged into a wider tunnel, gasping for breath as dust settled around them.

Ethan cradled Lily against his chest, checking her breathing. Her chest rose and fell steadily, her face peaceful despite their narrow escape.

CHAPTER NINETEEN

SCARS OF SURVIVAL

Ethan's legs burned as he carried Lily up the final stretch of the tunnel. Stale air gave way to something fresher - a breeze carrying hints of morning. The group emerged into an alley just as the sun's first rays painted Eldoria's eastern sky in pale gold.

The oppressive weight that had crushed the city for generations was gone. The air felt lighter, cleaner somehow. Even the shadows seemed normal, no longer writhing with evil purpose.

Lily stirred in his arms, her eyelids fluttering. The sigil on her arm had faded to a thin silver outline, dormant and powerless. She opened her eyes, blinking against the dawn light.

"Did we...?" Her voice was hoarse.

"We did it." Sarah helped Ethan lower Lily to her feet. "The curse is broken."

Marsh stood at the alley's mouth, her usual stern expression softened by exhaustion and relief. "Look."

They followed her gaze to the clock tower rising above Eldoria's skyline. The ancient structure that had dominated the city for centuries looked different now. Its dark energy was gone, the sickly glow that had pulsed from its windows extinguished. It stood as nothing more than stone and metal, stripped of its supernatural power.

Lily leaned against Ethan, touching the faded mark on her arm. "I can't feel it anymore. The pull, the whispers - they're gone."

The morning light spread across the city, touching places that had known only darkness for generations. Buildings emerged from the shadow, their surfaces catching the sun's warmth. Eldoria greeted the dawn as a free city for the first time in living memory.

The weight of their victory settled heavily on Ethan's shoulders as they approached the clock tower's base. Morning light cast long shadows across worn cobblestones, each step bringing fresh memories of those who hadn't made it.

"Twitch saved us." Ethan's voice cracked. "Just a kid, but he knew those tunnels better than anyone."

Lily touched the cold stone of the tower, her fingers tracing ancient grooves. "He showed us the way when we were lost. Even Marcus..." She paused, swallowing hard. "Despite everything, he fought Viktor to protect us in the end."

Sarah pulled out her worn notebook, its pages stained with tunnel grime. "So many names over the years. Andrea Bondy. Dr. Vane. Viktor himself, trapped and twisted by Alexei's power." She looked up at the tower's face, its hands moving with ordinary purpose. "We should mark this place. Not just as a reminder of the curse, but of those who died fighting it."

Marsh nodded, her usual commanding presence softened by exhaustion and grief. "A memorial. Something permanent. The city needs to remember, to heal." She reached into her jacket and pulled out Twitch's battered baseball cap, gently placing it at the tower's base. For a moment, she lingered there, her fingers brushing the stone as her expression darkened. "The curse is gone, but scars like this run deep. It'll take time for Eldoria to feel whole again."

Ethan watched as others in the street began to notice them. A few approached cautiously, faces bearing recognition of their losses to the Night Watch. An elderly woman laid flowers. A man set down a framed photograph. A child, clutching a stuffed toy, asked in a whisper, "Is it really over?"

"They're starting already," Lily whispered, wiping tears from her cheeks. She glanced at the clock tower. Its dark energy was gone, but the sight of it, stark and cold against the dawn, still cast a lingering shadow in her mind. "The healing will take more than just sunlight."

Sarah knelt and opened her notebook, beginning to write. Her voice trembled but grew steadier with each word. "I'll make sure every name is remembered. Every story told." She paused, looking around at the forming memorial, the tokens of loss and hope. "This isn't just history—it's how we move forward."

Marsh's gaze lingered on the tower as sunlight caught its stone surface. "We'll rebuild," she murmured, almost to herself. But as her hand brushed the scars left by centuries of darkness, a flicker of doubt crossed her face. "But some things can't be forgotten."

Ethan watched as more people ventured onto the streets, their movements hesitant like deer emerging after a storm. The usual oppressive weight of Eldoria had lifted, leaving behind an unsettling emptiness. Windows that had stayed shuttered for generations creaked open, letting in the morning light.

Sarah pulled one of the relics from her bag. The crystalline shard pulsed with a faint blue glow, feeble but still active. "This shouldn't still have power." She held it up to the sunlight, studying the energy that swirled within. "The curse is broken, but something remains."

"What do you mean?" Ethan's hand instinctively moved to his sister's shoulder.

Sarah's eyes fixed on the clock tower. "Alexei's influence centered there for centuries. That much dark energy doesn't just disappear." She traced her fingers over the relic's surface. "These artifacts are still drawing power from somewhere."

A small crowd gathered in the square, their faces a mix of wonder and unease. An old man touched the tower's base, yanking his hand back as if burned. "Still cold," he muttered, rubbing his fingers.

"The tower was more than just a focal point," Sarah said, flipping through her notebook. "Alexei wove his control into its very foundation. Even with him gone, the structure itself might retain echoes of his power."

Lily shivered despite the morning warmth. "I can feel it. Not like before, but..." She pressed her palm against the tower's stone. "There's something underneath, waiting."

More survivors appeared, drawn to the square. They moved silently as if afraid loud noises might reawaken the horrors they'd known. Some wept quietly; others stared at the tower with haunted eyes. The curse's absence left a vacuum, and the city seemed to hold its breath, uncertain of what would fill the void.

"We need to study this," Sarah said, her voice tight with concern. "The relics, the tower - there could be remnants we don't understand yet."

***

Marsh paced the tower's perimeter, her boots scuffing against the worn stone. Exhaustion lined her face, but her movements retained their military precision. "We need runners to spread the word through the districts," she said, scanning the growing crowd. "Sarah, your contacts in the press could help get accurate information out. The tower's visible from most of the city. We'll use it as a gathering point."

Her voice cracked slightly on the last word. She cleared her throat and squared her shoulders, but Ethan caught the tremor in her hands as she pulled out her police radio. "Central, this is Captain Marsh. The Old Quarter is secure. Send medical teams and crisis response units."

Static crackled, making the crowd stir uneasily. Marsh's jaw tightened. "Central, do you copy?"

"We're here, Captain," came the faint response. "Reports are coming in from all sectors. The darkness... it's lifting. People are returning to the streets."

Relief flickered in Marsh's eyes, but she didn't let it soften her tone. "Good. Focus on the worst-hit areas. We'll need supplies, and make sure you mark the tower as a safe zone."

While Marsh coordinated with her officers, Lily tugged Ethan aside. Her fingers traced the faint silver outline where the sigil had once burned on her arm. "When Alexei showed me those visions..." Her voice faltered. "I saw myself wielding that power. Reshaping the city. It felt..." She shuddered. "It felt right."

"But you didn't choose it," Ethan reminded her, his voice steady.

"I wanted to," Lily admitted, her whisper barely audible over the murmur of the crowd. "For a moment, I understood why people gave in to him. The power he offered... it wasn't just tempting. It was intoxicating." She glanced up at the clock tower, its shadow now ordinary in the morning light. "I could have become something terrible."

Ethan gripped her shoulders firmly, his gaze meeting hers. "But you didn't. You chose hope. You chose us. That's what matters."

Lily leaned into him, her breath shaky. "The tower doesn't feel the same anymore. Before, it was like this weight pressing down, suffocating everything. Now it's just... stone."

"That's all it ever was," Ethan said softly. "Alexei made us believe it was more, but his lies died with him."

Sarah pulled out her battered notebook, its pages stained with tunnel grime and marked with hasty scribbles. Her hands no longer shook as she wrote, each word precise and measured.

"We need to record everything," she said, glancing up at Ethan. "The symbols, the relics, the ritual - all of it. If we forget, someone else might try to harness this power again."

She turned to a fresh page, her pen moving with renewed purpose. "The tower should stand as a reminder. Not of fear but of survival. We could preserve the chamber below and create a proper archive."

Ethan watched as she sketched the ancient markings from memory, her strokes confident where they had once been tentative. Gone was the reporter who had trembled at every shadow. In her place stood someone who had faced darkness and emerged stronger.

"I've spent years chasing stories about the curse," Sarah continued, moving toward the tower's base. Her fingers traced the weathered stone. "But I was always on the outside, too scared to dig deeper. Now we have the truth, and we need to protect it."

She pulled Dr. Vane's journal from her bag, its pages dog-eared and marked with sticky notes. "These accounts, combined with what we witnessed - they're our shield against future manipulation. The city deserves to know what really happened here."

The morning light caught the determination in her eyes as she studied the tower's facade. "We'll need historians, archaeologists. People who can verify and document everything. No more whispered legends or half-truths. Just facts, evidence, and testimony."

Ethan leaned against the tower's weathered base, his muscles aching from the night's ordeal. The morning sun caught dust motes in its beams, so different from the oppressive darkness that had ruled these streets for so long. His gaze lingered on the growing crowd, then on the tower looming as a silent sentinel over a changed Eldoria.

The weight of their losses pressed against his chest. Andrea's face flickered through his mind—her determination, her faith in justice, her final moments. He'd carried that burden for so long, letting it shape his choices and his fears.

But now, watching Lily speak with Sarah, seeing Marsh coordinate relief efforts with practiced efficiency, something shifted inside him. They'd trusted him when he'd struggled to trust himself. Followed his lead through the tunnels, stood by him against Alexei's temptations, and shared in the sacrifices that had brought them here.

"We did it," he murmured, running his hand along the cool stone. The tower no longer hummed with spectral energy. It was just stone and mortar now, stripped of its supernatural power. Like the city itself, it could be reclaimed and rebuilt into something better.

His fingers brushed the scar above his eyebrow, a reminder of past failures. But for the first time in years, the touch didn't bring shame. They'd faced impossible odds, confronted ancient evil, and emerged not just alive but unified. Even Marcus, despite his betrayal, had shown glimpses of humanity in those final moments below.

Ethan straightened, his shoulders setting with new purpose. The guilt wouldn't vanish overnight—some wounds ran too deep for that. But he'd learned to carry it differently. It could be used as fuel for protection rather than paralysis. The city needed healing, and he could help provide that, one small act at a time.

The morning breeze carried the sounds of life returning to Eldoria's streets. Somewhere in the distance, church bells rang—not the doom-laden tolls of midnight, but clear peals of hope. Ethan allowed himself a small, tired smile, letting the sound settle over him like a benediction.

The morning sun pierced through clouds that had smothered Eldoria for generations. Ethan squinted against the brightness, his hand instinctively shielding his eyes. The light touched the city's spires and gothic architecture, transforming them from looming threats into mere buildings again.

Beside him, Lily drew in a sharp breath. Her face lifted to the warmth, tears gleaming on her cheeks. The shadows under her eyes spoke of exhaustion, but her smile held wonder. "It feels different," she whispered. "Like the air itself has changed."

Marsh sat on the stone steps of the tower, her leg bandaged hastily by a responding medic. She waved off the paramedic mid-treatment, her other hand pressing against her chest. "I'm fine. Just a scratch."

"Captain, you need—" the medic started but froze as Marsh doubled over, coughing hard. Wisps of blackened energy trailed from her lips and coiled like smoke in the air before dissipating into nothing.

Marsh straightened, her expression unreadable. "That's the last of it," she murmured, brushing off the medic's protests. "No curse left in me now."

Sarah knelt at the base of the tower, her reporter's instincts drawing her to something in the stonework. Her fingers traced faint lines carved into the foundation. "Look at this," she called softly. The others gathered around her. In the direct sunlight, ancient sigils flickered with a weak phosphorescence, barely visible against the weathered stone.

"They're still active?" Lily asked, tension creeping into her voice.

"Barely," Sarah replied, pulling out her notebook. "The curse is broken, but its marks remain. Like scars in the city's skin."

Ethan helped Sarah to her feet, and they stood together on the tower steps. The morning light bathed their faces as they looked out over Eldoria. Despite their exhaustion, despite the remnants of dark magic beneath their feet, hope filled the space between them.

Ethan's thoughts wandered to Nina, the last glimpse of her retreating into the shadows during the chaos. She had vanished, leaving questions that gnawed at him. Where had she gone? What was her plan now that Alexei's grip had shattered? The thought left a bitter taste, a loose thread in a tapestry they'd fought so hard to mend.

"We did it," Ethan murmured, the enormity of their survival sinking in.

Marsh, standing a few feet away, scanned the gathering crowd. Her gaze was sharp, assessing, already moving beyond survival to rebuilding. "No," she corrected, the faintest of smiles breaking her usual stern demeanor. "We're just starting."

CHAPTER TWENTY

LESSONS OF PAIN

Ethan stood at the edge of the square, watching as scaffolding rose around the clock tower's base. It had been a week since the curse had lifted, but the city was still finding its footing. The streets, once choked with fear, bustled with cautious activity. Shops reopened, children played, and the oppressive silence that had defined Eldoria for centuries had given way to voices filled with tentative hope.

Father Gabriel directed volunteers clearing rubble from the alleyways, his hands caked with dirt but his face shining with purpose. Marsh barked orders to a group of workers hauling timbers, her bandaged arm a visible reminder of the battle they had fought.

Lily sat on a crate nearby, her fingers idly tracing the faded silver outline of her sigil. "It doesn't feel so heavy anymore," she said, her voice soft. "But it's still there. Like a scar."

Ethan followed her gaze to the clock tower. Its shadow fell naturally across the square, unburdened by Alexei's malice. The bells had rung at dawn today—not the haunting tones of midnight's curse, but a triumphant peal that resonated across the city.

Sarah emerged from the crowd, notebook in hand, jotting down observations as she spoke with survivors. "They're calling this square Hope's Rise," she said with a small smile. "I don't think Eldoria's ever named anything after hope before."

Marsh winced as she adjusted her bandaged arm, but her voice carried across the square with unwavering authority. "Get those support beams to the east side. And someone tell Rodriguez we need more hands at the memorial site."

Her officers, still adjusting to daylight patrols, moved with renewed purpose. The night's terrors had left their mark—dark circles under eyes, hands that sometimes shook—but they stood straighter now, shoulders squared against ordinary challenges instead of supernatural horrors.

"Ma'am, we've got another group of volunteers from The Heights," Officer Wallace reported, gesturing to a cluster of well-dressed citizens clutching work gloves and bottles of water.

"Put them with Father Gabriel's team." Marsh surveyed the growing crowd, noting faces she recognized from the tunnels. Survivors, all of them. Some still bore fading sigils, others carried visible scars, but they worked side by side, rebuilding what fear had torn apart.

She gathered her senior officers near the tower's base. "We need structure. Organization. This isn't just about clearing rubble—it's about making sure nothing like this happens again." Her fingers brushed the bandage.

"I want teams. Survivors working with law enforcement, medical staff, community leaders. No more isolation. No more shadows for darkness to hide in."

The officers nodded, scribbling notes as she outlined patrol routes and community outreach programs. Marsh caught glimpses of their own healing wounds—Rodriguez's limp, Taylor's bandaged hand—but none complained. They understood what was at stake.

"And get me a full list of everyone who made it through that night," she added. "Not just the ones who fought with us. Everyone who carried a sigil and lived. They've earned their place in whatever we build here."

Her injured arm trembled again, a sharp reminder of limits she could no longer ignore. For a brief moment, she rested her good hand on Wallace's shoulder. "You'll be taking on more responsibilities. All of you will. This city's future can't depend on one person."

Wallace blinked in surprise, then nodded with quiet determination. Marsh straightened, her shoulders squared. There would be time for rest later. Right now, her city needed her to stand tall, showing them all how to move forward—but she knew the time was coming to pass the torch.

***

Ethan felt butterflies in his stomach as he approached the makeshift memorial at the clock tower's base. Fresh flowers and candles surrounded a collection of personal items—each representing someone who hadn't made it through that final night. Twitch's worn baseball cap sat front and center, its frayed brim catching the morning light.

Sarah placed a hand-drawn sketch of Viktor beside the cap. The man he'd been, not the monster he'd become. Marsh added her captain's bars next to a photo of Wallace's sister. Lily set down Dr. Vane's broken glasses, her hands trembling.

More survivors approached, each carrying their own tributes. A mother's locket. A child's stuffed bear. A brother's wedding ring. The pile grew, telling stories of lives cut short by centuries of darkness.

Ethan stepped forward, his voice carrying across the hushed crowd. "We stand here today because of their sacrifice." He gestured to the memorial. "Twitch—" His voice caught. "Twitch showed us the way when we were lost. Marcus fought through the curse to help us in the end. Every person represented here made a choice to face the darkness instead of hiding from it."

The morning sun cast long shadows through the square, but they were natural now, untainted by malice. Around them, the city stirred—shopkeepers sweeping away debris, children running freely, neighbors exchanging quiet greetings. Life was returning, tentative but resilient.

"For generations, this city lived in fear. We survived by turning away, by pretending not to see. But these people—" He touched Twitch's cap gently. "They showed us that our strength lies in standing together. In choosing hope over fear. In sacrificing for something greater than ourselves."

Survivors nodded, many wiping tears. Some reached for strangers' hands, sharing grief that needed no words. The clock tower's shadow fell across them all equally now, no longer a threat but a reminder of what they'd overcome together.

Ethan's gaze swept the crowd, his voice steady. "We honor them not just by remembering but by building something worthy of their sacrifice. A city where we face our darkness together. Where we protect each other. Where hope isn't just a word, but a promise we keep."

As the crowd murmured its agreement, a small child placed a single sunflower at the memorial's base. Its bright petals caught the sun, a vivid contrast to the somber tributes around it. Ethan smiled faintly, the gesture a reminder of why they fought—to preserve the future, not just to avenge the past.

Sarah's heels clicked against the cobblestones as she approached Ethan, her overstuffed notebook clutched tightly to her chest. The morning breeze tugged at its pages, threatening to scatter them like autumn leaves.

"Ethan, we need to talk." Her voice was low, meant for his ears alone. She cast a wary glance at the dispersing crowd, waiting until they were out of earshot.

Flipping open her notebook, she revealed pages filled with hastily scrawled diagrams and sketches. Her finger traced a pattern that looked unsettlingly familiar—veins of energy snaking through Eldoria's streets. "I've been tracking residual energy across the city. The curse—it didn't just disappear. It left scars."

From her satchel, she pulled a small, whirring device. Its needle jittered erratically as she turned it toward the tower, the sound sharp and urgent. "These readings shouldn't exist anymore. But they do. They're strongest near places like the tower and the chambers below—anywhere the curse held sway for too long."

Ethan's eyes narrowed as he studied the diagrams. The patterns mirrored the sigils they'd encountered in the chambers—fainter, yes, but disturbingly familiar.

"Alexei may be gone," Sarah continued, her frustration breaking through, "but his power seeped into everything—stone, air, maybe even us. It's like the city itself is contaminated. And look at this." She turned a page to reveal photos—shadows bending the wrong way, frost forming in strange shapes, blurred distortions captured midair. "Residual phenomena. It's weak now, but it's still here."

Her voice tightened. "We can't tell people everything's fixed when it's not. These energy traces... they're active. Eldoria isn't safe yet—not completely."

Ethan glanced toward the memorial, where families lingered, speaking softly, their burdens eased by the morning light. They deserved their peace, but Sarah's words gnawed at him. He knew she was right.

"How much time do we have?" he asked.

Sarah exhaled. "I don't know. But if we don't address this—if these scars fester—someone will exploit them. The curse might be broken, but its echoes could be just as dangerous."

Ethan froze, his gaze fixed on a flicker of movement—dark fabric vanishing around the corner into Fuller's Alley. His heart tightened, memories of Nina's fluid, calculated movements in the chambers below rushing back like a tidal wave.

"Did you see that?" he asked, his voice low and tense, gripping Sarah's arm.

Sarah turned sharply, following his gaze. "See what?"

"Someone in a cloak," Ethan said, his hand brushing his holster instinctively. His eyes scanned the alley, but whoever—or whatever—had been there was gone. "It reminded me of her."

Sarah's brow furrowed, and she shuffled through her notes. "Nina hasn't shown up anywhere. Not at the shelters or med tents. I've spoken to dozens of survivors, and no one's seen her since that night."

Ethan's jaw tightened, unease coiling in his gut. "If she's alive, she knows too much—about the relics, the rituals, the symbols." His voice dropped. "She nearly destroyed us."

Sarah's lips pressed into a thin line. "She was more than desperate," she said, her tone grave. "Everything she did in the chamber... that wasn't just instinct. She knew exactly what she was doing. Someone taught her—someone who understood the curse."

Ethan's gaze lingered on the darkened alley, a cold certainty settling over him. "If she's still out there," he said, his voice edged with steel, "she's not hiding for long. People like Nina don't just disappear. They plan."

Sarah opened her mouth to respond, but a distant call for volunteers broke the moment. Ethan glanced at her, his resolve hardening. "We'll deal with it if it comes," he said, forcing himself to turn away from the alley. "But not today."

The shadows in Fuller's Alley remained still, but an uneasy chill lingered as Ethan walked back toward the growing crowd. Whatever threat Nina posed, it wasn't over. And though he left the alley behind, the thought of her lurking in the city remained, a faint but undeniable echo of the darkness they had just escaped.

***

Lily ran her fingers over the faint outline of the sigil on her arm, its intricate design now little more than a shadow of the power it once held. Sitting on the memorial steps beside Ethan, she tilted her face toward the morning sun, letting its warmth soak away the chill of lingering memories.

"Sometimes I wake up reaching for it," she murmured, her voice barely audible over the hum of activity in the square. "That energy—raw, limitless. When Alexei showed me what I could become..." Her voice wavered. "It felt like it was mine. Like it always had been."

Ethan stayed silent, his steady presence an anchor as she worked through the words.

"It wasn't just tempting," she continued. "It felt... natural. Like I could finally fix everything—Eldoria, the curse, even myself. But then I saw what it cost him. What that power turned him into." She closed her fist, and her knuckles were whitening. "It wasn't strength. It was a lie, built on the suffering of everyone he touched."

"You saw through it," Ethan said, his tone steady. "You made the right choice."

Lily exhaled, her shoulders easing. "And now I know where the real power is." She gestured to the square, where survivors worked side by side to clear debris and rebuild. Children planted bright flowers in a fresh soil bed while volunteers handed out food and water. "This is what strength looks like—people helping each other, healing together. No magic. No shortcuts."

Ethan watched her stand, the haunted look in her eyes replaced by quiet determination. "What's next for you?"

"Everything I can," she said, her smile soft but resolute. "Organize shelter rotations, help record the real history of this city, and teach what we learned about the relics. Maybe even work with Father Gabriel. There's so much to rebuild, but this time..." She glanced back at the tower, its shadow now ordinary and unthreatening. "This time, we'll do it right."

Ethan watched as the morning light filtered through the stained-glass panels of the memorial hall, painting the worn floorboards with hues of blue, red, and gold. His old instincts tugged at him, whispering that he should leave—put the city, the curse, and its memories behind. But something stronger rooted him here, a quiet resolve that had grown in the darkest hours beneath Eldoria.

"I used to think keeping my distance made me stronger," he admitted, his voice low but steady. "That if I didn't care, I wouldn't lose anything."

Across the room, Sarah paused mid-sentence, her pen hovering over the page. She looked up, her expression curious. "And now?"

"Now I know that strength comes from standing with people." His hand settled on Lily's shoulder, a grounding touch. "We only survived because we trusted each other—because we didn't try to do it alone."

Lily leaned into his side, her gaze soft but steady. "You're staying, then?"

"Yeah." Ethan's eyes drifted to the wall of photographs, tokens, and candles honoring those lost to the curse. "This city deserves someone watching out for it. And you two deserve someone watching your backs. Whatever's still out there—Nina, the relics, whatever's left of Alexei's influence—we'll face it together."

Sarah snapped her notebook shut, a wry smile tugging at her lips. "Ethan Morrow, the lone wolf, joining the pack?"

"Not joining," Ethan corrected, his posture straightening. "Remembering I was part of one all along."

His fingers brushed the edge of his holster, not as a burden of past failures but as a reminder of his purpose—a tool to protect the people who mattered. "This city still has scars, but it's not broken. We'll help it heal. And if the darkness ever comes back, we'll be ready."

"Together," Lily echoed, her voice steady with conviction.

Sarah stepped closer, her presence a quiet affirmation. "Together," she agreed, standing beside them as the stained glass bathed them all in light.

Ethan watched as Captain Marsh pulled out her notepad, already organizing teams for the cleanup efforts. Her voice carried across the square, firm but encouraging as she directed volunteers toward the areas that needed immediate attention.

"Southeast quarter needs structural assessment," she called out, pointing toward a group of engineers. "Start with the buildings marked in red."

Sarah gathered her research materials, tucking Dr. Vane's journal carefully into her bag. "I'll be at the library," she said, adjusting her glasses. "Those symbols we found—there's more to understand about them. We need to document everything while it's still fresh."

Lily squeezed Ethan's arm before stepping away. "I'm heading to help with the community center. They need hands to clear debris and set up temporary housing."

"I'll check the foundation work," Ethan said, nodding toward the construction crews already gathering near damaged buildings.

As they separated, each moving toward their tasks, the morning light caught the clock tower's weathered face. Deep grooves marked its stone base where the curse's power had scarred the foundation. Faint traces of ancient sigils still glowed in the cracks, barely visible unless you knew where to look.

Wind whistled through the empty streets, carrying echoes of the past night's events. The sound curved around abandoned cars and scattered debris, a hollow reminder of what the city had endured. Paper and leaves skittered across the pavement, dancing through shadows cast by buildings still standing sentinel over their wounded city.

Ethan paused, taking in the sight of his sister's retreating form, Sarah's determined stride toward the library, and Marsh's commanding presence among the volunteers. The tower loomed above them all, its face now ordinary, its bells silent—yet the foundation stones still held their secrets, their faint luminescence a testament to powers not entirely forgotten.

Chapter Twenty-One

EPILOGUE

Sunlight spilled through the towers of Eldoria, casting long, warm rays onto streets bustling with life. Vendors arranged crates of fresh produce outside reopened shops, their chatter mingling with the rhythmic pounding of hammers as construction crews worked to patch crumbling walls and shattered windows. The scent of bread wafted from Paolo's bakery, its line of customers curling out onto the sidewalk—a sight absent for years.

Children's laughter echoed down Cedar Street, their soccer ball skittering between the legs of adults who paused to smile, their burdens lighter in the morning air. In the market square, neighbors greeted one another with cautious optimism, exchanging goods and stories under awnings that once sheltered them from fear.

The clock tower loomed over the square, its polished face gleaming in the sunlight. Below it, fresh flowers adorned the memorial wall, tributes left by survivors who lingered only briefly before returning to their tasks.

Each gesture—a shared meal, a lifted beam, a freshly painted wall—spoke of a city reclaiming its soul, piece by piece.

In Heritage Park, the carousel spun again for the first time in decades, its painted horses gleaming with fresh coats of color. The sound of its cheerful organ music carried through the air, blending with the chatter of families and the hum of the city's rebirth.

***

Ethan's pen scratched across the cream-colored paper, his shoulders hunched over the wooden desk. Streetlight filtered through his apartment window, casting shadows across the half-written letter. He paused, running his thumb over the scar above his eyebrow—a habit from his detective days.

"Dear Andrea," the letter began. His hand trembled as he continued writing. "You never gave up on finding the truth, even when everyone else walked away. I failed you then, wrapped up in my own doubts and fears. But watching Lily stand against Alexei, seeing her choose light over darkness—it reminded me of you."

He shifted in his chair, the wood creaking beneath him. The sounds of the healing city drifted up from the street below: voices, footsteps, life returning to Eldoria's veins.

"Your case files still sit in my drawer. I used to keep them there out of guilt, but now they're a reminder. You taught me that one person's conviction can change everything. That justice isn't just about solving cases—it's about protecting people, standing between them and the darkness."

The pen moved faster now, his words flowing easier. "I promise you, Andrea, no one else will face what you did alone. Eldoria's changing. We're building something new from the ashes of Alexei's curse, and I'll make sure it stays that way."

Ethan folded the letter carefully, creasing each edge with purpose. Rising from his desk, he placed it on the windowsill where the night breeze rustled its edges. He pressed his palm against it for a moment, then drew back, leaving the weight of his guilt behind with those written words.

***

As Lily handed another seedling to Vanessa, the girl grinned up at her, dirt smudged across her cheeks. "My big sister would love this," Vanessa said, carefully patting the soil around the roots. "She's the one who told me to come help today."

Lily paused, her smile softening. "Your sister sounds pretty amazing."

"She is," Vanessa said with a decisive nod. "Emily says the city needs all of us to make it better. She's helping paint a mural at the park today."

Father Gabriel chuckled, his weathered hands steady as he worked another patch of soil. "Sounds like your sister has a good head on her shoulders."

"She does," Vanessa replied proudly, brushing dirt off her hands. "Emily says one day the whole city will be beautiful again because of people like us."

Lily placed a hand on Vanessa's shoulder, her smile widening. "Your sister's right. Every little thing we do today builds a better tomorrow."

As Vanessa scampered off to help another child, Father Gabriel glanced at Lily, his voice calm and reflective. "The choices we make ripple outward," he said. "Even the smallest actions inspire others."

Lily nodded, watching Vanessa kneel to guide a younger child's hands with patient care. "And those ripples become waves. Emily's already started hers."

Reaching for another flower, Lily's sleeve slid up slightly, revealing the faint outline of the sigil on her arm. Once a mark of pain and fear, it had faded into a pale scar, like a memory of battles won.

Father Gabriel's humming filled the quiet pocket of the garden, blending with the children's chatter and the rustle of leaves. He knelt beside her, planting a seedling with practiced ease. His presence brought a calm that settled over the space.

"These will bloom in spring," Lily said, her voice carrying to the gathered children. "And every year after that. That's why gardens are special—they keep growing, keep giving back."

The children dispersed, tending their flowers with renewed energy, leaving Lily and Father Gabriel in a moment of peaceful stillness. She traced her fingers over a rose stem, careful to avoid the thorns.

"Sometimes I wake up thinking I can still feel it," Lily admitted, her fingers brushing the faint scars on her arm. "But then I come here, see all this life we're creating, and it fades."

Father Gabriel nodded, his kind eyes fixed on hers. "You chose to create rather than destroy. That choice saved more than just lives—it saved Eldoria's soul."

"I never thought I'd find peace in something as simple as planting flowers." Lily pressed another seedling into the earth. "But there's something powerful about building something that lasts, isn't there?"

"More powerful than any curse," Father Gabriel agreed, securing the plant alongside her. "Your strength wasn't in the sigil, Lily. It was in your heart—in knowing the difference between power and purpose."

***

Sarah's fingers traced the brittle edges of the ancient tome, dust dancing in the shaft of afternoon light that pierced the clock tower's archive. The leather-bound volume had been hidden behind a false panel, discovered only when she'd knocked over a stack of maintenance logs.

Her breath caught as she translated the faded text. The page detailed a mark different from the one that had branded Lily—not Alexei's curse sigil, but something older. The text called it the *Watcher's Mark*, illustrated with intricate drawings that seemed to shift in the dim light.

"This can't be right," she muttered, adjusting her glasses. The symbols matched none of Dr. Vane's documented patterns. These curved lines spoke of protection rather than binding, of resistance rather than submission.

She pulled out her notebook, sketching the unfamiliar sigil with trembling hands. Unlike Alexei's mark, which had pulsed with satanic energy, this one seemed to whisper of defiance. The text described it appearing on those who had stood against Alexei's predecessors, marking them not as victims but as guardians.

Sarah's pen stilled over her notes. If this mark had existed before Alexei's time, it meant others had fought similar battles. The implications sent a chill down her spine. She thought of Lily's scars, of the fading marks across the city. This wasn't just about one man's dark ambitions—it was about a cycle of power and resistance that stretched back centuries.

The tower's stones groaned around her as she carefully photographed each page. Her fingers brushed against symbols that seemed to resonate with something deeper than ink and paper. Here was proof that Alexei's influence had been opposed before, that others had recognized the darkness for what it was and fought back.

The archive's silence pressed in around her as she worked, broken only by the scratch of her pen and the distant ticking of the great clock above. Each revelation in the text raised more questions, suggesting layers of history still buried in Eldoria's shadows.

***

Nina's fingers traced the brittle parchment spread across the wooden table, her other hand absently touching the ritual dagger at her hip. Candlelight flickered across the basement walls of the abandoned monastery, casting dancing shadows over shelves lined with occult texts and artifacts.

The map before her showed Eldoria in intricate detail, but not as others would recognize it. Ancient sigils marked key points throughout the city - places where the veil between worlds grew thin, where power gathered and pooled like dark water. Her own annotations covered the margins, calculations and symbols that would make most scholars recoil.

She reached for a leather-bound journal, its pages filled with her cramped handwriting. Alexei had been a fool, too caught up in his own hunger for power to see the bigger picture. The curse he'd woven through Eldoria was just one thread in a much larger tapestry.

The candlelight caught the silver chain around her neck, revealing a pendant that matched one of the stranger sigils on her map. Unlike the mark that had branded Lily, this symbol seemed to drink in the light around it.

"They think it's over," Nina murmured, her voice barely disturbing the dust-filled air. Her fingers brushed over the clock tower's location on the map, where the parchment still pulsed with faint energy. "But they have no idea what's coming."

She straightened, surveying the artifacts she'd gathered. Each piece had been carefully chosen, patiently collected while others celebrated their hollow victory. The remnants of Alexei's power were still there, waiting in Eldoria's shadows - not destroyed, merely transformed.

***

Captain Marsh leaned on her cane, her knuckles white against the polished wood as she surveyed the faces of her senior officers around the conference table. Maps and reports covered the surface, each one marked with updates on Eldoria's recovery efforts.

"Davidson, you'll oversee the western district reconstruction. Roberts, coordinate with the volunteer teams in the north." Her voice carried the same authority it always had, even if her body still bore the marks of their ordeal. "Wallace, I want you to handle civilian outreach. People need to see badges on the street, need to know we're here for more than just emergencies."

Officer Wallace nodded, jotting notes in her leather-bound notebook. "What about the abandoned buildings near the old market?"

"Convert them," Marsh said, tapping her cane against the floor. "Food banks, shelters, whatever the community needs. This isn't about maintaining order anymore—it's about building something worth protecting."

She shifted her weight, hiding a grimace as pain shot through her leg. The injury from Nina's attack had healed, but the doctors said she'd always feel it. A reminder, like so many others in Eldoria.

"One more thing," Marsh straightened, her voice softening. "The remembrance ceremony. I want it done right. Every name, every story needs to be told. Not just the recent losses—all of them, going back to when this started. The city needs to heal together."

Davidson cleared his throat. "We've already started collecting the names, Captain. The community's been helping, sharing stories we never knew."

"Good." Marsh looked each officer in the eye. "You've all proven yourselves more times than I can count. This city's in your hands now. Make me proud."

The officers stood, gathering their materials with a new sense of purpose. Marsh watched them file out, remembering how each had stepped up during the crisis. They weren't just following orders any-more—they were leading, building bridges between neighborhoods that had once viewed each other with suspicion.

***

The last rays of sunlight painted Eldoria's buildings in amber and rose as Ethan made his way through the evening crowd. His boots clicked against the cobblestones, each step measured and purpose-ful. The air carried the scent of fresh bread from Paolo's reopened bakery, mingling with the metallic tang of construction work.

Something flickered in his peripheral vision—a darkness deeper than twilight's natural shadows. Ethan's muscles tensed, old instincts kicking in as he slowed his pace. In the narrow gap between Martinez's grocery and the old bookshop, the darkness seemed to pool and writhe, defying the warm glow of the newly installed street lamps.

The temperature dropped as he passed another alley, his breath forming a brief cloud in the air. These cold spots had become more frequent lately, appearing and vanishing like winter's ghost. Most people hurried past them, their steps quickening unconsciously, their conversations faltering mid-sentence.

The clock tower loomed ahead, its weathered stones catching the day's dying light. Ethan broke away from the flow of pedestrians, drawn to the ancient structure that had witnessed so much of Eldoria's history. His fingers brushed against the cool surface, feeling the subtle vibrations of the massive gears turning within.

Traces of old symbols still marked the stone, their power faded but not completely gone. Like scars on the city's skin, they served as reminders of battles fought and won—and warnings of those yet to come.

"I'll be ready," he said quietly, his words meant for no one but himself. Then he stepped back into the crowd, blending with the evening's flow of people heading home.

***

Sarah's footsteps echoed through the empty archive, her shadow dancing across ancient tomes and carefully preserved scrolls. The clock tower's massive gears rumbled overhead, marking time with the same steady rhythm they had for centuries.

Her desk lamp cast a warm circle of light across scattered papers and open books. She'd spent hours transcribing their experiences, cross-referencing them with historical accounts and Dr. Vane's meticulous research. Her hand ached from writing, but satisfaction filled her chest as she closed the leather-bound journal.

Dr. Vane's familiar handwriting covered the original pages, but now Sarah's neat annotations filled the margins. Diagrams of the sigils, detailed accounts of the ritual, and observations about the curse's nature - all carefully documented for future generations.

She ran her fingers over the journal's worn spine, feeling the texture of decades of use. Rising from her chair, Sarah approached the tall wooden shelves where other historical records rested. She slid the journal into place between a chronicle of Eldoria's founding and an account of the great fire of 1832.

The archive's silence wrapped around her as she returned to her desk, gathering her belongings. Her lamp clicked off, plunging the room into darkness broken only by moonlight filtering through high windows.

As Sarah's footsteps faded down the corridor, the archive settled into its nighttime stillness. On the shelf, Dr. Vane's journal pulsed once with a soft, silvery light, barely visible in the darkness, before fading away.